FINDING
COVER

www.mascotbooks.com

Finding Cover

For more information, please contact:
Mascot Books
620 Herndon Parkway #320
Herndon, VA 20170
info@mascotbooks.com

Library of Congress Control Number: 2019920079

CPSIA Code: PRV0520A
ISBN-13: 978-1-64543-371-2

Printed in United States

FINDING
COVER

A NOVEL

BECCA BREDHOLT

CONTENTS

INTRODUCTION

As soon as I was outside, a brick of strong wind blew right through me. I hadn't even thought about checking the weather this morning. For a moment, I debated darting back inside and grabbing my sweater, but a split second later large drops of rain were pelting my backside. I decided to make a run for my car. When this type of rain started, it only got worse the longer you waited. I looked down and ran. With each step, the sheets of rain came down harder.

I got to my car and reached for the handle to the driver's side door when somebody slammed up against me. Before I could turn around, the person grabbed my hair like a horse's mane and pulled my head back and down. I wanted to scream, but could not bring enough air into my lungs. He bashed my forehead against the roof of my car. Blood ran down my left temple and I collapsed to the ground, dropping my keys under the car. I tried to crawl underneath to reach them. The gravel from the pavement scratched the skin on my cheek. My hand landed on my car keys and I struggled to press the panic button.

His hands pulled me out from under the car by my leg. When my hand holding the keys was in plain view, his boot crashed down on my clenched fist. I let out a howling scream; it felt like my bones were being crushed.

"Help!" I screamed.

I heard cars driving by on Semoran Boulevard. I wanted to get up and run, but everything was blurry. My head was bursting with pain. The man latched on to the bottom of my shirt, twisting it to pull me up from the ground. I reached for the keys with my left hand, curling around the ends so they poked out between my fingers.

I tried to see his face, but the rain blinded me as I looked up. As he spun me around to face him, I kicked him in the groin and swung open my car door. I pulled the door shut as quickly as possible and fumbled for the ignition key. He punched the window with his fist, but it wasn't enough to break the glass. Slamming on the gas, my car flew into reverse.

My name is Crystal Vargas.

You might think this was the low point of my life. But you would be wrong.

PROLOGUE

CRYSTAL

June 10, 1998

I WAS PATHETIC, REALLY. White foamy waves greeted me at my very doorstep. A rosy orb of light sank into the azure horizon every evening from my window. And I couldn't stay. Another dreamer was moving back home because she couldn't make it in California. I didn't have the motivation to look for a job. I didn't care about much of anything. I was lucky if I made it to the shower in the morning.

Last night, my dad sat next to me at dinner talking to some missionaries about Sri Lanka, one of many places I had always wanted to see, but probably never would. I used to want to travel to exotic lands. I used to want to live in Southern California. I used to want my dreams to come true. I gave up.

In the twilight of my college graduation, I was in a state of clinical depression. My parents were worried about me. I'd stopped eating almost entirely. My 5'6" frame looked strange with only ninety-eight pounds left on it. I'd lost almost twenty pounds of my athletic surfer girl frame in a matter of months. In addition to eschewing food, I hadn't been able to write in my journal or read my favorite authors, which, to me, was worse than losing too much weight. Eating hurt. Reading hurt. Writing hurt. Even sleeping hurt.

When I moved to San Diego four years ago for college, I swore I would never move back to Orlando. Anyone with an ounce of ambition left Florida when they turned eighteen, if not sooner. When I left home, I'd had great expectations for my life. I was going to see the world and write about it. I wanted to capture new stories. I wanted to have adventures in strange lands where I didn't speak the language and the foods upset my stomach. I thought I had enough talent to do something truly special with my life—something that would impact other people long after I was gone. I was not going to get stuck in a cemented-over swamp where the heat rising off the pavement filled the sky with so much humidity it made the clouds darker and darker until they smacked the earth with huge bolts of lightning. It happened every day at three o'clock, as regular as the freaking Disney parade.

But I was stuck. Instead of launching from the precipice of all my liberal-arts degree had to offer, I found myself struggling to get out of bed. With no job, no money, and no place to live, my only option was to move back in with my parents, back to Winter Springs, a painfully small town that more closely resembled a retirement community, a manicured village devoid of culture and intellect. The kind of place that would always think like a small town, regardless of its size. The perfect place for a girl who had given up.

I really wanted to be disappointed with myself, except I didn't feel anything. In a few days, I would walk across a white platform, collect my journalism degree, shake the university president's hand, and then fly back to Florida.

There were four local coffee shops within a short drive of my college campus. Two of them stayed open twenty-four hours during finals and midterms, but only one of them had comfy couches and old recliners. The owners converted a midcentury two-story home on the corner of Rosecrans and Ingraham into a mecca of caffeine consumption. It was also the perfect place to study because it felt like you were at home in your own living room, except there was someone to bring you a latte. I loved curling up in their plum-velvet lounger before descending onto the bloody battlefields of 15th Century England. As I studied, the high-pitched blast of milk being steamed into metal frothing cups registered as little more than weak ambient noise in the distance.

While lounging on one of these comfy couches during finals week, I found a cigarette lighter on the ground. It had a bluish-purple background with a lightning strike on it. I took it as a sign and put the lighter in my pocket.

I didn't know what the sign meant, exactly. I try not to interpret signs when they happen because they tend to develop their significance later. Too often we try to extract meaning at the time the sign occurs instead of tucking it away and looking at it in a fuller context later.

Graduation day. The weather was perfect, as usual, and I found myself alone in it. As the sun set, I meandered away from the crowds and down to Point Loma's oceanside cliffs that jutted out like dark orange towers of Play-Doh from a cobalt blue sea.

I came across white lounge chairs arranged precisely two inches apart. The meticulousness with which they had been placed there bothered me, so I pulled chair one away from the flock. Not so perfect now.

By that night, I found a way to zip up my sad insides and put on a smile. I attended a celebratory graduation dinner with my roommate, Amy Charles, and her family, who'd come down from Ventura County. They'd taken me in like a second daughter, hosting me on long weekends when I couldn't afford to fly home but didn't want to stay on a deserted campus.

Amy had thin blonde hair that was straight as a board, even in damp weather. She was a few inches shorter than me and had wide-set hips like her mom. She also had annoyingly perfect skin, perfect blue eyes, and a flawless tan that magically lasted year-round. We'd lived together in an all-girls dorm for the last two years, but when my mood swings got to be too much for her, she'd moved into a single room across the hall. I guess I'd scared her the day I took a broomstick handle to all my perfume bottles.

Amy was normally a great listener, but I could tell I was dragging her down tonight as I droned on and on about my ex-boyfriend, Sammy. Sammy and I broke up in October. The break-up was mostly on his part. He moved back to Orlando from San Diego after following me out there the summer before my senior year. I never heard from him after he left.

I'd pretended to look for a job on my last visit home, but I was really looking for Sammy. I'd driven to some of the local clubs where his friends used to spin. Nobody had seen him for months. A couple of his friends thought he had overdosed somewhere in the Keys. I didn't believe them. He had been clean for more than a year the day I met him. When he moved, he'd left a hole inside of me bigger than all of Buena Vista.

"Men," Amy's mother declared at the dinner table, "do not fill the hole." Her shiny golden hair slid forward from her shoulders and she batted her blue eyes. "And that's what you've been trying to do." She leaned backward and flipped her hair over her tan shoulders. "You've been trying to fill the hole with men—I'd venture to say your whole life."

I smiled and nodded at her, but did not take her words to heart. I'm disinclined to take relationship advice from beautiful women. They have it so easy and probably don't have to work very hard at relationships like the rest of us.

Amy's mom reached out and took my chin sweetly in the palm of her hand. "Only self-love can fill that hole, sweetheart."

Whatever. Moms don't know much about true love. Amy said I would fall for anyone I could have a meaningful conversation with without ever noticing that I was the one bringing the meaning to it.

When I got back to my room later, Amy's door was open. She was sitting on her bunk bed surrounded by six pieces of luggage in matching pink Hawaiian orchid prints. Everything was packed except her TV and her bedding. A few loose toiletry items remained on her dresser, but she was driving, not flying, and didn't need to be as consolidated as I did.

"Want to watch *The Devil's Advocate* with me?" Amy yawned and scooched over to make room for me.

Being an only child from Orange County, she was accustomed to getting her own way. I didn't want to watch that movie right now. It shows how the devil tries to get at us from our weakest aspects, making us think we're getting everything we always wanted, and then watches us as we crumble trying to turn away from hell.

Amy owned every movie ever made about lawyers. She was going to law school in San Francisco in the fall. I told her all she needed to do was wear a short skirt in the courtroom and she would win every case. She tried to explain that her blonde hair and soft facial features were actually going to make it more difficult for her to be taken seriously.

I fell asleep before Keanu blew his brains out. Amy had to nudge me awake. I stumbled into my own room across the hall and slept for ten hours.

I wanted to order a drink. The flight from San Diego to Orlando was over four hours. To add insult to injury, the in-flight movie was *Good Will Hunting*, a story strikingly similar to how Sammy and I wound up together. Then again, it seemed like everything did in a way. Why couldn't I accept that our relationship just wasn't meant to be? Sometimes I thought I tried to use my sheer mortal strength to change the fate ordained by the gods.

I was exhausted. Too tired to even cry. I didn't understand my moods. I had a hard time dealing with my pain because I couldn't see where it was coming from. I would do anything to get rid of this feeling. The advice from Amy's mom came back to me again and again. If my need to be loved by a man was my weakness, what was I willing to give away in exchange for it?

The flight attendant was serving the row of seats in front of me. I really wanted to order a drink. A gin and tonic sounded so good, but my dad was picking me up at the airport. If he smelled anything on my breath, I would never hear the end of it.

Anthony Vargas, Tony to his friends, was a well-known motivational speaker who refused to hug his children in public or listen to us when we spoke. He would stay for hours after church talking with people at length about church policy. Then he wouldn't say more than two words to his wife and kids on the thirty-minute drive home. My sister and I would ask to listen to the radio, but he hadn't approved of our choice of music. Madonna, in particular, was strictly forbidden.

He was also extremely disappointed with my lack of academic achievements and felt awkward about my looks, making sure I wasn't allowed to buy or wear makeup, and my dresses had to cover my shoulders and knees. Secretly, I wished my father was an alcoholic. Then at least I would know that he loved me. But he had problems I didn't understand, like why he only hugged me from the side and never looked at me when I talked to him. It was bad enough I had to give him a minute-by-minute, play-by-play of every evening I was out of the house or I wouldn't be allowed out again. I wasn't even allowed to attend the school I'd wanted to go to because it wasn't a Christian college.

He was too intimidating to stand up to, though, which was probably what made him a well-known motivational speaker. He was tall and had handsome brown eyes. Amazingly, for a man in his early fifties, he didn't have any wrinkles. Just a few gray hairs. His perfect teeth, wide smile, and deep voice commanded people's attention. His dark suits and solid handshake earned him the respect of CEOs and college presidents, who were also his clients.

Maybe that's why I didn't protest when he made me get a nose job when I was eighteen. He'd said my nose was too big for my face and no guy would ever marry me with a nose like Bill Clinton's. The plastic surgeon took out a measuring tape and held it against the length of my nose, forehead, and chin. Apparently, these three sections of the face should all be the same size; mine were not.

"What would you like to drink?" The flight attendant jumped in front of me like an air mask falling from the cabin above.

"Water, I guess," I said reluctantly.

When I exited the airport, "the Florida sticky" suffocated me like a giant sheet of cling wrap. When you're away from the humidity for too long, you forget how quickly the thick, warm air swallows you up when you step outside.

Dragging two large black bags behind me, I searched for

my dad's car. A stream of old people with white hair and overly tanned elephant skin came flying out of their SUVs, scooping up their young family members who were walking out of baggage claim. To my right, I finally saw our good old 1985 white Oldsmobile waiting for me. For all the money Dad made, he sure drove a crappy car.

My dad got out of the driver's side wearing a light blue polo shirt and khaki pants. He didn't say anything to me. Didn't smile. Didn't make eye contact. He opened the trunk, put my luggage in, slammed the trunk, and got back into the car like a taxi cab driver.

Is it possible to love someone with whom you never make eye contact? I think God would have greeted me the same way—obligatorily faithful and unfailingly consistent. Or maybe that was the way I was feeling toward God.

Opening the passenger-side door, I plunked myself down onto the gray fabric seat. I took the black hairband from my right wrist and pulled my long dark hair up into a sloppy ponytail.

"Where's your surfboard?" Dad asked. "I was expecting you to bring everything home."

"I sold it," I said flatly.

There was a brief pause as we pulled out of the airport and onto Toll Road 427, a runway of smooth black cement down the middle of a swamp laid out under a bright blue sky.

"When do you start your new job?" Dad asked.

"Next week," I said, staring out the window through my dark Oakleys.

"You're going to need a car," he said, glancing over and down at me. "And some new clothes."

I looked at my flare-legged jeans and long beige tank top.

"People at engineering firms don't wear tank tops and sandals, you know." He thought he was being funny.

My dad would take me shopping for work clothes. It would make him feel good to think he was taking care of me.

As for the car, I had no idea how I was going to get one with no money. Dad would not help me in that department. A car was absolutely necessary. Orlando didn't have any public transportation to speak of, and nothing was within walking distance of anything else. Besides, you'd be a pool of sweat by the time you got to wherever you were going.

"So, are you excited?" My dad asked ignorantly. "New job, new chapter in your life."

"You know that I'm not," I snapped at him. "Why are you even asking?"

"Your mom and I are excited to have both our daughters home, that's all," said Dad. "We're proud to have two girls in college."

Maybe I was too harsh. He was trying.

"Speaking of, want me to pick her up from the airport when she comes in next week? I think they get back from Mexico on Wednesday."

"No, I'll pick her up. You focus on getting settled in. You're making a big life transition and she's still got two more years of school left. It's incredible that she was able to head into Point Loma with so many college credits as a senior."

I couldn't tell if he intentionally tried to make me feel bad or if it just came naturally. Dad brought up Lyssa's impeccable academic performance regularly, while I had been described as the "creative" one, like it was a handicap, from birth.

"The only reason she got to do that and I didn't is because we didn't travel in the summers when she was in high school," I reminded him. "Then she got all those AP credits and then didn't have to work her freshman year, like I did, and could take more classes."

"Don't be so bitter all the time, Crystal," said Dad. "It's not becoming of a polite young lady."

I stared out the window and watched the palmetto trees

zoom by. I'm not a polite young lady, I thought to myself. I'm a rip tide. You just can't see me.

"It wouldn't kill you to think about someone other than yourself for a while," he said. "Being a servant for the Lord will take your mind and your heart off your troubles."

"Thanks, Dad," I replied. "I'll keep that in mind."

We pulled up in front of our small townhome just inside a quiet golf-course community. The wide streets, walking trails, and "Yield to Golf Carts" signs were the dream of every retired person in America. Emphasis, sadly, on retired. Lucky me; this was where I was going to live.

My mom came strutting out to the driveway and hugged me. She was terribly excited to show me how she had redecorated the house—again. Guests were warned not to sleepwalk, since my mom was likely to rearrange the furniture at least twice before dawn.

I walked up to the quaint little front porch and went inside through the screen door. Doors in San Diego didn't have screens because they didn't have bugs like we did here. The palmetto bugs were so big they could carry your lunch away. Inside the house felt incongruously like a summer cottage on the coast of New England, with French doors in the kitchen and patio.

I liked our old house better, where we'd lived when I was in high school. It was a lot bigger and only a few blocks away from this one. It had double-wide sliding glass doors in each of the bedrooms that faced the backyard. I loved those doors. One summer, I pushed my bed up against the glass, so on nights when blue lightning pierced the sky, I could open both doors and breathe in the rain.

I could set my watch by the afternoon thunderstorms. Orlando's weather rarely deviated from May to August because there were only two seasons: hurricane season and non-hurricane season. I never complained about the heat. Sweat oozes from every pore, causing even the lightest linen clothing to cling to wet skin like a suction cup. I actually found comfort in its predictability, the way the morning sun microwaved the moisture in the air until the afternoon couldn't take it anymore.

Central Florida was known as the lightning capital of the world, where storms were brilliant to watch and dangerous to be caught in. The sultry humidity intensified to a broil, only to be relieved by violent assaults of rain and cracks of electricity that could be deafening. The hour before the storm was always the most intense and dreamlike. The wind would all but cease. The air would hang suspended and thick. Dark clouds were far, then near, then directly overhead, like a magnificent spaceship sucking up all the air so there was nothing left to breathe on the ground.

An introductory high-decibel clap of lightning would start the performance; next came a symphony of rain and thunder, until the scorching sun burst through the looming darkness heroically, painting the remaining clouds pink and orange for a breathtaking sunset that showed it had claimed victory over the sky before nightfall.

Oddly enough, after being home for nearly a week, my lightning was nowhere to be found. Something in the air had changed. I crashed in what would be my bedroom, playing with the lightning lighter, thinking it might conjure up a storm if I concentrated on it hard enough. But all the lightning had moved to San Diego. El Niño was flipping the weather on its head.

As California choked on the floods of El Niño, I was drowning inside as well. The antidepressants my doctor had put me on didn't seem to be working. I was supposed to gain weight because of them, but I was losing it instead. If I could handle my new job for a month or so, maybe I could ask if I could quit taking them. I had never planned to stay on them for very long anyway.

July 3, 1998

I hadn't made any friends at work since I'd started a couple of weeks ago. The only women at the firm worked in the marketing department or as receptionists. They were all in their forties and married with kids. I invited them and a couple of the guys from the mechanical department to come over for a party that my sister and I were throwing. I wanted to invite some of the guys from the engineering department, but they were in a totally different building I never went into, and I didn't want any of them to think I was hitting on them. Ugly guys never understood that it wasn't a personal invite and hot guys always missed that it actually was. The electrical engineering guys were hotter than the guys in mechanical. It was a small company, and almost all the guys were straight out of college like me.

The firm started with five guys, each with experience in one of the four disciplines: mechanical, electrical, fire protection, and plumbing. After they'd hired a ring of project managers to work under them, they'd recruited the brightest college grads from their Midwestern alma maters. It had not escaped my attention that they only hired men to be engineers. I was not really sure how I'd ended up in the marketing department of a small engineering firm.

During spring break, I had called some high school friends who still lived in Orlando. I'd told them I needed a job, something full time. Orlando was a big small town. Everyone was either a former classmate, a relative, or both. A girl from my varsity cheerleading squad in high school gave my résumé to her uncle, who worked at an engineering firm.

I'd interviewed with his firm over the phone. They'd needed a marketing coordinator right away. I had no idea what a marketing coordinator did, but it sounded easy. I didn't want to apply anywhere else. Easy was all I could manage. Marketing sounds creative if you've never done it. I found out it's not creative in the least. A lot of templates and cutting and pasting. I was already bored with it, but tried to act like it was challenging.

"Crystal," my boss called for me like an old lady might summon her small poodle.

Sandie Roche was the kind of woman who has always had an assistant, at home or at the office—probably since elementary school.

"Before you leave today, I need two of those spiral-bound marketing kits put together for a hospital proposal that's going out next week."

I could see Sandie as a high schooler, singling out the loneliest girl, waddling up to her with those saddlebag hips, and convincing her that indentured servitude was her best option. Sandie liked to push her stocky body around the office, flipping her thinning brown hair from one shoulder to the other. Someone needed to tell her that long dark business jackets and knee-length skirts did not flatter short women of her weight.

"No problem, Sandie," I replied with a smile. "Do they need a cover letter or do you just want the clear sleeve on the front?"

"Obviously we need the clear sleeve to put the cover letter in, Crystal. You should already know that by now."

My smile turned into a grimace as I went to the mammoth filing cabinets. Sandie had these huge metal filing cabinets installed when she'd started here four years ago. Each section came out of the wall like drawers in a morgue. She kept each element of the marketing kits in meticulous order—alphabetical by project, text facing left, top of the page toward the wall. It was my responsibility to make sure we always had several hard copies of spec sheets in their proper file folders based on project type.

For a firm that seemed to be doing well financially, I didn't understand why they couldn't just pay a graphic designer to create these so they looked professional. I could edit an existing document, but I was not an InDesign wizard.

This job was not fun, but it paid well. Soon, I would have enough money to rent a cute apartment on the edge of town and get the heck out of my parent's house.

"Oh, and Crystal," Sandie yelled around the corner, "did you ever find those slides that were sent down from the corporate office? They have been missing for almost two weeks now."

"I still have one more place to look," I answered. I was pretty sure I'd lost those slides two weeks ago.

"If you find them over the weekend, just leave them on my desk Monday morning."

If I find them over the weekend? Is she seriously expecting me to come into the office on a holiday weekend to look for slides that may or may not exist?

"Will do," I replied cheerfully, then rushed to finish the marketing kits, not even paying attention to their binding.

Before the clock struck five, I fled from the office as fast as my almond toe heels would carry me. If this is why people get college degrees, I'd rather go back to lifeguarding.

Every channel on TV was blaring with news about the deadly fires. Any hopes of hitting the beach that weekend disappeared amid the ashes strewn across Highway 44 in Flagler County. Even the air at the country club pool was too heavy to breathe. Not only did I miss my thunderstorms, but now I couldn't even go outside and enjoy the Florida sunshine. Instead, Lyssa and I sat at the kitchen table, spooning away at Mom's rocky road ice cream.

"I wish you would stop stealing my clothes," I said, looking at the jean shorts Lyssa was wearing. Her red, white and blue belt matched her strappy sandals and white halter top. She looked cute, in a baton-twirler kind of way.

"Whatever," said Lyssa. "These are mine."

"No, they're not," I replied with a sense of futility.

"It's good to see you eating again," my sister said, smiling to change the subject.

"I will never stop eating ice cream," I countered with a wink.

"Have you gained any weight since you moved home?"

Lyssa scooped large heaps of ice cream onto her spoon. She bit directly into the ice cream with her front teeth, sending shivers down my spine as I watched. She had no idea it was leaving marks of chocolate on the corners of her mouth. Lyssa never got embarrassed about stuff like that. If I had the slightest bit of something on my mouth or teeth, especially in front of a guy I liked, I would be mortified.

"Only about three pounds—not as much as the doctor said I would," I confessed.

"Do you feel better?" she asked. "I mean, not about living at home, but about having a job and meeting new people and stuff?"

"I like having a job," I said.

"Are you still taking Zoloft?" she asked, almost apathetically.

"Yeah, but I don't plan on taking it for long. I mean, now that I have a job, I have a reason to get out of bed in the morning, right? But I don't like meeting new people, especially where I work."

"You never have," she said as she finished her last spoonful. "Are there any cute guys there at least?"

"Yeah, sorta."

I didn't want to tell her about one particular engineer named Duncan who'd taken me to lunch on my first day. He had my favorite hair and eye color combination, where his dark black hair made his light blue eyes pop. He was older than the fresh crop of recruits and seemed like he had more life experience. I'd overheard one of the secretaries talking about him in the kitchen. Apparently, he was letting his parents live with him because they'd both lost their jobs. I didn't know any boys my age who would do that—mainly because they hadn't yet rented their first apartments, much less purchased their first houses. They were all too busy blowing their money on beer and video games.

Duncan also treated the women at the firm with respect. He knew all their names and their kids' names, and asked about the kids. It seemed like he was always thinking of someone other than himself. The fact that he was tall and had broad shoulders didn't hurt either. If I even mentioned his name, she would find a way to interfere, so I kept my daydreaming thoughts to myself.

"They're just not my type," I answered. "All white-collar businessmen. Bor-ing."

"No long-haired DJs or guitar players?"

I laughed and shook my head.

"Dad will be so disappointed," said Lyssa.

"So, how many hundreds of people did you invite over for the party?" I asked abrasively. Lyssa's friends were like vampires. Once you let them in your house, they wouldn't leave until they sucked you dry.

"Just a few," Lyssa replied as she left her ice cream dish in the sink for me to wash.

"Try to remember that we don't live in a big house anymore," I yelled. "We can probably only fit half of UCF in this place . . ."

I got up to rinse our spoons off in the sink.

"Is there anything special you want for our very independent Fourth of July weekend?" I asked. "I'm going to hit the store tomorrow for supplies."

"Oh! We should get sparklers!" Lyssa said, jumping so high in the tiny kitchen that she nearly hit her head on the overhead lights.

Sparklers were the only thing that came close to being a tradition in our family. We'd traveled so much for our dad's work that we were never in the same place twice for holidays. My sister and I had created other customs using whatever resources we had access to at the time. Like playing with sparklers on the Fourth of July in Europe in lieu of huge fireworks ceremonies.

One summer, our flight back to Orlando was delayed. We were stuck in the Atlanta airport, bored out of our pre-teen minds in the Delta Crown Room. The attendant found us with lit sparklers in the coat closet. I had never seen a black woman turn so white. The worst part was sitting on the hard, scratchy airplane seat when our flight finally departed. My parents had whacked my butt black and blue, and the polyester seats provided no relief from the stinging.

"This state is in the middle of the worst drought in its history," I explained to Lyssa. "You can't even light a cigarette without getting arrested."

I wasn't entirely exaggerating. Reporters from *TIME, Newsweek,* and *The Boston Globe* were flooding the state. Rumors circulated that this was the worst summer anyone had seen since Black Friday in 1985.

"Then I guess a few packs of smokes for my friends are out of the question," she replied sarcastically and bounced out of the room.

My sister complained about this house being much more difficult to sneak out of in the middle of the night than our old house. Now I could see why. It's not just smaller. The master bedroom was right by the front door, and the back door led to a snake-infested swamp of a backyard in the summer. I wondered if my parents picked this house for that very reason.

In high school, Lyssa threw legendary parties when my parents were out of town. For as much of a bookworm as I was, she was a raging partier. She knew almost everyone in our school, and everyone in school knew our address. One time, I came home to find two giant skid marks down the middle of our semi-circle front lawn and about 200 people inside drinking, smoking, and making out. I'd even found some poor blonde girl passed out in my bathtub upstairs with what went down as strawberry margarita and came up as a chunky red pattern down the front of her shirt.

Tomorrow night's soiree was probably going to be much tamer, but my sister always found a way to get me into trouble when my parents were out of town. For this Fourth of July weekend, our mom and dad had decided to visit the Adirondacks, leaving me in charge of the townhome and its contents—the groceries, the cleaning, the mail, and one mischievous sister.

1

LYSSA

July 4, 1998

CRYSTAL WAS TAKING FOREVER TO GET READY. The party was starting in thirty minutes and I still didn't know what to freaking wear! My sister would throw on a white tank top and jeans and still look amazing, which was super annoying. She was so pretty; she didn't even have to wear makeup. Sometimes the gene pool can be so unfair. Dad's crazy idea that she get a nose job in high school to make her even prettier was insane. I'd thought her nose looked fine. But now it was smaller, sure, and conventionally pretty, but somehow that one minor imperfection had made her look even more beautiful.

All the guys used to drool over her in high school, when bib tops were popular, because you could see her six-pack abs and perfectly tanned skin when she wore them. I couldn't form a muscle if my life depended on it. And, having been born with my mom's pale skin, I would go from whitefish to red lobster in less than ten minutes if left in the sun unshaded.

"Crys!" I shouted at the top of my lungs.

I needed her to be dressed and downstairs already so she wouldn't notice if I took anything from her closet until it was too late. Nothing in my closet was going to work. I needed Crystal's cute college clothes, but she would never let me borrow anything to wear to a party.

"Crys," I yelled again, this time a little softer. "Are you in the shower?"

She didn't respond.

I tiptoed into her room and slid open the top drawer of the white wicker dresser, expecting to see a bouquet of crop top options, but it was empty. So was the next drawer. And the next.

I quickly scanned the room. Where were all her clothes? Did she leave them in San Diego? I ran to the closet and slid the mirrored bifold doors wide open with a hard push. I was running out of time!

A few lonely dresses hung on white plastic hangers—not the overflowing rummage sale rack of clothing I was used to seeing in her closet. When I looked down, I noticed her luggage on the closet floor. She still hadn't unpacked. This was very strange. I didn't have time to hypothesize. I needed an outfit, stat.

Aha! A cut-off concert shirt. Perfect. I had no idea who The Ramones were, but it was a cool shirt. I was totally going to steal it.

"Lyssa!" Crystal yelled from downstairs.

Funny how much yelling went on in a two-story home, no matter how small or large. Nobody could be bothered to walk up or down a short flight of stairs.

"WHAT?" I replied. I waited to shout down to her until I was clearly in the hallway and by no means in her bedroom.

"Your friends arrived," she said. "Get your butt down here."

Crap, I still had to do my hair and I didn't get to look at her shoes.

"Coming!" I yelled back, even though I wasn't.

I heard Britney Spears playing in the living room and smiled. Crys hated that music. Tiffany must have showed up early.

I got dressed and ran downstairs and into the kitchen. She'd caught a ride here with Duke, our stocky skater friend we've known since kindergarten. He was stuffing the fridge with wine coolers and cheap beer as I came in.

"Wassup, doll," Duke said and gave me a wink and a nod.

Tiffany and Duke would normally never ride together because Duke's girlfriend got so jealous of Tiffany. Our senior year, Duke and Tiffany went to prom together, but just as friends. Duke's girl never got over it. I bet they're fighting again.

"Heya," I said as I breezed past him and headed for the kitchen table. I thrust my black eyeliner pencil and brown eyeshadow case in front of Tiffany.

"Please, Tiff, you're so good at this!" I said, batting my un-mascaraed lashes.

Tiffany grabbed the makeup and pointed to a chair. "Sit."

"Drink," said Duke, slamming a strawberry kiwi wine cooler in front of me.

"No lime?" I asked.

"Limes are for tequila shots," he said. "We'll do those later."

"Is that my shirt?" Crystal asked. "Were you going through my stuff?"

"Busted!" laughed Duke.

"Shut up, Pee-wee," said Crystal. "I know your big brother and I'll call him to pick you up right now if you even think of taking her side."

"You weren't wearing it," I said.

I'd been using that line of defense since sixth grade. She

would let me get away with wearing this now, but I knew I would have to pay for it later in one way or another. That's the upside and downside of having a sister who wore about the same size.

"Don't spill your stupid wine cooler all over it," said Crystal. "I can't get another one of those. Besides, you don't even know who the Ramones are, do you?"

"They're a band," I said, matter-of-factly. It made Tiffany laugh, at least.

"You know, Crys," said Duke as he cracked open his third beer in thirty minutes. "You actually should call my big brother. He probably still has the hots for you."

"No way, Pee-wee," said Crystal. "I don't date frat boys."

"Ya, she only dates DJs who are also drug dealers in Miami," I piled on.

"Gimme that shirt back," said Crystal. "Like, now."

Crystal jokingly tried to take the shirt from my back right there in the kitchen in front of my friends. I hated when she embarrassed me like this. It was almost as if she had to do it to remind me she was the big sister.

I tried to squirm away. She pulled the back of the shirt up so high my bra was exposed. I wrestled away from her, but then she took me down to the floor with the shirt now nearly up over my head. Duke started cheering and I started laugh-crying out of anger.

"You're ruining my eye makeup!" I cried.

The doorbell rang, thank God.

"Saved by the bell!" I said.

"Your favorite show!" Crystal shot back.

Tiffany and Duke stood there looking at me, snickering.

"I'm going to have to redo your makeup," said Tiffany. "Sit back down."

I didn't remember the next couple of hours after that. Did I start with those tequila shots? Did I eat dinner? Lunch? Yes, yes, I did. Taco Bell, and I regretted it.

"Who is that hot guy talking to your sister?" Tiffany asked.

Her words were slurred. I wondered if mine were too.

"What hot guy?" I asked. I could feel a wine cooler burp coming. "She just invited her stodgy coworkers over tonight."

"That one," she said, pointing in a not-so-subtle way towards the back patio.

He was easy to spot, even on the over-crowded deck. A very tall, dark-haired guy with thick shoulder muscles that showed through his white t-shirt was leaning hard into my sister. He used one hand to prop himself up against the wall. His other hand was holding a can of beer. Who did he think he was, some kind of 1980s rock star? What a jerk.

"Oh, this is going to be good," I said as I grabbed Tiffany by the wrist and dragged her through the throbbing living room.

"What?" said Tiffany, barely able to keep up as she tried to squeeze through the bodies.

Jeez, how did so many people fit in this little townhouse? I was inches from Tiffany's face, but we could barely hear each other, even when we yelled.

"She's going to crucify this one," I shouted. "I want to hear it all go down."

"How do you know?" Tiffany asked.

"Because he's so not her type, it's laughable. And she's still heartbroken over Sammy."

"Whatever happened with him? Did he really just vanish?"

Tiffany was slurping down her wine cooler through a straw. I wasn't so sure that was a good idea.

"Crystal said there's a rumor he overdosed in a hotel in South Beach."

"Oh my God," said Tiffany. "In that case, this guy looks too clean cut for her, for sure."

"Yeah, she's going to mop the floor with this one," I said. "It's going to be awesome! Trust me."

"Hey, Tiff!" said Duke. He pushed his way through the crowd towards us. "You're not leaving, are you?"

"Um, the front door is that way," said Tiffany, and pointed in the exact opposite direction of where we were going.

Duke looked around, confused. "Good, 'cuz it's time for those tequila shots!"

He pulled Tiffany away from me and back towards the kitchen. I turned to follow them, but the room started spinning. I stopped for a minute and blinked a few times, trying to settle the movement. I'd heard that if you look down or close your eyes and spin in the opposite direction, you should be able to make it stop.

It wasn't working. People kept bumping into me and it was so hot in our tiny living room. I opened my eyes wide and took a deep breath. I tried to focus on the giant oil painting of a sailboat on the far side of the room. My mom loved sailing, but my dad was basically afraid of the water.

Some guy bumped into me and spilled his drink down my shirt. Crystal's shirt.

"Crap!" I yelled.

Crystal is going to kill me over this for sure.

Who were all these people? It felt like I didn't know anyone in my own house, like I had walked in on someone else's party. A nerd's party. Were these all Crystal's work friends? Was this what corporate America looked like from the inside? Pasty farm boys in Brooks Brothers polos?

Normally, I would have been thrilled to have more guys

than girls here, but these engineer geeks outnumbered my cute girlfriends two to one. These guys did seem to hold their liquor better than my friends, though. Nothing was broken or stained. Yet.

"Oh, my God!" an orange-skinned woman in her late thirties screeched at me as I turned to follow Tiffany and Duke. "You must be Crystal's sister, Lisa! You look just like her. Are y'all twins?"

"It's Lyssa, actually, like Alyssa, but just the Ly—" I started to say before she blindly cut me off.

"I'm Tina," she said, heaving her ginormous orange boobs forward at me. "I work with your sister at the firm."

She said The Firm, like she was referring to the movie. Pretty sure it's not that serious or elite.

"Oh, so nice to meet you," I said. "You know, she's like, so excited about her new job. Hey, you don't happen to know that guy she's talking to on the patio, do you? I don't think I've seen him before."

"Oh, that's Duncan, the office stud," Tina said, then jabbed my stomach and laughed at her inside joke. "He's super friendly with all the receptionists. He even knows all our kids' names and asks how they're doin' all the time."

"The office stud?" I replied.

I didn't want to know any more, but she kept talking.

"Yeah, he's such a great guy; he even let his parents move into his house when they lost their jobs. I mean, it's not like he doesn't have the room for 'em. Plenty of room for all his toys, too."

"How do you know he has toys?" I asked, now positive he was a child molester.

"Oh, we used to date a while back," she said with a wink that almost made me vomit. Then she burst into a shrill laugh and fell forward, possibly from the weight of her huge, overly-inflated fake boobs. "Oh, honey, I don't mean sex toys! Is that what you were thinking?"

No, but clearly you were, I thought, as I continued working to make the room still.

"You should have seen your face just now. What a hoot! Ah, no, no, I meant his cars, motorcycles, jet skis . . . stuff like that."

Looking more closely at Tina now, I saw that she definitely fake-baked in addition to bleaching her hair with over-the-counter products. Duncan dated this type of girl? My sister was way too good to even be talking to him.

"Lyssa!" I heard Duke shout over the crowd from the kitchen. "Get your butt in here!"

Why are people always demanding my butt?

"Sorry, you'll have to excuse me," I said, thankful for an escape. If I had stayed there another minute, I definitely would have puked right in her Grand Canyon of cleavage. "I'm needed in the alcohol dispensary. Nice meeting you."

I lied. I totally lied. It was not nice meeting her. And it was not nice having Duncan leaning all over my sister. Sammy might have been a drug-dealing loser, but I would have paid a million bucks to bring him in here to get this sleazebag off her.

Duke was spilling the tequila all over the countertop in the kitchen. Some of it ended up in shot glasses, but most of it did not.

"Dude! You're making a mess!" I yelled. "I'm not cleaning this up."

"Drink!" said Duke, pushing a half-filled shot glass my way.

I pushed it back. "I don't feel good. My stomach hurts."

"You got cramps, little lady?" asked Duke.

"Gross," I said. "But yeah, it does feel kinda like a cramp. I'm going to go lay down."

I headed toward my parents' room since it was the closest one. I passed people who were leaving the party. I heard one of the engineer nerds say they were headed down to Orange Ave and we should all go.

That's all bars, you dolt. My friends are barely twenty years old. Most of the fake IDs we had when were sixteen had been taken away by our parents or the police.

A sharp pain pierced my lower abs and I felt my forehead break out into a sweat. This was the worst time to get my period. Maybe it would go away if I drank some water.

I went back into the kitchen and started filling up a glass with water from the fridge.

"You don't look so good," said Tiffany. "You should go lay down. Here, I'll come with you."

"Yeah, me too," said Duke.

We shot him the look of death and he laughed it off.

Once in my parent's room, Tiffany had to almost lift me onto the bed. It hurt to move. It hurt all over now. This didn't feel like period cramps. I dripped with sweat all over my body. I couldn't get the water down. I took a deep breath and closed my eyes.

Just go to sleep, I thought. Sleep will make it go away.

"Augh!" I cried and shot open my eyes.

The pain! Oh my god! I'm dying!

"Tiff, Tiff, wake up," I said.

I nudged at her limp body as hard as I could. Tiffany was passed out hard. Even if I woke her up, she would not be able to help me. I loved Tiffany dearly, and we had been friends for a long time. She had the deer-in-headlights look down pat. Every time we got into trouble at school, she'd managed to get out of it with her sincere reaction of shock and disbelief. This included the time we were skipping second period to go to New Smyrna and the principal stopped us as we were bounding down the backstairs to the parking lot. I was in full denial that we were headed to the beach. He pointed out that Tiff clearly had her bathing suit top on, with its fluorescent yellow strings tied up tight at the nape of her neck, visible under her high ponytail. She'd acted so shocked that he'd pointed that out, or was it that she was shocked she had her suit on already? Either way, he'd let us go.

I started crying and decided to search for my big sister. She'd know what to do.

I rolled myself onto the floor. I couldn't even stand up. I started crawling toward the bedroom door. Shoes. I needed my shoes. I needed to go to the ER.

I pulled the door open and crawled on my hands and knees into the foyer, only to run into Duncan. Why was he still here? Why was he holding a garbage bag?

"Lyssa!" I heard Crystal shout. "Do not throw up on the carpet! We just finished cleaning this whole stupid house."

So, that's why he stayed. To help her clean up after his friends. Smart.

"Take me to the hospital," I said, soberly and matter-of-factly.

"Well, I'm not surprised," said Crystal. "How many types of alcohol did you mix tonight?"

"I'm not drunk," I said, still crawling across the floor. "I need to go to the ER."

"Should I get her some water?" Duncan asked.

"Just go back to sleep," Crystal said. "You'll feel better in the morning."

A shooting pain hit me in the stomach and I let out a howling scream and curled up on the floor.

Crystal's angry face dropped off and a look of true concern came over her as she rushed toward me.

"What's wrong? Where is the pain?" she asked.

"My stomach," I said. I held my lower abdomen, trying to show her where it hurt, like I was a kid again.

Crystal was always quick on her feet in emergencies—not always in day-to-day living, but always when someone's life was on the line.

When I was about eight years old, our family rented a small sailboat at a resort. We got stuck about ten yards offshore when the wind died. Against my mom's warning, my dad wrapped the line around his hand, twice. When a gust of wind shot out of the sky, he couldn't release the rope fast enough and the mainsail caught the brunt of it. The whole boat capsized.

Dad's glasses went flying. Mom's head was struck by the jib, and I found myself directly underneath the capsized boat in an air pocket created by the hull. I could hear Crystal shouting instructions to my dad. Moments later, she was right there with me, underneath the boat, without her life vest.

"Take a deep breath, and don't let go of my hand, okay? I'm going to get you out," she'd told me.

And she had. She got all of us back to the shoreline. No wonder she'd won all those swimming medals. She was a mermaid.

"I'm going to roll you over onto your back," said Duncan. "And I need you to lie straight with your hands by your side."

I didn't have the energy to argue. I rolled over like an armadillo in traffic. Duncan grabbed my left ankle and raised it up forty-five degrees.

"Tell me if this hurts," he said. He used the flat palm of his right hand to smack my heel. I doubled over in pain, screaming.

"Get her to the emergency room," said Duncan. "Her appendix is about to rupture."

"How the heck do you know that?" Crystal asked, as if learning the answer was more important than getting me to the hospital.

"I was pre-med before becoming an engineer," Duncan said.

"Can somebody please take me to the freaking hospital?" I shrieked.

Duncan scooped me up in his arms like a damsel in distress, which I kind of was at the moment. Crystal took the shoes I was clutching in my hand and ran for her purse and keys.

"We'll take the Olds," she said firmly.

Duncan laid me gently across the back seat and closed the door. I heard him say something to Crystal, who had already started the car. I couldn't hear what they were saying. Why isn't she backing up out of the driveway? Why are we still sitting here?

"Crys-tal!" I yelled as loud as I could, but it hurt to scream.

"I'm going!" she yelled back at me. But she wasn't. She was still speaking with Duncan.

"Go!" I cried.

"I'm going already!" said Crystal, this time actually backing out of the driveway.

The drive to the hospital felt like an eternity.

"Hey, Lyssa," Crystal said. "How ya doin' back there, sis?"

I couldn't muster a response. I just wanted to close my eyes.

"We're almost there," she said.

I could barely breathe.

"Lyssa!" Crystal yelled.

I heard the panic in her voice. I'm so sorry, Sis. I can't speak. I can't even speak. I started to cry, and then everything went black.

2

DUNCAN

July 5, 1998

I LET GO OF THE CLUTCH ON MY BIKE AND ROLLED IT INTO THE PARKING LOT OF THE ER AHEAD OF CRYSTAL'S CAR. There was nobody around, so I grabbed the attention of the first person I saw just through the automatic sliding glass doors.

"Pardon me, sir," I addressed a short man in scrubs pushing a gurney. I followed him, grabbing his arm to get his attention. "A girl is pulling up in a white Oldsmobile in less than one minute," I gasped, then waited to catch my breath. "Her sister needs attention immediately."

"What happened?" the man in scrubs asked.

"I'm not sure, but I think her appendix may be rupturing. Please, get a wheelchair, would you?"

As the man ducked inside, Crystal's car horn blared beneath

the awning. The hospital's yellow outdoor lights rolled over the white motorcar's front fenders as it pulled up. Scarcely had the passenger door opened before Lyssa came tumbling out. Right behind me was the man with a wheelchair.

"Can you hear me?" the man asked Lyssa.

Crystal's face was wrenched with panic.

"How long has she been like this?" he asked Crystal.

"About two stoplights," she replied as she replaced a sandal fallen from Lyssa's limp foot. "I don't know."

A nurse came out to wheel Lyssa inside. Crystal started after them, but the man instructed her to move her car. Crystal looked so lost and helpless.

"Give me your keys, Crystal," I said. "I'll park your car. You go inside with your sister."

Crystal stared at me with a blank look on her face. A few pieces of her hair had strayed from her ponytail, and her white hooded sweatshirt dropped from her tan right shoulder. She had been crying. God, she looks sexy.

"Crystal, dear," I said gently. "Give me your car keys."

Her eyes widened. She cupped her right hand over her mouth.

"They're in the car," she mumbled through her fingers.

"Did you lock the door?" I asked.

"I don't remember!" she yelled.

She ran her hands through her long dark hair and appeared on the verge of tears. I gently laid my hands on her shoulders and turned her towards me.

This is the kind of moment you seize. The kind of opportunity that presents itself very rarely, so you must take it. She's vulnerable and she wants you to be the hero. Lead her through this and she will fall for you.

"Okay, Crystal," I said calmly. "Just go inside. I'll take care of it."

She hesitated briefly, but then ran inside to her sister. That's a good lass.

I held my breath while I tried the driver's side door. It was unlocked, keys still in the ignition.

Why does her family drive such a little shit of a motorcar? I thought they had money.

I drove the car around back and parked it far from any other vehicles, not that we needed to worry about someone denting this car. It's more a habit of mine, protecting my cars. They were something to be proud of, something worth showing off. This car was only worth hiding.

I left my helmet in her passenger's seat. That way she would have to walk me out here to say goodbye and I might have another one of those magical moments alone with her.

Crystal was truly an enigma. Beautiful. Strange. Sharp, and yet naïve. She might do nicely after all.

As I walked back inside, the black entryway rug crunched beneath the soles of my new trainers. Looking down, I saw bits of black gravel stuck in the grooves of the shoe. Blast. Even if I got the stones out, the blackness ruins the white rubber.

Scanning the room for the girls, I noticed the waiting-room queue jammed with Fourth of July accidents. Bloody Americans. A pathetic lot of juvenile boys with burned hands and such. I finally found Crystal and Lyssa in the smallest excuse for a room. More like a broom closet, it was.

"Could they not have put her in a nicer room?" I asked a passing nurse, who simply gave me a dead stare.

The lights were off and Lyssa's bed was pushed against the far wall. She was out like a church candle in a Scottish wind. Crystal sat in the room's only chair, next to a small footstool. I stepped in the room gently, closing the curtain behind me.

"Shh!" Crystal joked. "They offered us a suite on the twelfth floor with free cable and a balcony, but I thought the three of us would feel more comfortable in a room the size of our pantry. Anyway, I filled out the paperwork and gave them our insurance, but the nurse hasn't even taken her temperature yet."

"The waiting room is packed like sardines," I muttered. "Could be hours before anyone examines her." Having spent a good deal of time doing electrical engineering for hospitals, I'd become somewhat of an expert on the medical routine. "Let me see if I can procure someone."

Looking down the corridor, I spotted the nurse's station. It was rather antiquated, with one black and white monitor and a computer running MS-DOS. Hadn't seen that in years. A rotation chart hung on the wall next to the house phone. Appeared as though a nurse named Angie was coming on shortly. Shaking my Omega watch down my wrist, I studied the time. She'd be here any moment. Angie wouldn't know how long we'd been waiting. I logged in to the terminal and pulled up the charts. I printed out a new one for this rotation and logged back out.

I wrote in Lyssa's room number next to Angie's name, then quickly hung the chart back. Suddenly, a rather plump woman with a name tag reading "Angie" came around the corner. I ran up to her, wringing my hands.

"Pardon me, miss. Is your name Angie?"

"Yeah, why?" came the reply from a pinkish, swollen face. Her blue eyes were set deep behind thick spectacles.

"They said to come get you soon as you arrived. There's a girl in this room here. She's really poorly."

Angie looked bewildered. "Who said that?"

"Quickly, please, there's no time," I said, leading her through the curtain. "She's over there."

The nurse mumbled below her breath. Waddling over to Lyssa's bedside, she looped her pudgy fingers 'round Lyssa's tiny wrist bone and lifted her watch up into the light.

"Is my sister okay?" Crystal rose from the chair, looking

over the nurse's shoulder. Angie's eyebrows rose up above her silver frames.

"I'll be right back with your sister, honey," Angie told Crystal. "We're just going to do some tests."

Unlocking the wheels on the bed, she took Lyssa and backed out of the tiny matchbox-sized room.

"What kind of tests?" asked Crystal.

"We'll start with a pelvic exam and get some blood work."

"Pelvic exam?" Crystal shouted. "But she's not pregnant."

"We can't rule anything out just yet," said Angie.

"Well, you can rule out pregnancy! I think..." Crystal replied, but Lyssa and Angie had already vanished down the hall.

I put my arms around Crystal and pressed her head against my chest. "Needn't worry, Crystal. I'll take care of you."

"Thanks. Thanks for helping with all this," Crystal said, pulling away from me. "I don't know what happened to me back there."

Guiding Crystal back to the chair, I seated myself on the small footstool. Crystal pulled at her hair band, sliding out her ponytail. Her dark hair fell down her back, revealing where the sun had bleached the ends of it to a light blonde color. I liked Crystal's wide smile and bright eyes.

This girl captured my attention the first day we took a lunch break together. Her thin legs were too small for her stockings, which gathered a bit 'round her ankles. I hadn't had the heart to tell her she had a small piece of spinach stuck in her teeth. Every time she spoke, it was so serious. She was beautiful, so I'd thought about what it would take to win her over. I didn't want to mess it up.

"Even though I have worked in hospitals, I hate being in them as a patient," I said.

"I don't know anyone who likes being in them," she replied.

"Well, the first time I was in hospital, other than being born, of course—I mean, we're all in hospitals when we're born, well, most of us anyway. Sorry, got a bit carried away there." Ugh. Sod it! I was nervous. I paused. "Right. Well, long story short, the first time I was in hospital, I was declared DOA by the doctors. My mom was hit by another driver. My brother was just a baby in the back seat and flew about fifty meters out the window."

There. I think that came out right. Girls usually love this story. With Crystal, for some reason, I felt more pressure to be precise.

"Oh my gosh. How did you make it?"

"My veins collapsed. There was no' a drop o' blood in 'em."

Before I could finish my story, nurses wheeled Lyssa's bed back into the room. This time, she had an IV in her arm and a drip bag pumping her with liquids. With the color drained from her face, I started to see a resemblance in the two sisters. Their eyes were the same. Crystal's were a darker green and Lyssa's were a unique blue-green I'd never seen before. Both girls were quite thin.

"We're keeping her from dehydrating," said the nurse. "But we can't give her any pain medicine until the doctor sees her."

"And in what year will that take place?" Crystal snapped. "We got here at midnight and it's almost 3 a.m."

"It'll be just a few minutes," the nurse said and waddled out of the room, closing the cheap, faded cream curtain behind her. The metal curtain rings scraped along the rod in the doorway.

"Do you want to call your parents?" I asked, remembering that they were out of town.

"I don't know how to reach them," she said. "I left their numbers at home."

"Tiffany's still there, right? Maybe she'll pick up if we call," I suggested, proud of my ingenious plan.

"Is there a phone I could use?" Crystal asked.

"There's a phone in the nurse's cubicle. I know how to dial

out because I install those phones for my clients. Give me the number and I'll have a go."

"I don't have anything to write with," said Crystal.

"No need," I said. "I'm good with numbers. Trust me. Throw it at me."

"Is this your way of getting my phone number?" asked Crystal.

"If it is, it's the most elaborate effort, for which I truly deserve it, don't you think?" I said.

Crystal smiled that wide smile at me. I reflected her smile with my own.

I was able to get through to Tiffany. I then left messages for her parents.

"Well, there's good news and there's bad," I said, reestablishing my place on the now-painful footstool in Lyssa's hospital room. "Which do you want first?"

"The bad news," she replied.

I would've guessed she was a bad-news-first kind of girl. Not like the type I normally went out with.

"The bad news is Tiffany says your mom's bed smells like vomit. The good news is I got your parents' numbers and left messages for them at their hotel."

She looked unimpressed. Cracking this lass was going to be harder than swimming the English Channel. All the guys at the office assumed I had slept with her by now, but there was more to Crystal than met the eye. She wasn't just cute. She was clever. And tough. I hated to disappoint the guys at the firm, but I was pretty sure I could get more from this girl than just a one-night stand. Something told me she wasn't a goer like that anyway.

"Lyssa," Crystal said, leaning over her sister. "Lyssa, Mom and Dad are on their way back. Can you hear me? Are you in pain?"

Lyssa didn't answer.

I placed my hand on Lyssa's forehead. It was not warm.

"She doesn't seem to have a fever," I said. Cocooning her into her blanket, I adjusted it around her arms so it wasn't tugging on her IV. "Now that looks nice and neat, doesn't it?"

"Why are you treating her like she's your sister?" Crystal asked. "You've only just met her tonight. It's almost like you're some kind of guardian angel or something."

"I've always wanted a little sister," I told her. "But all I got was a lit'l breather."

"I'm sorry, but the way you've said a few things tonight, it just sounded weird. Could you say that last part again?" Crystal asked.

"I said 'all I got was a little brother,'" I repeated.

"No, you said it with an accent. You said 'breather.'"

Oh no. I'm too tired to hide it.

"I did?" I asked, hoping to change the trajectory of this conversation.

"Are you from England?" she asked with a happy look on her face. She looked as if I had just told her she won the lottery.

"Wow," I said. Couldn't hide the lot from this one. The accent seemed to impress her, like it did most women. Couldn't use it every day because people tended to ask too many questions. I'd figure out an angle for Crystal later, when I was not so groggy. "You guessed it right. Most people say Boston."

"No, you're definitely from England. It's kind of a relief, actually. Explains why you're always wearing soccer clothes. But I can't tell where in England. It sounds northern, but your As are weird."

How long has she been listening to my pronunciations?

"I'm from Durham," I told her, praying she hadn't been there before. How did she pick up on that? Her intuition was a bit frightening. "Have you ever been to England?"

"I've only been to London, Manchester, and Haworth," she said. "But, please, go on with your story. You and your brother were 'in hospital' . . ."

Shit. She picked up on that, too.

"The accident happened in London," I said. "Unfortunately, my brother didn't make it."

"I'm so sorry," Crystal said, putting her hand on my shoulder.

"Thanks. It's still hard for me to talk about. My mom's car ended up in the Thames. We were taken to the Queen's hospital straight away. My mum used to be a nurse. Long story short, the Queen's doctor was on his way out for the day. When he saw my mom, he agreed to help. He brought me back to life again. My spleen was removed and I have a huge, embarrassing scar down the front of my bloody chest."

Lifting my shirt, I ran my finger down the line of pale, melted skin, now hidden by the black hairs on my stomach. "Mum said my eyes even lost a shade of blue."

I could tell she was captivated by my story. I couldn't take my eyes away from hers. Crystal was listening to me so intently, she hardly noticed a doctor entered the room.

"Hello," said a tall blond man in a raspy voice. He was holding Lyssa's chart and his white duster hung open over his blue scrubs. "So, I hear you've got pain in your abs."

He was talking about Lyssa, but he was looking at Crystal. An attractive man, early forties, no wedding ring. Damn. Do I have competition already?

"Yes, doctor," said Crystal. "What are you going to do?"

The doctor went 'round to Lyssa's right leg, lifted it up, and smacked the bottom of her heel the same way I had. Crikey! Couldn't have planned that any better, could I? Lyssa curled up in pain, wailing.

"We need to get her into surgery right away," said the doctor. "Her appendix is about to explode."

Crystal shot a glance at me as if she'd just discovered I was Superman. Angie came into the room and wheeled Lyssa back out into the hallway. I put my arm around Crystal's shoulders and led her out of the room. We started to follow, but the nurses told us to go back to the waiting room. Surgery would last about an hour if things went well. They would come get us when they were finished.

"There's not much we can do now except wait," I said. "You must be starving. Should we go and get some food?"

"I'm not hungry, but I would love some coffee," Crystal said, staring down at the floor as she walked.

"Well, you know Denny's has the best worst coffee," I said, trying to be funny. It didn't work.

She leaned on my shoulder as we left the hospital. I felt invincible. I wanted to be everything to her. I wanted to absorb her warmth, her strength. She should belong to me.

3

CRYSTAL

July 5, 1998

I WOKE UP IN DUNCAN'S BEDROOM AS IF AN INTERNAL ALARM HAD SUDDENLY GONE OFF INSIDE ME. It was daylight. I needed to get back to the hospital. How long have I been asleep?

"Hey, Sleeping Beauty. How was your catnap?" said Duncan, who entered with a coffee mug and some toast. He set the mug down on a cheap wooden rolltop desk that was pushed up against one of the four white walls of the room I found myself in.

"What time is it?" I asked. "When did I fall asleep? How long have I been here?"

"Whoa! Calm down, Crystal," said the handsome, broad-shouldered guy who towered over me. "It's only two o'clock. Your sister's only been out of surgery for maybe an hour." Duncan sat down on the bed's gray side panel. "Do you want me to take you back to the hospital?"

"No, thanks," I replied. "My car is here. I'll be fine."

Duncan reached for the coffee and put the plate of toast down on the floor in front of me.

"Was this a waterbed?" I asked. The frame of the bed had gray padding like the edges of a waterbed, but it was a regular king size mattress. There was no headboard, which I also thought was strange.

"I've had this bed forever. I love how low it is to the ground, but I wanted a regular mattress," he said, touching the padded side panel.

"What happened to the headboard?" I asked.

"I didn't like it, so I just took it off," said Duncan.

"Oh," I replied.

Duncan took hold of my hand, interlaced his fingers in mine, and led me out of the room. I followed him down the small hallway to a Berber-covered staircase. I wanted him to slow down so I could see the rest of his house, but I didn't want to appear overly curious. The fact that all the doors were shut made me wonder what was behind them. Bedrooms? Bathrooms? Closets?

As we headed down the narrow staircase, a ferocious-looking black cat was unraveling the Berber with her claws. The panther-like creature paused from her project long enough to show me her wide face and cold green eyes.

"Careful," said Duncan. "That's Luscious."

"Oh, I love cats," I said, bending down to offer a peaceful greeting.

"I wouldn't do that if I were you."

"Why not? Animals love me."

"That's no ordinary animal."

I got the feeling he was right, and I left the cat alone.

The downstairs living area had very little in the way of furniture. Like the upstairs, it was painted all white.

This must be what a bachelor pad looks like, I thought.

I had seen boys' apartments in San Diego, but those were college guys. This was a real single-family house owned by a real adult. It smelled like old people though.

A tiny bistro table sat in the dark kitchen on a linoleum floor. The cabinets were a flimsy, dark wood. Duncan led me through the tiny kitchen out to the garage.

Duncan's garage was a playground of tools, auto supplies, and out-of-place gardening equipment stacked next to a washer and dryer. Amazingly enough, Duncan managed to squeeze in two automobiles and his motorcycle with room left over to walk between them.

I had seen his hunter-green car at the office before, but hadn't recognized its make. As I passed by it, I slowly leaned over, trying to read the cursive lettering on the rear right side of the trunk. Alfa Romeo. What the heck was that? I wanted to get a better look at the blue muscle car, but I needed to get back to the hospital.

"Listen, thanks for everything you did last night," I said, finding it difficult to get in my car and leave.

"You're welcome," said Duncan. He stood close to me and put his hand on the corner of the open car door. "I know you would do the same for me. Your sister and her friends were really nice to me at the party. You know, the party you didn't invite me to." He laughed.

I felt awkward. He seemed so grounded—a cinder block you could tether a kite to in a hurricane. I lingered.

"Seriously, though, I hope your sister is doing better. I've always wanted a little sister; you should take good care of her. I know you will. You're a great sister. I can tell."

An awkward pause passed between us.

"Well, listen, drive safe, and if you need anything, you know how to reach me."

I nodded, but I really didn't know how to reach him. Before driving away, I told him I would see him at work the next day. A small part of me, a part I didn't want to acknowledge, wanted to see him before then.

The hospital looked different in the daylight. As my body walked back into the emergency room, my mind wandered somewhere else. The thought of Duncan's calming voice and gentle touch stayed with me.

An old pear-shaped lady stood behind the front desk. I gave her Lyssa's name and she pointed me toward the elevator at the end of the shiny white hall. My sister had been moved to a recovery room on the second floor.

When I found her room number, I pushed open the wide brown door and saw my mom standing at the foot of Lyssa's bed. Crap. When did she get here? Does she know I was in a guy's house by myself?

A middle-aged doctor, different from the one last night, stood on the other side of the bed with his hands holding the stethoscope hanging around his neck. Lyssa, still pale, was awake.

"You're alive!" I said and leaned over to plant a kiss on her forehead. "Thank goodness. If you had died, they would never have left me in charge of the house again."

I stayed leaning over Lyssa and whispered to her softly so my mom couldn't hear. "Duncan is my angel."

Then, I turned around and hugged my mom. She looked exhausted.

My mom and I have the same dark brown, almost black hair.

Hers used to be long and wavy like mine, but my dad made her cut it short and bleach it blonde. The lighter color made her look younger, though. I always wondered what she would look like if she'd left it alone. Her dark eyebrows had high arches and her lips were beautifully thick, like Angelina Jolie's.

As I stood facing her, I realized we were currently the same height and almost the same weight. She kept going on and off these crazy diet plans. Her pale blue pantsuit hung from her frame, and she wore a silk scarf under the collar of her blazer. Her face held full makeup at all times. Today was no exception, even though she probably hadn't slept in two days.

"The doctor was just telling me how she barely made it into surgery before her appendix exploded," Mom said, on the verge of tears. "I couldn't get here fast enough. Your dad is still at the hotel. He can't leave until he finishes his business meetings. Are you okay? Have you eaten?"

The doctor made some notes on a clipboard, smiled at my mother and me, and quietly left the room.

"I've eaten, so let me go get some food for you," I said.

"Wanna see my scar?" Lyssa's scratchy voice caught us both off-guard. "He said you won't be able to see it if I'm wearing a bikini."

My stomach turned as she peeled back the oozing white bandage to reveal a thick incision with Frankenstein-sized stitches. It looked gross. I suddenly felt horrible for thinking she was drunk when she crawled out of our parent's bedroom.

"Lyssa, don't do that," my mom ordered. "We want it to heal properly, so just leave it alone. How many pain meds did they give you? You're talking nonsense, sweetheart."

There was a knock at the door and I could hear Tiffany's high-pitched voice.

"Heeey," she said, pushing the door open.

I had completely forgotten she even existed. Seeing

her reminded me of how long ago I had left our house for the hospital.

"How's my girl?" Tiffany asked. She was wearing the same red halter-top and jean miniskirt from the night before.

Lyssa smiled for the first time, and I breathed a sigh of relief. I know I'm hard on her, but I honestly don't know what I would do without her.

Since my parents are not close to their siblings, my sister and I never became close with our cousins. Every vacation and holiday was just the four of us. My sister was my only companion. If we didn't want to hang out with Mom and Dad, then we had to hang out with each other. We explored train stations in Germany and walked to every cheese shop in France. Sometimes we had to share a bed while traveling, which was fine until Lyssa hit twelve years old and her legs shot out like beanstalks. After that, there was no room in the bed for the both of us.

"Did that hottie Duncan guy bring you guys here last night? I didn't see him when I left your house this morning," said Tiffany.

This girl needed to shut her trap immediately.

"Who's Duncan?" asked Mom.

"Duncan's just a guy from work, Mom," I said.

"He wasn't at the house while we were gone, was he? You know the rules."

Tiffany, Lyssa, and I exchanged glances, biting our lips.

"Well, is he as cute as that doctor?" Mom asked. "He was checkin' you out, Crystal."

"Honestly, Mom, I don't even remember what the doctor looks like," I replied.

"Duncan's the guy she talked to all night while I was dying," Lyssa piped in. "Everyone's paying more attention to Crystal, and I'm the one who just had surgery."

"You heard us?" I asked, truly surprised.

"Every word," Lyssa replied with a mischievous grin.

"Crystal," my mom said, grabbing my chin gently with her hand. "If Lyssa needs to be here overnight, I'll have you bring me a change of clothes later."

"But, Mom—" I interrupted.

I knew what Lyssa had overheard and I was positive she was going to tell our mother. The two of them would always gang up on me when it came to my dating life. I stopped trusting my sister with private information when I was fourteen years old.

One evening, I came home from swim practice and found them both reading my diary out loud to each other, laughing hysterically. My sister had discovered it and gave it to my mom under the pretense that I was breaking curfew and writing about it. I think they both made up that excuse so they could make fun of my boy troubles.

"No buts," my mom barked. "Just go. I'll call the house later."

As I left the room, I thought about how quickly I had gone from feeling like an adult to feeling like a child again. How can a guy like Duncan ever take me seriously if my family keeps reducing me to a teenager every time I'm around them? And why do I care so much about what he thinks?

4

DUNCAN

July 25, 1998

Bugger! Humidity's making my hair stick up again. Didn't want to look like a poof on my date with Crystal. I'd even taken the time to shave again, right before leaving to pick her up. Something told me she didn't like facial hair, not even a little. If this was going to work, everything had to be just right.

Despite the moisture in the air, it hadn't rained in weeks, which was great for the Cutlass and the Alfa. I bought the Alfa two years ago from my best friend, Drew, even though it was a rebuilt title. I hated owning cars that everyone else had. I hated owning anything that everyone else had. Maybe this was why I was drawn to Crystal. The more unique, the better, no matter how expensive.

Since I needed something a little posher in my collection, I chose to buy the Alfa from my car buddy, Drew. Crystal seemed to be impressed by this car when she saw it, so I thought I would use it on our first date. I pulled into her parent's driveway and closed the sunroof. I took my cell phone from the center console and noticed a piece of lint caught under the leather. I delicately removed it and opened my door to throw it out. I believed organization and cleanliness to be signs of self-respect. Cars also performed better when they were well looked after. Nothing on or in the Alfa was ever out of place.

As I approached their front door, I realized their home was actually a duplex. The vaulted roof was split down the middle inside and formed two small townhomes. The fragrance of Crystal's perfume lingered near the front door. Her mother answered the bell.

"Hello, Mrs. Vargas," I said, using my best Northern British accent. The cat was already out of the bag with Crystal, and mums always liked this accent anyway. British accents denote manners, better ones than these American wankers display.

"Hello, Duncan. It's nice to meet you."

As she leaned over to open the screen door, Crystal ran up, pushing past her mom and the partially-open screen door.

"Bye, Mom," yelled Crystal, darting past me. "See you later. Don't wait up."

Crystal was wearing low-cut jeans and a white tank top with a coral necklace. She had straightened her hair and wore very little in the way of makeup. She was breathtaking.

"Ready to go?" Crystal asked me. Her perfect white teeth made her smile look even brighter.

"Only if you are, sweetheart," I said, not sure what was going on here. "Nice to meet you, Mrs. Vargas. Lovely home."

"Please, call me Donna. It was nice to meet you, too, Duncan. Don't keep her out late. She has to get up early tomorrow."

She closed the screen door and I turned to catch up with Crystal, who was almost running to my car.

"Here," I said, jogging around to the passenger side door. "I insist on getting the door for you."

She giggled like a child and bowed in a mock curtsy. Manners were one of the easiest ways to a second date. Americans, on the whole, were lazy and clueless about civilized culture. All I had to do was pull out a chair or open a door, and chicks thought I was a knight in shining armor. Slip in a British accent at the right time, and they practically tore their clothes off in front of me.

"So, where are we going?" Crystal inquired, studying the inside of the car.

"I took the liberty of booking a table at a small bistro in Winter Park."

I opened up the sunroof and started up the air conditioning. I knew it would seem silly to have the sunroof open, but I liked the feeling of the wind in my hair, even if I had to burn through some extra air conditioning.

"Winter Park?!" Crystal said with a hint of panic. "Am I dressed okay?"

I used the invitation to look her up and down again. Her curves were perfect. I was guessing a C-cup, but without the big American butt that usually went with it.

"It's more about how you carry yourself than what you're wearing. But, yes, you look great."

She was in amazing shape, like an athlete, but still slender. Girls that beautiful could wear anything anywhere.

I turned onto Highway 17-92 and hit a red light. It felt too quiet in the car. Most girls would have told me their life story by now. I wanted to start up the conversation, but I couldn't decide which cover story would impress her the most—the one about my motorcycle, the hotel my parents used to own in England . . .

"What CD are you listening to?" she asked, interrupting my thoughts.

"You can change the music if you want. I have more than a

hundred CDs in a leather-bound case behind your seat there."

I reached for the button to eject the CD, but she had already found it. The CD slowly backed its way out of the black dashboard and into her hand.

"The Police? The whole CD? What is this, a time machine?" laughed Crystal. "You should at least put your favorites on a mixed CD. I mean, don't get me wrong, I absolutely love '80s music, but the whole *Outlandos d'Amour* album? A bit much, don't you think?"

Parallel parking in front of the restaurant on Park Avenue was a must. I only saw three Mercedes, one of which was a black SLK. An Audi TT sat next to a 740 BMW, blue with gray interior. Tacky. My Alfa, while not as expensive as these, certainly looked just as posh. People always stopped to examine the unfamiliar Italian emblem on the grille.

Winter Park itself was a status symbol. The brick street was lined with locally owned boutique shops; there was a public park on the north end next to the train tracks and cafes on the south end near the Rollins campus. During the spring and summer, most of them opened their doors, allowing for dining al fresco on the sidewalk. It made for great people watching, which was one of my favorite pastimes. I would sit outside with a beautiful woman, a blonde if possible, when I came here.

Occasionally, a Lamborghini or Ferrari would cruise by or park in front of one of the restaurants. The men driving those cars always stared at the woman seated next to me because I always got the pick of the litter.

"Duncan!"

I looked up and saw the restaurant owner, Alfredo, coming out to greet us. He was a little round man wearing a white button-down shirt and black bow tie. He extended both his arms to me as we passed the hostess stand. He gave me one of his firm handshakes and a smile.

"So good to see you," said Alfredo. "And who is this lovely signorina with you this evening?"

Alfredo knew I brought a different girl here almost every weekend, but he never slipped. Italians. They could pull it off—the cars, the women, the restaurants. I just didn't like how fat they all became as they aged.

"Your table, sir. Enjoy your evening."

Perfect, the small table in the back by the piano. A white lattice behind the piano was covered in ivy and white Christmas lights. If I knew Crystal's type, and I was confident I did, she would think all this was so romantic.

Pulling the small dark wooden chair out from under the white linen-draped table, Alfredo revealed the long-stemmed red rose awaiting Crystal on the seat.

"This is for me?" Crystal picked up the flower and buried her nose in the bud.

I slipped twenty dollars into Alfredo's palm and watched as Crystal smiled and took her seat.

"I can't believe you know the owner. That's so cool," she cooed as she reviewed the menu.

Her nails were short, manicured, no polish. Her hair looked completely natural as well, no styling products or hair clips. Natural girls were so much lower on the maintenance scale, but it was harder to buy them expensive things when you were trying to make up with them. She reached into her pocketbook and emptied two small white pills into her palm.

"Oh, are you sick?" I asked. Crystal didn't strike me as one to openly down happy pills on a first date.

"Some would say . . ." said Crystal. She didn't look up before popping the pills in her mouth and drinking from her water glass.

"Mind if I ask what's wrong?" I inquired.

"It's Zoloft. I'm taking antidepressants. My doctor put me on them when I lost the motivation to eat."

"You look fine to me," I told her. I had no idea what Zoloft was, but I was sure she did not need to put on any weight. "Besides, I don't believe in those kinds of doctors. You should stop taking pills. You're fine." I imagined her sitting next to me at company parties, smiling, looking cute and thin and young.

"Is that your professional diagnosis, doctor?" Crystal teased. "Oh wait, you were pre-med, but you changed your mind. Guess I'll listen to my real doctor for now."

Had I said that? That was brilliant of me. Not true, exactly, but brilliant of me to say at the time. I saw that heel trick in a movie once. Still can't believe it actually worked.

"Crystal, not that I'm not entirely grateful to be sitting here with you, but what made you change your mind about me? When we first met at the office, you never spoke more than two words to me, and one of those words, if I recall correctly, was 'dork.'"

"What you did for my sister the night of the party was . . ." Her voice went quiet. "No one I've ever dated has treated her like that, like she was his own sister. I know you said you always wanted a sister of your own, but it was more of the way you stayed with me the entire night. You never even thought of leaving us at the hospital by ourselves. Even after I didn't officially invite you to my party and I treated you like crap around the office, you still acted like an angel that night. I know I called you a dork to your face at the office, but that's not at all how I really felt, especially after that night at the hospital."

I reached out across the table and put my left hand on Crystal's right hand.

"And, there's one other thing. It's silly though." Crystal smiled and sheepishly tucked her hair behind her left ear.

"What is it?" I asked.

"I've always had a thing for guys with British accents. We traveled there a lot when I was growing up, and I had a feeling

I was meant to be with one of those guys. Not some dumb American guy. They are so uncultured."

My cell vibrated in my pocket. I took it out and looked at it. I wanted her to see that I had the latest technology, a Motorola flip phone. Maybe she'd be impressed if she thought it was the office. I turned it off and looked up at her.

"Did you need to answer that?" she asked.

"No."

"Why not?"

"You're beautiful." The words came out before I was conscious of them. She and I would make a handsome couple. We both had dark hair and light eyes. I stood about six inches taller than her.

"What?" She looked as surprised as I felt.

"I said you're beautiful. Or don't you know it yet?"

"Does that mean you accept my apology?"

"No apology necessary, Crystal," I said and reached for her hand across the table. "You are right about a lot of things regarding me. I am arrogant. And I am a dork, truly."

The waiter came to take our order, and I let Crystal order first. She asked for a house wine and a Caesar salad. I always got lamb if they had it, along with a Jack and Coke. When our drinks came, she asked if she could have a sip of mine. I knew she was twenty-two, but for the moment, she seemed younger. More innocent.

The date was going better than I had anticipated, so I took the liberty of ordering dessert. Tiramisu, one with two spoons. It was still early when we finished dinner, and Crystal wanted to walk down to the Rollins College campus. I had always wanted to see what the inside of that chapel looked like, so we agreed to head that direction.

"Oh, I almost forgot something."

I went to my car to put away my sunglasses. These were $300

Oakleys, and I didn't want to forget them somewhere. I took the hard case from the glove compartment, unzipped it, and took out the black sock. Gently sliding the glasses in the sock, I placed them back into the hard case and properly placed that back into the glove compartment. It was a small glove box, so the case had to fit in at just the right angle. Then I locked the car and we were off.

Just as we reached the campus, the heavens opened and it started pouring. We rushed up the steps to the chapel doors, only to find them locked. Too tired to make a run for it, we sat under the portico, just out of reach of the heavy sheets of warm rain.

"How strange," said Crystal. She pulled her hair back into a ponytail, using the black rubber band that never seemed to leave her wrist. "It's been dry as a bone for weeks and now it's monsooning. I'm so glad my Florida summer rain is back."

"You're the only person I know who likes this rain," I said. "You're the only person I know . . . fill in the blank, Crystal. You're not like a lot of girls I know."

She laughed, flattered, but a little embarrassed or unsure what to say.

"Sorry you didn't get to see the inside of the chapel," she said. "It's really pretty."

"Oh, you've seen it before?" I asked.

"Yeah, I took a tour of the campus when I was looking at colleges," said Crystal. "I really wanted to go here, but my parents made me go to a Christian college. And they wouldn't let me live off campus, so I had to find a place with on-site housing."

"Sounds pretty strict," I said.

"You have no idea," she said. "They do have an MFA program here. I was thinking about applying."

"At the risk of sounding stupid, what is an MFA?" I asked. "Sorry, I'm only familiar with engineering degrees."

"It's a Masters in Fine Arts, the highest level for creative writing," she said.

I could tell this was important to her.

"You should go for it," I said. "There's nothing stopping you now, right?"

"Well, besides money," she said with a laugh.

"I'll help you with that," I offered. I wasn't even sure why I said it.

"Really?" she glowed. Her smile was breathtaking. "I mean, I would pay you back . . ."

I wanted to kiss her. The rain was slowing down and I reached for her hand, but then stopped. I looked at her and got lost in those green eyes.

"You're beautiful, Crystal." I heard the words come out before I could filter them. "I would do anything for you."

She let out a light-hearted laugh.

Great, I thought. I've made a fool of myself.

"There it is again. Your accent is coming out. Why do you hide it?"

"It only comes out when I'm tired or I've had a bit to drink. The guys at work teased me about how I pronounced things. I got tired of them asking me to say 'schedule' or 'petrol', so I just started talking like them and eventually they left me alone. There are a couple of your words I still can't say, though, like 'water'."

She laughed.

"See! That's what I'm talking about."

"No, I'm not laughing at your British pronunciation. I'm laughing at your attempt at an American way of saying it. You sound like a drunk John Wayne."

I leaned back and gave her my best contorted facial expression. "Whale, howdy there, little laddie. How's about a cup o' cold wauder?"

"Oh, that's terrible, Duncan! Please stop."

"Well, they're your Western films, not ours. I can't help it if they're terrible."

We finished laughing and sat there staring at each other until it became almost uncomfortable. She curled her knees up to her chest and looked out at the curtain of rain bordering the chapel's archway where we sat.

"Actually, my pa really likes Westerns. They're part of what makes your country so great, you know."

"I do know. That's what I don't like about American guys. They have no appreciation for what this country is all about and what it offers those of us who are fortunate enough to be born here."

"I couldn't have said it better myself. The guys I . . . I mean, we work with, they have so many opportunities, and they don't even know it. If they earned the same salary in the UK as they do here, they could not afford to drive new cars or own homes at their young ages. Two of the guys in my department just went in together and bought a four-bedroom home in Lake Mary."

"Well, you own your house," said Crystal. "That's pretty good for a twenty-six-year-old guy."

"You're not like most girls your age," I told her, truthfully. "Hell, you're not like most girls my age, certainly not like the other pretty ones."

"I've been fortunate enough to learn that success in life is great, but only half as great if you don't have the right person to share it with. Being with somebody who knows the world is bigger than they are is important to me. It's always been my dream to travel and see parts of the world I haven't been to yet . . ."

"Oh, I can show you places you've never seen."

"Oh my gosh, really, where? Like in England? Scotland? Africa?"

"Africa? Why would you want to go there?"

"Because I want to go everywhere."

I took her face in my hands and pulled it close to mine. I looked her in her green eyes and told her exactly what she wanted to hear from me in that moment: "I will take you anywhere you want to go in a hot second."

"In a hot second," she repeated.

She smiled at me and I leaned in to kiss her.

We must have kissed for a while. The rain let up a bit and the mosquitoes began swarming about. As we headed back to the car, I grabbed her hand and wove my fingers in with hers, except for the pinky. That would be our thing, part of what made us special to each other.

5

LYSSA

July 26, 1998

CRYSTAL HADN'T LIVED AT HOME FOR FOUR YEARS. Yet, the minute she returned to the family dinner table, we all slipped right back into the same roles, like some kind of Tom Stoppard play set in suburbia. The topics changed, but the performances were the same. Mom always cooked the meals by herself. I set the table because it required the least amount of effort. Crystal usually cleaned everything up, and Dad didn't have to do anything, because he paid for the food on the table.

When I was in high school, the four of us always ate dinner together unless my dad was out of town, which was often.

"Are you coming with us or not?" my father shouted to Crystal across the dinner table, not looking up from his plate of meatloaf and macaroni.

"No," she said firmly. "I'm staying here."

"Does your mother know this?" he asked, shifting his gaze from his plate to his glass of iced tea.

"Yes," my mom answered for herself. "I said it was okay because sometimes her boss makes her work on the weekends."

The last weekend in July was quickly approaching, and my dad wanted us to go to Amelia Island for three days. Mom would have to start teaching in a few weeks. It was the last chance for a final family getaway.

"May I be excused?" I asked out of habit.

"No," Dad replied. "Finish your supper."

"I'm not hungry," Crystal said. She stood up and carried her full plate of meatloaf to the sink and let it crash into the other dishes there.

"Can I please be excused?" I asked again, looking across our small round kitchen table.

"Tony, why do you do that?" Mom said.

"Do what, Donna?" Dad shot a look at my mom and put his fork down on the table. The corner of his left collar was curled under a bit on his gray golf shirt. I was surprised Mom let him leave the house like that.

"Push her away," my mom retorted, still picking away at her dinner.

"I'm not pushing her away," he countered. "She's the one who doesn't want to spend time with us. Those pills are not making her act any better. She doesn't even finish her plate."

The phone rang like a bell signaling the end of round one. I ran to pick it up. It was Tiffany. I told her to hang on while I went upstairs. I snuck out of the kitchen, clutching the cordless phone under my arm.

"She's an adult now, Anthony," said my mom, now clearing the rest of the plates from the table. "She can make her own decisions."

My parents were going to keep fighting about Crystal; they no longer cared if I left the dinner table. Everything was always about Crystal.

"It's just one weekend, honey," my dad said emphatically. "I thought she loved the beach."

Mom turned on the faucet and began washing the dishes.

I was safely out of the war zone and walking up the stairs.

A loud clink of dishes joined the sound of the running water. Dad must have thrown his dish in the sink like a toddler throws down a toy that's bored him.

"Well, just as long as she's not staying home so she can hang out with that Duncan character—whom, by the way, I have yet to meet," my dad continued. "When she was in high school, the rule was that the boy had to pick her up here so we could meet him. When did that change?"

I stood frozen at the top of the stairs. I placed one hand on the railing, barely breathing as I listened. Whenever my parents started to argue, I gave my dad until the count of five before he left the room, hung up the phone, or slammed the door. He always had an award-winning exit and an epic period of silent treatment would follow.

"She's not in high school anymore, Anthony."

Five.

"That doesn't mean we can't hold her to the same rules."

Four.

"Her apartment will be ready in less than a week."

Three.

"What are you going to do, Tony?"

Two.

"Make it a rule that she come with us to the beach for a weekend?"

One.

"While she's under my roof, she'll go by my rules. And

that's final!"

SLAM.

The sound of my parents' bedroom door slamming shut downstairs gave me a slight jump, even though I knew it was coming.

I tiptoed toward my room and noticed Crystal's door was slightly open. She was face down on her bed, crying.

"Hey, Tiff, can I call you back?" I hung up the phone and knocked on my sister's door until opened all the way.

"Hey, Crys, can I borrow some clothes?" I asked. I felt like I needed a reason to enter.

We used to steal each other's clothes so much that when she left for college, we went out and bought duplicates of our outfits so we wouldn't have to part ways with anything we loved.

"I forgot how much I hate living at home," said Crystal. "I'm just glad the Bible says to honor your father and mother, but nothing about having to love them as well."

She rolled over and stared at the ceiling. I started looking through her clothes, which were now hung neatly in her closet. She noticed I had the cordless phone from downstairs and rolled her eyes.

"Is that thing surgically attached to your body?" she said.

"No, but my appendix was and that's gone now, thanks to you."

"I did not rupture your appendix."

I pulled out a black tube top and started trying it on. It didn't look as good on me as it did on her. I had no boobs to hold it up. I started to try on something else.

"What are you looking for exactly?" she barked.

"Did you and Duncan have sex?" I asked. I was dying to know. We never talked about this kind of stuff. We always seemed to be within earshot of Mom and Dad in this small townhouse.

"I can't believe you just asked me that," Crystal complained. "If we don't talk about it in this house, it doesn't happen, remember?"

"Then there is a lot that doesn't happen," I replied, now picking through Crystal's shoes on the closet floor. "Remember when we weren't allowed to say 'butt' or we would get in trouble? Ha!"

"So many rules to break," Crystal said laughingly.

"So little time," we both said in unison, as we had said so many times before.

I wobbled over to the bed in some high heels and fell down next to my sister. She sat up next to me and I pulled her hair around to the front of her neck.

"Look, Crys, please don't waste your time on this guy. He's a poseur. He dates girls like that Tina chick who works in your office. He's not even your type."

There was an awkward silence. I wanted to tell her that sex was not all it's cracked up to be, but I didn't know if she already knew that yet. I wasn't sure if I should bring up what happened to me in the back seat of Duke's car while he and his girlfriend were inside at prom. I was drunk and didn't even remember the guy's name. Josh, maybe.

"Have you had sex?" asked Crystal. "You know, since, what happened."

It was like she was inside my head.

"I don't get what all the hype is about, so don't get your expectations up."

Another awkward moment passed.

"It's good that you waited, Crys," I said. "I wish I'd had that chance."

Crystal reached over and hugged me. I hugged her back and closed my eyes. A small tear ran down my left cheek and I tried to wipe it away before she sat back and could see it. I didn't want her getting all upset. She felt responsible for every bad thing that happened to me, even though she would never admit it.

We both took deep breaths and smiled at each other.

"So, tell me, honestly, why do you hate Duncan so much? He may have saved your life. He stayed with you at the hospital." Crystal had grabbed a small white throw pillow and curled up with it tucked in her lap.

"No, Crys," I said. I kicked off the heels and turned to face her. "He stayed with you at the hospital. He's trying to help himself. He didn't care about me. He only cared about impressing you." I grabbed the little white pillow from her lap and threw it into her face. "And what was with that weird accent anyway?"

"You heard that?" she said.

I stood up and reached for a cardigan from her closet. I didn't want to tell her how gullible she'd sounded that night. I couldn't figure out what it was about this guy that impressed her so much.

"I heard almost everything," I said. "So does Duncan know you're a virgin?"

"Yes, I spray painted it in the men's bathroom at the office so they would all know. Now, please get out of my room."

I reached for the jean skirt like a thief, stashed it under my arm, and bolted out. My sister and I were both expected to behave like good Christian girls, but it never took for me; I was pretty sure Crystal was just faking it, too.

Being raised by Christian parents can be a confusing experience. They don't drink. They don't curse. They don't smoke. But they seem to fight just as much as any couple who does. There were a lot of "thou shalt not" rules, especially for girls.

I stopped going to youth-group activities in high school because they were nothing more than continued gossip sessions from the cafeteria. My parents would drop me off in front of the church and pick me up a couple hours later. Luckily, the youth group was so big, no one noticed that I snuck off with one of my friends to smoke cigarettes at the Circle K down the street.

Once I was safely in my room, I closed the door. Our doors didn't have locks. Dad had them all removed. I threw Crystal's clothes on my bed and hit play on my little purple Conair stereo. My Backstreet Boys CD blasted across the room. Tiffany and I got to see them downtown last year in concert. She even got a kiss from Nick Carter. Personally, I thought Howie was cuter.

My sister was blaring Pearl Jam across the hallway. Her music was so depressing. I skipped to the song "Everybody" and turned the volume way up. I wondered if my parents could hear our music battle from downstairs. No one pounded on my door telling me to turn it down, so I let it play.

I stayed upstairs until I thought the entire house was asleep. Then I snuck downstairs to get some ice cream. Walking into the kitchen, I passed by my dad, who was walking out. We looked at each other for a split second, then looked away.

"You scared the crap out of me," I said.

"Don't use that kind of language," he replied.

"Good night," I said.

He kept walking without saying a word and slammed his bedroom door shut behind him.

"Yeah," I said to the closed door, "I love you, too."

6

CRYSTAL

July 29, 1998

DUNCAN AND I SAT ON A SMALL WHITE STONE BENCH IN THE MIDDLE OF MY MOTHER'S SIDE YARD GARDEN, SURROUNDED BY BRIGHT PINK IMPATIENS. We'd spent the whole weekend together at my parents' house while they were in Amelia Island. I wasn't looking forward to them coming back tonight.

"Why don't we just go now?" Duncan asked.

"You mean just get in the car and go?" I laughed.

"We both know we're meant to be together," he insisted.

"But we've only known each other a few weeks," I said, even though I loved the idea of running off with Duncan. It would make my dad furious. "Where would we go, silly? We don't have the money to fly to Vegas and there's nothing like that around here."

"Let's get married in the chapel at Rollins then," Duncan replied.

"Knowles Memorial Chapel?" I gasped.

He lifted my hand up and kissed the top of it while staring at me.

"Is that a yes?" he pleaded.

I tapped my fingers against my forehead. It was so hard to resist him when he used his accent. What would have been a monotone string of consonants and vowels from the lips of anyone else turned into an enchanting melody when he spoke.

"Please, join me, Crystal. I've never felt this way about anyone. I promise, I will never break your heart. I will never leave you alone. You will always have my full attention . . . I love you."

A quick clap of thunder caught us both off-guard. We looked up to the sky and got doused with a sudden downpour of rain that seemed to be limited to the surrounding garden. We didn't move.

I was soaking in what he told me. I wanted it so badly, my heart physically ached. He was offering me everything without holding back. I was ready to jump in with both feet. I was so tired of guys leaving me, or never fully being with me in the first place. If I married him, then he definitely couldn't leave me. The Bible said marriage was forever, and this was exactly how I wanted to feel, forever.

"Should we find cover?" Duncan asked, but the sun was still shining. It was like being in an outdoor shower with my clothes on. I loved it.

Neither of us moved. The raindrops gathered on our eyelids, spilling down over our faces until we looked like statues unaffected by time or weather. I grabbed my long blue skirt and, stepping up on bench, tilted my face upward toward the sky. I lifted up my arms and held them out like strong wings.

"What are you doing?" laughed Duncan.

"Drinking it all in!" I said.

Duncan pulled me down off the bench and swung around.

"Crystal, run away with me and be my bride."

I looked down into Duncan's pale blue eyes, rain dripping down from our foreheads. He was exactly who I always knew I would marry—someone who was more mature than the guys my age; someone with dark hair and blue eyes; and on top of it all, someone with a British accent and a mysterious past. And he was crazy about me like no other guy had ever been crazy—obsessed, can't-stop-looking-at-me crazy. I needed that most of all.

Why shouldn't I marry him? I knew I was only twenty-two years old, but I wasn't like other girls my age. I never had been. My parents' friends always said I had an old soul, as if I had been through one lifetime already. I didn't need an apartment or a job to make me feel mature. After living with almost 500 other girls in two different dorms over the last four years, I felt like I'd had all the independence I needed.

As a matter of fact, I thought it was better to get married young. More important to share a lifetime of memories with one person. If I waited until I was forty, then my life would be half over.

I had heard people talk about turning thirty and being settled in their ways and struggling to merge their lives with someone else's. Marriage at my age was definitely preferable. This way, Duncan and I could grow into our habits together, so they merged instead of competed. I really felt like I was ready to settle down. I still planned to travel a lot, but now I didn't have to do it alone. This was better.

I wrapped my arms around his neck. I could barely speak through my smile. "Yes! Duncan, take me away!"

He hugged my waist and began twirling me around.

"I love you so much," he said, still hugging me. "Why should we wait when we know right now that we want to be with each other for the rest of our lives?"

Duncan set me down on the ground and began kissing me with all his might.

"I love you, Duncan," I whispered in his ear. I couldn't wait to marry this man.

"Thank you, Crystal. I love you, too. Thank you."

A bolt of lightning cracked through the sky and we made a mad dash for the screened-in porch. My heart still pounding, Duncan took my face in his hands to emphasize the importance of what he was about to say.

"Crystal, you know that you'll always be safe with me, don't you?"

"Yes, I really feel that I am. Why?"

"I just wantcha to know that. It's very important to me." Duncan almost looked like he was going to cry.

"I know, Duncan. I know. Are you okay?"

"I've never been better. You've made me the happiest man alive. I just can't believe you love me so much. I can't believe we haven't known each other for very long, and yet it seems like I've known you since I was a lad," Duncan said, never taking his gaze away from mine.

"I know. I feel like I've known you since I was a lad, too."

He let out a laugh from his gut. "Crystal, you couldn't be a lad. You're a girl. You were a lass."

"I know. I was just trying to say I'm right there with you."

"Sure, right," he said and kissed my forehead. "Now, what do you say we get you into some dry clothes?"

"Honestly, I'm on such a high right now, I forgot I was wearing clothes."

"Well, we could fix that, too."

I raised myself on the balls of my feet and kissed him. Balancing myself by pulling on his shirt, I stopped kissing him but continued to look into his eyes. I began to unbutton his shirt from the top down, never lowering my feet, never losing my balance. Duncan backed away suddenly.

"What's wrong?" I asked.

"You've got superhero strength in your toes, and I've got an eighty-year-old man's knees. I can't even stand up right now. I feel like my legs are going to give out on me and my stomach is doing flips."

I pushed him backward into the wicker chaise lounge in the corner of the patio and peeled my saturated shirt from my skin. I loved that I could do this to guys. I left them gasping for breath while they lay on their backs and stared up with amazement. I always knew how far I could go physically with a guy without going all the way.

"Is that a tattoo?" Duncan asked as he stared at my shoulder.

"It's a dolphin. It's below the Northern Cross in the summer sky. I wanted a dolphin tattoo, but I wanted mine to be different from everyone else's. So, when I took astronomy in school, I saw this through my telescope and decided to get the six small stars that make up the constellation."

There was also nothing I loved more than being on the ocean at night. I wanted so badly to go on a cruise for my honeymoon. I wanted it more than I wanted a wedding dress or even a wedding. Some girls planned wedding days; I had been planning my honeymoon since I was sixteen years old.

"So, it's like a secret then, is it? I mean, nobody else would know that."

"It's also a secret because my dad would kill me if he found out I got a tattoo. He's still pissed about my belly button ring, and I got that done like four years ago."

"Did it hurt?" Duncan asked.

"The tattoo or the ring?" I looked down and gave my belly ring a little pull.

He winced. "Either? Both?"

"Nah, neither one hurt really. I have a pretty high tolerance for pain. I tore my knee up in high school. I had surgery on it and was back on my surfboard a few weeks later."

"You are so amazing, you know that? I've never met anyone so smart and talented."

I smiled and began kissing him. The rain continued outside, pouring down from the gutter like a mild waterfall. Humidity hung in the air, blanketing us in wetness. It had only rained twice so far that month, both times when Duncan and I were together. The lightning continued to flash around us and made the moment even more romantic.

The phone next to Duncan's non-waterbed bed frame rang loudly in my ear. The room was pitch black. I groped for a light switch in unfamiliar territory while the loud ring assaulted my ears again and again. Duncan leaned over me from the other side of the bed and picked up the receiver.

"Hello," said Duncan. "Who is this?"

I found the nightstand lamp and turned the light on. Duncan winced at the brightness. I glanced at the alarm clock. It was two o'clock in the morning.

"Ya, she's right here," Duncan said and handed me the phone. "It's your father."

I sat up straight, took a deep breath and then put the receiver to my ear, prepared to get an earful. And I did.

If I didn't come home this minute, I was going to be homeless, broke, and no longer his daughter.

Something in me snapped. I was done. Done with being treated like an irresponsible child. I didn't care if he really was going to throw all my clothes out on the lawn.

"I'll be home in the morning, Dad," I said, surprised at my own audacity.

"You'll be home now. You will apologize and you are not allowed to see Duncan again, or else."

"Or else what?" I almost laughed.

"Or else you can't come home at all."

He wasn't bluffing. I knew some families fight like this, but they made up a day later. My dad and his brother got into a fight in 1978 and hadn't spoken since. If I told him no, I would be exiled from the Vargas household.

I didn't need them anymore. I had a new refuge and I was going to make my own household.

"Then I guess I can't come home at all," I said. And then I hung up on him.

I would probably pay for that brazen move the rest of my life.

7

LYSSA

August 1, 1998

WHETHER THEY KNEW HER FOR A DAY OR A YEAR, BOYS WERE ALWAYS CHARMED BY CRYSTAL. When I was twelve years old, our family went to Cocoa Beach for a long weekend. Our dad had a speaking engagement at one of the hotels. As always, he combined a work trip with a family vacation. We stayed at a Hilton hotel on the beach, which was nice, but it wasn't anything fancy.

Crystal was swimming in the hotel pool. She wore a one-piece black bathing suit that had a thick Tarzan-style strap over one shoulder. A cute blond teenage boy came over to watch her as she practiced her back dives into the deep end of the pool. There was no diving board, so Crystal just stood on the side of the pool, and with perfect posture, she raised her arms straight above her head, cupped her hands together, and arched seamlessly backward into the water. She'd barely made a splash. That boy must have watched her for hours. She was as oblivious to her admirer as she was to her own beauty.

Even as she stood before me on her wedding day, she was more beautiful than she'd ever been and she still couldn't see it. I wanted to grab a mirror and hold it up before her and scream, "Look! Look how amazing you are! Look at what a big mistake you're making!"

Crystal's perfectly tanned skin was absolutely glowing against her white dress. It was the first dress we'd pulled off the rack at the store. It had a halter neck with a fitted waist and a princess-like full tulle skirt. Her long dark waves of hair were pulled up in a hundred little bobby pins, exposing her flawless back. I fluffed up the skirt and tucked the comb of the veil into the back of her bun.

Crystal didn't always have the greatest fashion sense, but she was always unique. Her prom dresses were red-carpet-discussion worthy. My favorite was the Cleopatra dress she wore to her senior prom. It had gold sequins in a half-moon shape under her neck. She never acted like hot stuff, but she was a hard act for a younger sister to follow. I didn't know if I was as much envious as I was proud. Proud, at least, until today.

I had a knot in my stomach as I stood next to Crystal, holding her white rose bouquet in the nave of the chapel. The cream arches leading up to the altar stood tall on each side like angels guarding us under their golden halos. I always thought I would be her maid of honor. Just not like this. We didn't even get our hair and nails done together today.

Yesterday, when I told Mom and Dad that Crystal and Duncan were eloping, I didn't think they believed me. They should have known better. I think their disapproval only fueled her insistence on doing this. Dad told her to have a nice life and Mom just cried for hours.

"Alright, Lyssa," said my mom as she looked at me with her fully made-up face. "What do you know about Duncan? Why are they getting married so fast? Is she pregnant?"

My father never chimed in. He paced back and forth, looking down at the kitchen floor. His face was bright red.

"Is she on birth control? And if so, who gave her birth control?" My mom drilled me relentlessly.

"I don't know any more than you guys do," I argued.

They'd finally given up when they realized I was as clueless about what Crystal was doing as they were. The only thing we could all agree on was that we didn't like this Duncan guy and we certainly didn't want her marrying him.

I told my parents that I couldn't quite put my finger on it, but something was definitely wrong about this guy. The way he talked to my sister in the hospital room was so cheesy and fake. His accent was weird. He was obsessed with his cars, but they weren't even cool cars. None of this fazed Crystal, though. She wanted to be with him. And when she put her mind to something, not even the National Guard could stop her.

"Your sister has always lived according to her own rules," Dad said. "If she makes this bed, she'll have to lie in it." And with that, he made his famous exit.

I didn't like what they were doing either, but I couldn't let her go through this alone. So, I decided to be there for her—a witness to the train wreck.

The minister who stood in front of Crystal and Duncan, reading their vows, was a rickety old man with bright white hair that was whipped back like cotton candy. He read from a small leather-bound Bible.

"Now," said the minister, "Duncan, will you repeat after me? I, Duncan, take thee, Crystal . . ."

Duncan wore an expensive dark suit and extremely shiny wingtip shoes. A million guys would have given anything to be with her—guys more deserving than the jerk she was marrying today. I couldn't even try to like him. Not after hearing him smooth talk her while I was laying in the hospital with my eyes closed. He was so phony. How could she not tell?

In the front row of ebony pews sat an old man and woman with hard features and tons of wrinkles. The man had a white beard and mustache. Like Santa, but angry. I could only assume those were Duncan's parents.

"Now," the minister continued, "Crystal, will you repeat after me? I, Crystal, take thee, Duncan . . ."

There were two large candelabras behind the minister. For a split second, I thought about knocking one of them over and making a run for it. Unfortunately, burning down a chapel probably wouldn't even stop her at this point. Her mind was made up.

"Duncan, will you place the ring on Crystal's left hand?" the minister said, turning toward the man to my sister's right.

Duncan slipped his hand into his jacket pocket and pulled out a platinum wedding band embedded with square diamonds. Everyone in the room leaned forward as he slid the band down her finger, resting it gently on top of her two-carat, princess-cut engagement ring. How did he get her a ring in two freaking days? And where did this guy get his money? There was no way engineers made enough to afford what he had.

"Crystal, will you place the ring on Duncan's left hand?" the minister asked, looking at Crystal, who then turned and looked at me.

"What?" I whispered.

"The ring," she whispered back. "I gave you the ring."

Oh crap, I thought. Crystal gave me one thing to do, and I had totally forgotten.

"One sec," I said and ran to get my purse.

"Here it is," I exclaimed, holding up the thick white gold band. I ran back to Crystal and she took it from my sweaty palm.

"Sorry," I whispered, but she didn't respond. Her trance-like state prevented her from noticing anything other than Duncan.

My dislike for him grew by the minute. He was ruining everything. Crystal and I were supposed to have adventures together after I graduated. We had it all planned out. We were going to stay with our friends in London, then visit our family in Denmark, maybe even stay with them all summer. Crystal could go with me to Paris, since I was fluent in French, and we would make friends all over Europe. Instead, Tiffany and I were going to France for her birthday, but I wanted to go with Crystal.

"You may now kiss the bride."

I couldn't look. Was it already over? Where was the part about "if anyone has a reason these two should not be married"? Did he skip that part?

An old woman in the back of the room hit the tape player, and the bridal march crackled from the cheap speakers. Crystal and Duncan kissed and my stomach churned.

"Can you please smile, Lyssa?" Crystal asked. "Let's get some pictures!"

"Isn't she just lovely?" The old woman from the front row came up and stood beside me. She had a slight British accent. "And don't they make a lovely couple?"

I just forced another smile.

"I'm Lyssa," I said, introducing myself. "Crystal's sister."

"Right you are, dearie. I'm Gale, Duncan's mother, pleasure to make your acquaintance."

She had an ugly cream-colored dress on and flat white shoes. Her white beaded purse looked like something a grandmother would carry. Her handshake was like a dead fish.

"Pleasure to meet you as well," I replied.

Crystal and Duncan stood at an antique writing table, signing papers with the minister. The angry little Santa man came up to me next.

"I'm Howard, Duncan's father," the man said with a Scottish accent. He was wearing a gray suit and dark blue tie. His teeth were very yellow.

"Hello," I said with another forced smile.

Wow. This wasn't awkward or anything.

"Well, we're going to get piss drunk," said Howard. "It's Scottish tradition that I treat."

Crystal bounced by us with a smile and wave, then headed out the door like she was running an errand and would be back in a few minutes. I didn't even get a hug.

Suddenly, I heard a shriek from outside. When I ran out the wooden, castle-like entrance in the back, I saw Crystal standing in front of a brand-new white convertible Mercedes with tan interior. Her dream car.

"You bought me this car!" screamed Crystal. "Oh my gosh! I love it! Thank you!"

"Nothing but the best for my wife from now on," said Duncan.

I stood there with my jaw on the sidewalk and waved like a stranger bon voyaging a crowd aboard a cruise ship. Duncan was spoiling and kidnapping my best friend, and there was nothing I could do to stop him.

Crystal turned and waved from the front seat. I had a feeling that was the last I would see of her for a long time.

8

DUNCAN

August 25, 1998

"Great news, Duncan," Chuck bellowed, leaning back in his Herman Miller chair.

I hated those bloody chairs. Didn't think they were nearly as comfy as the leather ones. I raised my eyebrows at him and ran my hand through my thinning hair. Chuck was more than ten years my senior and still had a head full of thick hair. Bastard.

"We got the Parson's account in Vancouver—and it's mostly electrical work, so that's big for you. Congrats!" Chuck beamed like an idiot.

Sod it! Five years I'd been at this firm and they had never tried to send me outside the country.

"Excellent," I said with a smile.

"We will need you to do the site inspection. You can choose

one guy from your team to go with you. We're also sending Mike from mechanical and Joe from fire protection and plumbing."

Chuck had the corner office and was the only one of the owners who had a window. Had to special order his stupid blinds. Even his credenza had to be purchased from an entirely separate catalogue. I knew this because I was smart enough to chat up the secretaries. They knew everything about everything at this firm.

"That's great boss, but, you know, I have been slammed with the Mercy Medical Center. Don't think I'll be able to make it. We can just send Doug."

I stood up straightaway to head out of his office before he could yap out another word. I didn't move quite fast enough.

"Mercy's only a one-time job, Duncan. This Parson's account is a multi-year, multi-million-dollar opportunity. And I'm pretty sure we got it because of your systems engineering fee proposal. They were impressed." Chuck leaned forward, smoothed down his tie and picked up the receiver on his desk phone. "Get your passport ready. You leave in a week."

I smiled and backed out of his door, closing it behind me. Got to find a way out of this one. As if it was not hard enough leading a team of eight guys who barely knew what they're doing. Now I'd been given a higher profile, higher risk assignment with completely new security codes. Damn it.

I passed by Doug's cubicle to see what he was working on. If I were to send anyone in my stead, it would be him. Each of the guys on my team had a separate cube. The carpeted walls were light gray and rather tall, since most desks had more than one monitor. I could easily see my team's row of cubes from my office door.

"Hey, Doug, how's it going?" I said and leaned in his entry-way, resting my arm lightly on the carpeted wall.

Doug was in his late twenties, sandy blond hair, slightly shorter than me with a bit of pudge around his belly.

"Hey, man, I was just coming to get you," said Doug as he rolled back from his monitor and pulled up some drawings. "I need you to sign off on this change order. We had to move a few outlets around because the architect forgot to put bathrooms on this floor."

"Really?" I asked.

"No, but I thought it sounded good. Just your typical changes. Nothing major."

Doug handed me a pen and I signed in the lower right-hand corners. When people see my signature, they think I'm a doctor. I used to practice doing my initials when I was project manager. I also practiced doing the other PMs' signatures.

"Cool, man. Thanks," said Doug.

"Sure thing," I said, handing him back his pen.

I had a couple of Montblancs in my office. I'd never let anyone use them except Chuck. If Doug were a little smarter, he'd get a special pen for me to use.

"Hey, listen, I need you to do me a favor. Remember that fee proposal I did for the Dubai account?"

"Yeah, man. That thing was huge," Doug said as his eyes widened.

"Well, long story short, we got it," I told him.

"No way! That's awesome."

"Yeah, so look, you've done such a great job with Mercy. And when we were in South Florida during the hurricanes, you really stayed calm under pressure and came through for the team."

"Just doin' my job, boss."

"Because you did such a great job, I want you to go on the site visit to their Vancouver location next week to kick them off."

Doug nearly fell out of his chair. "Seriously, the Parson's job?"

"Yes, seriously. But don't tell the other guys. I don't want to hurt their feelings. But you are the best man for the job. So, well done."

"Wow! Thanks! Hey, but what about wrapping up the Mercy job? I still owe them some drawings."

"Don't you worry about those. Just get your passport ready."

I shook Doug's hand and walked back into my office, shutting the door. Sweat marks stained the pits of my white shirt. All I wanted to do was go home, eat some Weetabix, and go to bed, but I made certain Chuck saw me working late.

When I eventually got home, Crystal was watching TV. Some kind of dinner food sat on a plate wrapped in foil. I wasn't hungry. Wished she'd go to another room so I could watch the telly in peace.

"Hey, Duncan," Crystal said, barely turning toward me. "How was work?"

"I don't want to talk about it. All I do all day is talk about work."

I put my briefcase in its place beneath the bar. I loosened my tie and grabbed the remote from Crystal's hand.

"Hey!" she whined. "I was watching a show."

"Let's find something we can both watch," I said. I started flipping through the channels and stopped on a football match.

"Very funny," she said. "So, Duncan, what do you think about getting a hotel room on the beach this weekend?"

"Nah," I said, not looking at her. "I gotta work this weekend."

"That stinks," Crystal said, getting up from the couch.

"What's your problem? Shouldn't you be in a good mood? You started your new job this week, right? How's the travel magazine?"

"It's great. I love it actually," Crystal said, taking something from the fridge. "Everyone is really nice and my boss is super cool."

"Ha, probably 'cause you haven't pissed him off yet." There

was nothing on TV. Maybe I'd put in a movie. "Get me a glass of milk, will you, darling?"

"What's that supposed to mean?" Crystal asked.

"It means you have a problem with authority, Crys. I give it four weeks before you have a problem with your boss."

"That's not true," Crystal shouted from the kitchen as she pulled the milk carton out of the door.

"Do ya have my milk yet, lass?" I got up and put a DVD into the five-disc changer on the wall.

"Coming," Crystal said as she brought my milk over and sat down.

"It's not in my frozen mug," I said. "You know that I keep a beer mug in the freezer? Don't you know what it's for by now? I'll give you a hint: It's not for beer."

"Oh, right. I'm sorry." Crystal got up and fixed her mistake. "By the way, I'm going out for drinks tomorrow after work with some friends."

"Fine. Just don't spend any money. Now, be quiet. I want to watch my movie."

Crystal put the mug down in my hand and walked upstairs. I thought I would get a moment of peace, but then Mum and Pa rolled in. I could hear them fighting in the garage before they even opened the door to the kitchen.

"It's your bloody fault!" said Mum. "If you hadn't ruined everything, we wouldn't be crowding up in this newlywed home. I don't feel comfortable living with a stranger now."

"Like ye' ever did anything to help," said Pa. "You cook dinners and drink too much wine. How does that help us any?"

"Well, it certainly wasn't my idea to burn down the bloody hotel!"

There was a pause, and then I heard a glass shatter on the kitchen floor. When I turned around, Mum came stomping through the rooms, arms folded with her angry face on. She didn't look at me. She just pounded her little feet up the stairs. I heard a door slam when she got to the top.

"Getch your arse back in here and clean this mess up, you old moo!" Pa yelled from the kitchen. He called Mum "old moo" even when he wasn't piss drunk. Sometimes he would call her "old moo," slap her bum, and kiss her on her cheek. Just his way of showing affection, I suppose.

"Clean it up yourself, your Royal Highness," Mum shouted back through the closed door upstairs.

Schtupid bloody parents. Don't know why they're being so loud. Pa could shout Scottish slang loud enough to wake the dead. Mum's short little Welsh comebacks were never as loud, but twice as mean.

"It were you who threw the bloody thing," said Pa.

I was going to duct tape their mouths shut if they didn't pipe down.

"What the hell are the pair of yer tryin' ta do?" I shouted from the couch. "Do ye' want the whole bloody neighborhood hearin' ya fight?"

I went into the kitchen and saw a mug shattered on the kitchen floor. Least it wasn't my mug. Mine woulda been more likely to dent the wall, since it was made out of stainless steel and all. I bought it after a friend had loaned me his camping mug. When I saw how fantastic the steel worked, I had to get my own. I loved my mug because it kept my tea hot at work. Two Red Rose bags, two heaps of two percent milk, and four or five spoonfuls of sugar. The perfect cup of tea. Couldn't start my day without it.

I grabbed a broom from the pantry and shoved it in front of Pa. "Stop yer screaming and clean it up. 'Less you want to go back ta livin' in yer bloody car."

"I'll kill myself before I do that again," said Pa.

"Suit ye'self, then. It's hard enough keepin' a low profile

'round here without the two a you blowin' a gasket."

It wasn't even eight o'clock and they were both already drunk as piss. Despite her fragile 5'3" frame, Mum could knock back a whole bottle of white zinfandel in a couple of hours. Pa went through cans of Natural Light like water.

Back when they had money to burn, they used to drink the good stuff. Now, they looked pathetic. I hated living with them. Couldn't turn them out in the street, though, them being my parents and all.

"I'm going for a smoke," grumbled Pa. For a little man, he was a big hard-ass. He could do something as simple as tuck his undershirt into his jeans and it looked like he was inciting a brawl.

"Keep your fags outta my garage," I shouted.

"Och, pish it up yer kilt," said Pa.

I wondered if he'd even heard me. I wanted to follow him and make sure he didn't get his stupid ashes near my Cutlass. I had to buy a car cover, they smoked so bleeding much out there. That damn smell got into everything.

Mum came back down to the kitchen and started whimpering after Pa was gone.

"I don't know why you let him get to you like that," I said.

"He's just a schtupid drunk now, your father is," she said and wiped the tears from her face. "He was never like this when we had money."

I helped her empty the trash bin. She put on her apron and started to make supper.

"Now then. What would you like? I was thinkin' of some bangers 'n' mash. Do ya think we have enough 'tatties?"

"Dunno, Mum. How would I know? You're the one who does all the shoppin'."

A little while later, I stepped out into the garage. Pa stood at the top of the driveway. He puffed away on a fag and stared out across the street at our neighbor's closed garage door. There was a single mom living there with her two daughters. Normally we don't talk with the neighbors, but she smokes and Pa had borrowed a few from her after one of the last hurricanes knocked power out to the whole shopping center and gas station in our area.

Pa was back to wearing jeans every day. Not the three-piece-suit gentleman I remembered from back home. Not having any work did that to a man. He'd never really gotten tangled up in the family business. He tried running an insurance racket when the tables went against him. Got away with a lot of it to an impressive degree. But when his brother wanted in and he wouldn't let him, the shit hit the fan. We had to come here, the hottest, stickiest city in America.

We lived in a quiet community, which was smart. Modest homes with big full oak trees lining the streets. Old people not bothering anybody. Neighbors thought I lived with my parents when it was actually the other way around. Didn't bother to correct people on it, though. Fewer questions that way.

"How's work, Pa?" I asked, coming out into the garage from the kitchen.

"Can't find enough of it, son. I'm gettin' old. Labor's too hard to do by me'self. Yer neighbors are cheap. I went to install a new sink and cabinetry in Ms. Woolfson's downstairs bathroom. She wouldn't gimme the advance to buy the crap from Home Depot."

"Their kids have money," I said. "Her oldest is a doctor. Drives a brand-new Mercedes."

"Children don't care for elders here in the States like they do at home," said Pa.

He tossed his fag into the street and lit another one before it hit the ground.

"Listen, Pa, don't lose your temper when Crystal's around, alright? This isn't like home where you can knock a woman around and nobody gives a shit."

"Go piss yourself," he said and stared down a red Mustang that drove by.

"Seriously, Crystal is different, Pa. You say one wrong thing to her and I'll give you such a shiner that Mum won't recognize you."

"You just try it, son," he joked and turned around. He pretended to jab me in the belly. "She's a U.S. citizen, right? That should be enough. It's not like the INS is coming after anyone who isn't a Mexican working the back kitchen anyway."

"Did you ever think I may actually love someone? You ever think about that?"

"You? Ha! That's a pisser," Pa laughed. "Is her family wealthy?"

"I don't think so. Her dad drives a cheap motorcar."

"Too bad," Pa said and sucked on his fag.

I could see that look from behind the smoke. I had disappointed him. Pa threw down his fag and got right in my face.

"Don't go getting all romantic and decide to let her in on where our money's comin' from, you hear me?"

I nodded. We were on the same page there. She should make things easier, not more complicated than they already were. Still, I should have found a girl with family money that could help in case things went all sixes and sevens.

"Don't we have ten grand coming in from Donaldson? You delivered four IDs over a month ago."

"You let me handle that end," I said.

"Just keep doing what you do best on those computer thingamajigs," Pa said in his angry little way.

Pa flicked his cigarette into the street like he was pissed.

"We're still gonna need more funds for the new machines. I can't keep reusing the old ones. We'll get caught that way."

Pa gave a forced laugh and shoved his chunky hands down into the front pocket of his jeans.

"Then that beauty of yours better fork over her salary, or you can rent her out. Either way, that's on you to figure out."

I got the message. We needed more clean cash to set my parents up for good. If Crystal wasn't going to be a source for it, Pa would expect me to find another one, which was incredibly stressful on top of everything else. I hated being stressed. Made me see red.

Pa turned away from me and walked back in the house. I watched the end of his cigarette burn in the middle of the road and tried to think of how to source funds or machines or both.

When I went inside and started jogging up the stairs, I looked up and saw Crystal at the top of the stairs. She had been crying. Bloody hell. Women.

"What is wrong with your parents?" Crystal whispered. She must have heard them fighting in the kitchen earlier.

"Nothing," I said. "You should hear 'em when they're going hammer and tongs."

I walked past her, headed for the bedroom. Done dealing with this crap, I was.

"What?" Crystal followed me into the bedroom and shut the door behind her. "You've got to ask them to leave. We're married and we need our privacy. Besides, they've been mooching off of you long enough," said Crystal. She jumped onto the bed and curled up like a little girl.

"Where they gonna go, Crystal? They've got no money and

no work. But you wouldn't know anything about that, would you? You've always had money. Your parents have always had money. Mum's not worked since I was in boarding school." My head began to throb. "Look, I have a headache. Can we talk about this later?"

"Fine, but just for the record, my parents didn't always have money. That's why they don't show it. It's all in the bank."

"Good for them," I said, lying down on the bed with my eyes closed and thinking about what she had just told me.

"I'm going downstairs to help your mother."

"When you come back, bring me some aspirin, will you?"

Crystal kissed me on the forehead and left the room. Downstairs, I could hear her and Mum in the kitchen. I left the door open so I could listen.

"Can I help with anything?" Crystal asked.

I could hear Mum open and close the oven as Crystal posed the question.

"Oh, no, dearie," said Mum. "You don't worry your pretty little face about anything. It's all cleaned up now. Good as new. Now, I'm just going to put on for a spot of tea and maybe get some dinner going for us old fogeys."

"Well, let me at least set the table," I heard Crystal say. She wasn't catching on to Mum's brush off.

I heard the clanking of silverware, cupboards opening and closing. I thought this might be more entertaining than watching the telly, so I stayed still with the door open to keep listening. Mum wasn't going to let Crystal in to what was now her kitchen, much less our lives. But Crystal was such a persistent lass, I wondered how far she could push it.

"Where's all my silverware, the stuff I bought?" Crystal asked.

"Oh, I moved it back over there," said Mum. "It's too difficult to reach on this side of the kitchen."

"Oh," I heard Crystal say as she slammed the drawer shut.

"If you like, you can dice those li'l onions for me."

"Sure," replied Crystal. "What does dice mean?"

"Did your Mum not teach you how to cook?"

"Not really. Unless you want me to microwave a hot dog or boil spaghetti."

"Does your Mum not make dinner in your family?"

"I wouldn't call her a chef."

"Well, what did your Mum teach you?"

"She taught me how to navigate the Eurail and exchange currencies in my head, in addition to navigating local tourism bureaus."

"That's not going to put a hot dinner on your plate, now is it?"

Something on the stove began to sizzle like bacon. Mum had forgotten to watch the kettle.

"Oh dear, the whistle must be broken on this damn thing. Och, that's hot."

"Here, let me get the tea bags," Crystal said. "Does everyone want tea? Do you take two bags like Duncan, or just one?"

"Just one is plenty. His Royal Highness will probably just have beer," said Mum, "Oh, look dearie, we don't serve tea with the bags still in it."

I could smell the frying sausages. They must have been nearly done.

"Why do you call Howard that? I mean, I heard you call him 'your Highness' a couple days ago, or 'your lordship' or something like that."

"I suppose it started out as a sign of respect. My mum always showed respect to my father, and, och, he doted on her, he did. Lately, it's been a bit tongue in cheek though, dearie. Crystal, would you mind bringing the bean 'round here for a moment?"

"A bean?" Crystal asked.

"I forget what you call it."

It's a garbage can, you twitty old mum, a garbage can.

"Oh, a bin, like a garbage can," said Crystal.

"Yes, sorry. Sometimes I get a bit muddled up."

They both started laughing. That was strange. Was Mum warming up to her?

"That's okay. I love your accent."

"You do? Oh, that's nice. I always thought it sounded a bit sing-songy."

"No," said Crystal. "It's lovely. I'm surprised you still have such a strong Northern pronunciation, having been in the States for so long. You've been here for what now, twenty years?"

"Oh, it's been longer than that, love," Mum replied.

Bugger! I wish she'd shut her yap. I should probably go downstairs before Mum says too much. They weren't supposed to like each other.

"Must be twenty-five years now."

"So, you were here a long time before Duncan was. I thought you all came at the same time, in like 1989 or something."

"Oh, no. Duncan was still in boarding school when his lordship and I came here. We tried putting him into that Patrick's Air Force Base school, but the boys picked on him so, what with him being almost two years younger and already in high school. Had to pull him out, send him back before he got the shi—"

"Mum," I called down from upstairs. She was feeding Crystal the wrong story. "Not telling embarrassing grammar school stories now, are you?"

"Course not, love. All these embarrassing stories are from your secondary school."

Crystal had put the tea into tiny teacups. I laughed out loud.

"We're real Brits, Crystal. We don't drink tea from tiny china cups," I said.

"I didn't think you wanted to use your work mug at dinner," Crystal said, carrying two plates to the TV room.

"And we don't drink our tea with the bag still in it," I shouted after her. Bloody Americans. "You're going to have to train her a bit better, Mum."

"Well, you could have given me something more to work with. Her mum doesn't even cook."

"Aye, but isn't she beautiful, Mum? Come here, Crystal," I said, hugging her, kissing her on top of her head. "I love you. You know that, right?"

Crystal nodded.

"What exactly is bangers 'n' mash?" Crystal asked.

"It's good. It's sausage and potatoes."

"Oh, I don't eat red meat."

"Well, I'm not a fan of these potatoes, so you can have mine and I'll eat your sausage," I said and kissed her again.

While I was still kissing her, Pa came up to us.

"Uh oh," he said. "Gale, you betta come here and show these bairns how it's done."

Mum shuffled 'round to Pa, who kissed her square on and reached 'round, slamming his cupped hand on her bum. Mum let out a bit of a squeak. Crystal must have been embarrassed, because she shoved me away and darted to the couch. Gave her a nice smack on the arse, I did, as she walked away.

"That's how you do it, son," Pa said.

Mum fumbled to straighten her bifocals, which Pa had nearly knocked off her face.

"Right, then," said Mum. "Let's eat."

9

CRYSTAL

August 29, 1998

"IT MUST BE HARD, SEEING HER AT THESE COMPANY FUNCTIONS," SAID AMANDA BAKER, SECOND WIFE OF THE FIRM'S FOUNDING PARTNER, TEDD, WHO WAS ABOUT TWENTY YEARS HER SENIOR.

Half-naked in her tiny beach outfit, Amanda was mid-day drunk and using her cocktail glass to point out Tina across the room. "I mean, wasn't she engaged to Duncan last year or living with him or something?"

My oversized sunglasses hid well the sudden bulge in my eyes. I hated these company gatherings, but I attended for Duncan's sake. All the guys got drunk and all the women stood around in their $300 bathing suits talking about each other. This particular soiree was at Tedd's luxury home on Lake Eola. He had a huge outdoor patio with a hot tub that spilled over into the large kidney-shaped pool. There was even a sand volleyball court and dock where he kept his fishing boat.

I still didn't know many of the 100-plus employees at the firm, nor did I care to. Duncan, of course, knew everyone. He was playing with two small children near the shallow end as if they were his own. I knew he was having a blast here, but the least he could do was rescue me from Amanda Baker. Her hair was flawless, her skin was perfect, and her claws were not retracting.

"You do know they were living together, don't you?" Amanda persisted and took a sip of her margarita; her collagen-plumped lips squeezed the life out of that poor straw. "Oh, look how well he gets along with her kids," she nodded in the direction of the pool. Duncan was picking up a little girl and tossing her into the water. "You know, that is so sweet, Crystal. I wish my husband was that good with little kids."

"Whose kids are those?" I inquired.

"Those are Tina's kids, honey," she smirked.

I knew Duncan had dated Tina, and likely all the other receptionists at the firm. The rest was news to me. I had only been married for a month, but I wasn't about to let this over-tanned hyena create the first division in my marriage.

"And where is your husband, Amanda?" I asked. "I don't think I've actually met him yet."

"Oh, he's inside watching the Gators pre-season. Boys will be boys." She smiled and took another large sip.

I didn't know how she could drink alcohol in this heat. Especially since she weighed all of 110 pounds.

All the owners' wives looked like they were made by Mattel. Most of them were in their mid-forties (except Amanda), but you would have never guessed it, seeing them in bikinis. Her only job was to look this good.

The managers' wives weren't in such great shape. The next rung down on the corporate ladder apparently didn't make as much money, so the wives had jobs as teachers. Engineers seemed to like marrying primary school teachers. I wondered what the connection was.

Secretly, I was afraid of the owners' wives. Something about them evoked an uneasiness and jealousy in me at the same time. I didn't feel as though I would fit in at any level of the female hierarchy of girlfriends or wives in this social circle.

The owners' wives drove BMWs, had weekly or daily tennis practice, and looked like former Miss USA contestants every hour of the day. They possessed every social grace and every couture item for the appropriate occasion. Despite the fact that they consumed twice as much wine on a daily basis as I could in a week, they never appeared to be intoxicated—except Amanda.

The managers' wives were gathered in a huddle on the steps of the pool. I had no idea what they were talking about, but I was willing to bet it was more interesting than shooting the breeze with Catwoman.

I excused myself from Amanda and found a place to stand among the girlfriends, who were by the volleyball net. These girls were less intimidating. They were all dating the recent recruits. When the recruits get hired, these girls move here with them and become elementary school teachers.

While approachable individually, they were a clique as a group and tended to ostracize me. I had a hard time piercing their circle. I had nothing in common with them. They were built like true farm girls. Some of them were wearing one-piece bathing suits, a few were in bikinis, but most were wearing shorts and tank tops. Strange, I thought, for a pool party. They were pale as dolls, not wearing any makeup, and they'd had the same hairstyles since junior high. And they always drank beer instead of wine or mixed drinks. How Midwestern of them.

One girl introduced herself to me when we first got there, so I stood near her. Everything about this short brunette seemed to be very round; even her name, Opal, started with a round letter.

A light breeze blew in from across the lake. It provided a peaceful view from the backyard pool.

"It's nice out today, huh?" Opal asked.

"Yes," I replied. Maybe she hadn't been here long enough to realize Florida was like this every day. "Very relaxing."

"Have you met the other Wisconsin girls?" Opal asked.

I shook my head.

"This is Jamie; she's Kurt's girlfriend. They've been together for two years. That over there is Elisha. You've been with Doug for what now, Lish, one year?"

"Fifteen months," Elisha replied.

"That's right. And this is Dana. Her and Steve just got together like six months ago now, but she doesn't live here. Just visiting."

I smiled a hello at everyone. "Nice to meet you all," I said, wondering what the heck to say next.

"Whose girlfriend are you?" Jamie asked innocently. Jamie was the tallest in the group and the only one with blonde hair.

"No, dumbass," said Opal. "She's Duncan's new wife. They just got married a month ago."

I didn't tell Opal when we had gotten married. I didn't have to. Word spread like wildfire at the firm.

"Oh my god, girl. Congratulations!" said Elisha. "He's super hot."

"Can I see your ring?" Jamie asked. "Kurt and I have been lookin' at rings for months now and we can't find anything we both like."

I couldn't believe girls would go shopping with their boyfriends for rings. Wedding and engagement rings were gifts. You shouldn't shop for your own gift. Besides, if you had to tell your boyfriend what you liked, that meant you didn't know each other well enough and probably shouldn't be getting married in the first place.

I pushed my left hand forward into the circle of pale Wisconsin women, proud of my ring and suddenly embarrassed by my unmanicured nails.

"That's a huge rock!" said Opal.

"It's only two carats," I said, not entirely sure what that meant. "Duncan said he chose a princess-cut for me because I was his princess."

They all cooed. My ring was another sign that Duncan and I were meant to be together. He told me the store had only one princess-cut diamond ring left, and it just happened to be my size. He hadn't even known my ring size when he got it.

"Where did you get your band? It's beautiful," said Jamie.

"I don't know," I said. "Duncan picked out everything and surprised me."

They all shrieked.

"I would kill Kurt if he ever did that."

In the middle of a round of laughter at her comment, Opal leaned over to me.

"Kurt probably didn't care either way about the rings," Opal whispered carefully in my ear. "He just doesn't want to get married yet."

The laughs died off quickly and Jamie looked at Opal. I tried to cover for her.

"Well, I like everything Duncan picked out," I told them. "He's actually better at this jewelry stuff than I am."

"How did you guys meet?" asked Jamie.

"At the firm," I said. "I'm not there anymore, but Sandie made him take me out to lunch on my first day."

"That's so sweet," said Opal. "I didn't realize you worked together. How long were you there?"

"About two months," I said. "I just recently started a new job, since Sandie fired me for marrying one of the engineers, ha, ha."

I tried to make a joke of it, but they didn't laugh. I knew what was coming next.

"So you only knew each other for like a few weeks?" Jamie asked, not in a judgmental way, but more like a math equation she was articulating at the same time that she was working it out in her head. But Opal's face definitely looked judgey.

"How romantic," sighed Jamie. Opal and Elisha exchanged not-so-subtle glances, and I looked up to see where Duncan was. Normally I would have defended our rushed timeline, explaining how all the signs pointed to us being meant for each other. At the moment, however, I wasn't feeling it. There was no sign of him. Where is my Prince Charming when I need him?

"I'm going to get a refill," I said, trying to hide my half-full cup of water.

"If you want anything other than beer, I think you have to go inside," advised Opal.

I thanked her and headed toward the house. On my way, I took a few steps down into the pool to cool off. The intense sun felt good, but this cool water felt even better. I got out, grabbed a towel, and continued my trek inside. The last thing I wanted to do was drip pool water on Amanda's new hardwood floors.

I walked through the sliding glass door that led into the great room. Glass doors lined the entire back of the house, folding in on each other so the occupants enjoyed an unobstructed view of the lake and pool.

I heard Duncan's laugh come from the direction of the kitchen. I was headed that way when someone came out of the bathroom and clipped my left shoulder. The impact caused some of my water to spill onto my leg and the floor. I quickly stepped to my right and the water under my foot was like grease on the hardwood. My ass went straight to the floor, my left wrist breaking my fall.

"Oh my god! I'm so sorry," said my assailant.

I looked up. Of course it was Tina. She reached out a hand to help, but I didn't trust myself not to pull her down to the floor with me.

Tina had large, fake, perfectly tanned boobs propping up her stars-and-stripes bikini like two well-pitched tents. Her long blonde hair was in serious need of conditioning, and I hated the fact that she, too, had her belly button pierced. I had mine pierced my freshman year of college, before it was trendy. My ring was so small that I couldn't take it out on my own, even though other girls traded out their barbells and studs to match whatever outfit they were wearing. Tina wore a gold half-moon with a diamond on each end. It made her stomach look tanner than mine.

"I'm okay," I lied, struggling to stand up on my own. I must have made a loud thud when I landed, because four people, including Duncan, ran out of the kitchen toward me.

"Oh my god, princess. Are you okay?"

I was already halfway up by the time he put his arm around me. "I'm fine," I said.

"So, Tina, I guess you've met my new wife," said Duncan.

"Your wife?" Tina asked, only it was more of a statement. Why did she look surprised? Everybody else knew by now. It wouldn't surprise me if she did know, but was trying to create drama.

Tina was divorced and shared custody of her three kids with her ex-husband, but nobody had ever met the father. I didn't know how she managed to have her nails done and highlights renewed every five weeks on her salary with three kids.

Sandie had introduced me to Tina my first day at work, but we hadn't spoken since. Tina seemed just as surprised to hear about me becoming Duncan's wife as I had been to hear about her having lived with Duncan.

"Didn't I tell you? Crystal and I got married last month."

The other three women who had emerged from the kitchen

with Duncan exchanged knowing glances and slid out the back door.

"Wow. That was fast," said Tina. She shifted all her weight to her back leg. Duncan failed to notice her subtle and indignant stance. "Didn't you just start working here in July?" She stared me up and down.

"The end of June," I said, not that it mattered.

"No, you didn't tell me, but congratulations to you both." Tina threw me a fake smile. "I guess this means you got over your commitment issues," she said, and forced a laugh.

Duncan laughed, too, and Tina turned to go back outside. As soon as she closed the door, I smacked Duncan on the arm.

"Ouch. What was that for?" he whined.

"A couple of things," I said through clenched teeth. "Can we please leave now?"

"Why? We haven't even eaten yet."

"Okay, we'll eat first, but then can we go? I really did hurt myself in that fall."

"Awww," Duncan said with a hug and a kiss on the top of my head. "Okay. Take a soak in the pool and I'll get us some hot dogs. Then we can go."

"Oh, Duncan, remember, I'm not eating meat right now."

"Yeah, but that's just easier to bring over. If you want something else, get it."

"Okay, never mind," I whispered.

I loved how he automatically thought of doing things for both of us, like getting the hot dogs. We had been only been together two months and he was already thinking in pairs.

I eased my sore bottom into the pool, and when I looked up, I saw Sandie walking in with her husband. Wonderful. My executioner has arrived. Now, the party was officially over.

The marketing department never mingled with the engineering boys. Sandie was not particularly thrilled with my marriage to one of them. I'd disappointed her in some way, even though she was the one who'd insisted I go to lunch with Duncan.

Sandie had donned a large brimmed straw hat and big sunglasses. Her navy blue wraparound top matched her long blue shorts. A straw purse almost as big as her hat was slung over her left shoulder. Bright red lipstick framed her fake broad smile. I hoped I wouldn't have to dress like that when I was in my thirties.

None of the owners' wives got up to greet her. They just smiled and waved from their seats, then turned back to their conversation. I sank lower into the pool and prayed she wouldn't see me.

"Hey, Sandie!" Duncan, bearing two hot dogs, went up and kissed her on the cheek. "Glad you guys could make it. What can I get you two to drink?"

No! What was he doing?

"I'll have a chardonnay, thanks, Duncan. Hubby here will have a beer."

Duncan shoved a hot dog under my nose without looking at me. I turned my nose up at it.

"Don't be a pain, sweetheart. Just eat it," Duncan whispered forcefully into my ear. "I'm going to get Sandie and her husband a drink. I'll be right back."

"Okay," I surrendered. "I'll just sit here, alone."

I sat there with an aching bum and shoved a gross hot dog in my face while trying to avoid the spawn of Satan in the straw hat.

"Hurry back," I said with a phony smile.

If my sister were here, she would know what to say. Lyssa could be thrown into any kind of social situation and shine like the sun. When she spent a semester in London, she walked into the U.S. Embassy and got herself an internship by turning the foyer into a nightclub. When she left, the rugby team threw her the biggest party on record. I think she still gets fan mail from England.

Elisha walked up and extended her arms for a hug goodbye.

"Bye, sweetie. Doug and I are leaving."

I gave her a hug and they were off. Opal came by next, on her way out.

"Hey, we're having a girls' night out next weekend. You should come."

"That's very nice of you to invite me, Opal. Call me. I'd love to go."

"Yeah, you're the local," she said. "You could actually show us around."

"Sure thing," I said half-heartedly. There wasn't a single dance club on Orange Avenue I hadn't been to at least a dozen times.

By the time Duncan returned, I was a prune and his hot dog was cold.

"You ready to go yet?" he asked.

"Very funny," I replied.

Duncan handed me a towel and wolfed down his hot dog while I dried off and put on my board shorts. I couldn't see behind his tinted Oakleys, but I knew he was watching me dress. Duncan threw on his T-shirt and started tucking it into his shorts.

"Honey, don't do that. Nobody in Florida tucks in their shirt."

"The guys at my firm do," he replied.

"The guys at your firm are dorks. I bet they also wash their hands before dinner and call women ma'am."

"What's wrong with having manners?" he asked.

"Nothing," I teased. "It's just out of place for men in Orlando."

We said goodbye to everyone and I successfully exited without having to face Sandie or Tina again.

For some reason, we didn't speak on the ride home. The sun had made us sleepy, and the afternoon thunderstorms never came to relieve the air of its broiling temperatures. I couldn't wait to get home and take a nap with Duncan.

When we pulled up to the house, Duncan's dad was smoking a cigarette in the garage. He moved so we could pull the Alfa Romeo into its parking spot. Howard's white truck was parked at the end of the street, where Duncan had told him to keep it.

"How was your party?" Howard asked, not looking at us.

"It was fun," I answered.

"Crystal, can you put our towels in the dryer? I'm going to back the car out into the driveway so I can wash her."

I wanted to ask Duncan if he could wait to wash the car until after an intimate nap, but I was too embarrassed in front of Howard.

"Sure," I said and went inside.

The house looked immaculate. The bistro table in the kitchen had been cleared off and cleaned. The avocado-colored countertops were spotless, and the white fridge looked as if it had recently been wiped down with a wet sponge. Gale was watching television on the burgundy sofa and stitching up a hole in Howard's jeans. She gazed up at me over the metal-framed bifocals resting on the tip of her very petite nose.

"Oh, Crystal, dearie, I didn't hear you come in." Her accent was so soothing. "I was just fixing Howard's trousers. Did you want to watch the telly?"

I wanted to correct her about trousers being called jeans, but decided against it. She and Howard had been in this country for more than twenty years. If she still insisted on calling them trousers, who was I to correct her? Besides, I liked how she said telly.

"No, thank you."

"If you're hungry, I can heat up some food for you. There's leftover porkchops in the fridge."

"No, thank you," I repeated, not sure if I had forgotten to tell them I didn't eat meat. "I'm going to jump in the shower."

A hot shower always felt sinfully good after a day at the pool. It took away the sting of too much sun on my skin, so my clothes didn't feel itchy. When I got out of the shower, I lathered on some aloe, wrapped myself in a towel, and laid down on the bed.

Why was it taking Duncan so long to wash his stupid car? I could go down there in my towel and lure him upstairs, but that might scare his parents to death—or make them so uncomfortable, they'd want to leave. Hmm. Maybe I will go downstairs in my towel.

I decided against it and rolled toward the closet to get dressed.

Duncan's clothes hung on one side of the closet and mine on the other. I stood there, staring at his side. It was always so neat. Each suit jacket and matching pants set hung on a special wooden hanger, arranged from light to dark. Then came his white button-down shirts, then his polos, and finally, his gray T-shirts.

The inside of Duncan's closet was as meticulous as his cars. It was funny, because he completely ignored the rest of the house. The bathroom sink was always full of hair and a black swirl at the foot of the bed marked where his cat slept.

I needed to talk to Duncan about his parents. Gale seemed sweet, but I hated coming home to Howard's judging eyes and her impeccably clean kitchen. I felt like a guest in my own house. I didn't even know where my own silverware was anymore. There was no way they felt comfortable in a house with newlyweds.

Not that you could even tell Duncan and I were married. This should have been the happiest time of our lives, but living like this was no honeymoon. I wanted us to go away together, but every time I brought up the idea of a mini-vacation, he got upset about missing work.

I didn't understand why it was okay for me to give up time with my family, none of whom had spoken to me since the ceremony, but it was not okay for him to give an inch. I had even stopped going to my church, my one refuge. It used to be the place where I really felt God was near me, but I hadn't been to worship in weeks. Duncan had convinced me that I didn't need my parents, didn't need Zoloft, and didn't even need God, because all I really needed was him. But I was never alone with him.

10

DUNCAN

August 1, 1999

"Bloody good martini, isn't it?"

Crystal and I sat at a tropical pub overlooking Sunset Square. For our first wedding anniversary, she'd talked me into going to Key West. Didn't get a honeymoon when we ran off that weekend, being so last minute and all. This was the first chance we'd had for a break.

Didn't tell Crystal, but I was letting my parents stay at the house while we were gone. Little apartment they moved into was so bloody small. I should know, it was my old flat. Same owner still ran the place. Nice man, kinda stupid. Just told him I needed the flat for a few months while we renovated our house. That way, we were able to avoid the background checks. It also made Crystal happy, which was nice.

"It's not as good as those banana daiquiris we had at the pool, but I love a good chocolate martini," she said.

Crys' cheeks were red as roses from lying around in the sun all day. The magazine she worked for now was letting her write a travel article. Good set up, it was. We got all this free stuff and discounted rates. She did all the work; I enjoyed all the benefits. Rooms were posh. Drinks were free. Could get used to this—VIP treatment and all.

At first, I wasn't happy about her leaving the firm. She hated Sandie and hated her job. But she was earning a packet for her age. So, I talked her into toughing it out a bit longer. Guess a bit too long. Sandie fired Crystal after the two of them had words in the copy room. Whole office heard it. Crys was pretty upset.

She wanted to write a letter of complaint to the owners, something about discrimination because of her getting married and all. Probably had a case to make of it, but I talked her out of it. Would've spoilt my chances for a promotion. Plus, I advised her, she was going to have to spend every Christmas and holiday party with these people, so it was best to just not make a big to-do about it.

"It's pretty cool that we get to be here on vacation and you don't have to take days off from work," I said.

"Well, I am working. It's a wonderful assignment, but it's still work. I have to interview the bartender and the hotel manager. Can you believe that bathroom? It's the biggest tub I've ever seen."

"I agree. So, how long do you think you can go without getting fired from this job?"

"This is different," said Crystal. "I'm in the right industry now. I have no idea why I took a marketing job. I don't like meeting new people and have this terrible habit of saying what's on my mind instead of just flattering other people to get what I want. Plus, I can still do this and get my MFA from Rollins. I'm really excited about starting next month. I even got my books already. Can you believe there's an entire semester available with Edward Albee? He went to Rollins . . ."

The setting sun stopped just above the pier. I put my shades on, it was so bright.

"What's the matter?" Crystal asked. "Too cool to be seen with me?"

"Sun's killing my eyes. Want to switch seats with me? Sun'll set in a few seconds and I'll take them off again. Want another drink?"

"No, I don't want to be hungover when we go snorkeling tomorrow." Crystal swallowed the last of her martini and a wait- ress in a Jimmy Buffett T-shirt came to take it away.

"Teresa," I stopped her before she jetted away. "Fetch me a Jack and Coke there, love? If it's not too much trouble."

"Why do you do that?" Crystal asked

"Do what?"

"Break out your English accent for waitresses."

"It's not English, it's British, and you're imagining things." I laughed.

"Yes, you do it all the time."

"Stop acting like a loon. It's not pleasant to be around," I said, taking the last swig of my drink. "And about that snorkel- ing tomorrow, I don't think I can go."

"But that's the main focus of the article," she whined. "Why don't you want to go? It's not costing us anything."

"I have trouble breathing through those tubes because of my sinuses. Besides, people get snot all over those masks and then you put them on your face. Maybe we should get our own masks. I did want to see how far underwater I could go with my Omega, though."

I looked down at my new watch. Pa used to have an original Submariner. Even Bond switched to Omega in 1995. That's when

I got the Seamaster, the first civilian version of a watch made to look like those worn by our sailors in World War II.

"They have sterilizing buckets. The masks get rinsed off after every use. I think it's a waste of money to buy our own, since we never go snorkeling, but if it'll change your mind about going, then fine. It's not like we go swimming together at home anymore. Actually, we don't even hang out together anymore."

"Crystal, don't ruin a perfectly good sunset."

A large sailboat cruised past, blocking the bright orange sun for a brief moment. Below in the town square, dozens of people gathered round for the sunset and the live music about to ensue.

"I'm not trying to ruin anything. I'm just saying how much I miss spending time with you. Remember when we would both come home from work and you would make us shepherd's pie? Sometimes you even had fresh flowers on the table. I loved that. That's all I'm saying."

Teresa came back and set my drink down.

"Thank you so much, Teresa. Oh, I'm sorry, just one more thing. Those people down there in the square, they're carrying their drinks in the open, aren't they?"

"Yes, they're part of the Sunset Block Party. You buy one ticket for twenty dollars, then it's all you can drink at those four bars down there."

"Is it available every night?" I asked.

"Just Thursday through Sunday. But yeah, you should check it out."

"Maybe we should do that tomorrow, Crystal." I meant it sincerely, but she looked pissed off. "What's wrong?"

"I was trying to tell you something, and you started up a conversation with the waitress."

"I'm sorry, love," I said, taking her hand. "I'm listening. What were you trying to say?"

"I was saying that we hardly ever spend time alone together

at home anymore," Crystal whined.

I let go of her hand.

"This isn't about me traveling, is it?" I asked.

I'd spent much of the year on the road for work. Being that I was the only electrical engineer with a background in computer science, the owners had seen fit to send me out to fix Y2K problems. Clients in both our hospital and educational divisions started buying our preparation services left and right. Seems everyone in the States was freaked out about a potential computer glitch that could set some software systems back to 1969 when the year 2000 rolled around. Most of it was rubbish, but people pay for security.

"Crystal, I know it's a lot of travel for one year. But 1999 is almost over. And I'm still hourly, so I'm getting time and a half for these trips."

"Really? Where's that money going, because I'm not spending it."

"Well, the Alfa needed a new transmission, and you know how much it costs just to buy the oil for that thing," I said. "And to be honest, darling, you are spending most of it on school, which you really don't need."

"You said I could get my master's degree," she said, her face looking rather serious. "I love the campus. It's beautiful. So Florida. I feel like I belong there. It's really important for me to do something like this right now, both personally and professionally."

Last thing I want is her getting more educated.

"Look," I started up again, leaning across the table so she'd see how serious I was. "If I can do this Y2K stuff for our clients, and our big clients start to like me, I'll have a better chance of moving up in the firm. You think it's easy competing with these guys who all went to school together? They all get to be chummy and invited to watch American football on each other's large-screen TVs. This overblown millennium meltdown could be the best thing for me."

I did like the travel, though. Got myself a new laptop from the office. Negotiated my way into first-class seating. Always had clean sheets in hotel rooms. Everything nice and sterile at the places I stayed. Clean, like the hospitals I was used to working in for my clients.

"Maybe I'll get a cat." Crystal said the most peculiar things sometimes.

"We've already got a cat."

"I want a cat that isn't trying to eat the flesh off my face at night while I'm sleeping."

"Come on, Crys, she's not that bad." The drink was getting to me. My American accent was fading. "She's only drawn blood twice."

"She's right out of a Stephen King novel, Duncan!"

"Alright, princess. We'll get you a kitten. My cat would love to have some fresh meat 'round the house."

"Stop it." Crystal pushed my arm. She took some money from her purse and left a tip on the table.

I downed my drink and picked up my Oakleys. The sun had set. The bar was filling up with a new crowd, and I was ready for some new scenery, like more hot waitresses.

"I heard someone at work say their cat had a new litter. Maybe if you're a good girl tonight, we'll take a look at them next week."

Crystal stood up and adjusted her skirt. I laughed and smacked her bum.

"Gross," she said, slinging her purse over her arm.

Every guy in the bar turned, watching her leave. Crystal never wore makeup. That was part of what I liked about her. She was wearing one of those tops that exposed her back. She had put onsome weight since we got married, but that skirt she had on hid it nicely.

Losing the sun didn't cool the air much. I hated the feel of sweat on my neck and back.

"Does my hair look alright?" I asked as we merged into the bustling crowd flowing down Duval Street.

"Yes, it looks fine," she said and took my hand.

"You didn't even look," I replied.

Crystal abruptly stopped in the middle of the sidewalk. A woman behind her walked smack into her, stared at her, and walked 'round.

"I'm looking now. It looks fine. If you want, you can use some of my gel after you get out of the shower."

We started walking again. I interlocked our fingers like I did that night at the bistro. She pulled away.

"I don't want it to look wet," I said.

"The gel just keeps it from frizzing," she explained. "Without, you know, making it look all ghetto."

Two really hot chicks crossed in front of us. I strained to not turn 'round and check them out. I could get used to this place. Made me sweaty and all, but girls wore even less clothing here than they did in Orlando.

Cars were blocked from driving to this end of the road. Music blaring from the pubs on either side turned the street into one big party.

"Can we go in here?" Crystal asked. "I really want to dance."

Loud, rhythmic thumps of music shook the windows along the front of the club. Bright flashes of strobe lights bounced over black walls inside.

"I don't want to dance," I told her. "My knee hurts."

"Come on, please? It means a lot to me."

"I said no, Crys."

"Duncan, I arranged this whole trip. Now, please come inside with me. We can do like at home with the guys, where you stand at the bar and I'll just dance in front of you."

Crossing the street without her, I started toward the hotel. I was done for the night.

"Fine," she said. "I'm going in without you."

"Some honeymoon this turned out to be," I shouted back at her.

"Have fun in the hotel room," she shouted even louder. "By yourself!"

The crowd around her began staring at me. I wasn't going to tolerate this from any woman. I marched right up to her and took her arm, firmly.

"Come on."

"Where we going?"

"Back to the hotel."

"I don't want to go back yet!"

She stopped dead in her tracks.

"Stop being a bitch, Crystal. I've had enough of this." I pulled her off the sidewalk. She lost her balance, falling down into the street.

"You're hurting my arm." She kept talking, but I heard none of it. I squeezed tighter and kept walking.

I heard Crystal whimpering in the bathroom as I crawled into the white sheets of our nice king-size bed. The door to the bathroom consisted of nothing more than white shutters that opened from inside. I stuck my finger through a slit in the door to force it open a bit.

"Where's my beautiful Crystal?"

Peering through the shutters, I saw her sitting on the edge of the tub, freshly showered, wearing nothing but a towel, head in her hands, crying.

"I've got some whipped cream out here with your name on it. Oh, my mistake, it's your name written in whipped cream. Care to take a peek?"

"Go lick yourself."

Guess she was a wee bit upset.

"Come on, Crys. Let me in so I can apologize properly."

Hearing the lock turn, I gave the door a push. She returned to the edge of the tub, grabbing tissues along the way.

"Don't cry, love. I'm sorry."

"It's just really hard for me," she said between sniffles. "I'm trying to be positive about this whole trip. It's a pretty crummy excuse for a honeymoon. I mean compared to the seven-day cruise I really wanted." She took a deep breath and blew her nose. "All I ever wanted was a honeymoon on a tropical island—even more than a wedding, more than a house, more than anything."

"We are on a tropical island."

"Key West is not a tropical island."

It was the most clearly enunciated sentence she'd said the whole night.

"Yes, it is."

"Maybe like a hundred years ago."

"Look, your pa was so pissed at us, he wouldn't've bought us the cruise tickets anyway."

"Yes, he would have, if I hadn't messed things up."

"Come lie down on the bed. I'll give you a foot massage. That'll make you feel a bit better, won't it?"

She is such a buzzkill sometimes—more like all the time, lately. I should try to see if Tina will meet me for a drink when we get back.

Crystal came out of the bathroom and slumped down on the bed next to me, her long brown hair trailing out beside her beautiful head. I drew a line with my finger from the top of her forehead around her square jaw and down her neck. She closed her eyes and I spread my whole hand out going down her body. I got just below her stomach when she grabbed my hand.

"Why can't we go on a cruise to the Bahamas?" Crystal asked.

I quickly went from bothered to miffed. I should just tell her and get it over with. All those Jack and Cokes were making it hard to come up with a plan. If I told her, Pa would be rightly pissed. If I didn't, she would keep being a tremendous bother about it all.

"Look, Crystal, when my parents and I came to the States, we were struck with more tragedy. I haven't wanted to tell you about it, but it's the reason why we can't go overseas right now."

I looked up at her to see how she was taking what I'd said so far. Her eyes looked sympathetic, so I kept going.

"Duncan, you're my husband," she said so innocently. "You can tell me anything."

"I don't like to talk about it, so I'll tell you, but don't tell anyone else. You have to promise."

"I promise."

"When we landed in the airport after we first arrived from England, we were robbed."

"Oh my gosh!" Crystal exclaimed.

"It was horrible. We were jet lagged and weren't paying attention, I guess. Mum's bag with all our passports and paper-work was stolen from the luggage trolley."

"That's horrible, but I'm sure customs was able to file a report, get you in touch with the embassy here so you could get them replaced."

"No, actually, they were no help. We didn't have the money right then to replace them."

"But that was what, like, nearly fifteen years ago? I'm sure you've been able to get a new one since then."

"Unfortunately, Pa let his E-2 visa expire. It sort of put us on the outs. And I didn't want to put my parents on customs' radar, so we just stayed. I was able to get a job and now everything is fine. I just can't leave the country, that's all."

"But we're married now, we can get this fixed tomorrow!" Crystal sat up on the bed and looked at me eagerly.

"No, Crys, just drop it."

"No, I won't drop it. I can fix this!"

I grabbed her right under her jaw and pulled her mouth to mine to kiss her pink lips. Then looked into her eyes and squeezed her throat, which fit nicely between my thumb and ring finger.

"We're going to drop this. Do you understand?" I said and then let go of her.

I laid back on the bed and turn on the telly. Pretty sure the mood had passed. Was alright with me, actually. Keeping up with her was downright exhausting. This girl was a lot more than I'd bargained for.

11

LYSSA

June 1, 2000

As I waited in my car at the airport, I saw wave after wave of people spilling through the automatic doors; not one of them approached my car. My classmates would be surrounded by tons of family and friends this weekend, and all I had were my parents and Tiff—who wouldn't even be here if my dad hadn't purchased her plane ticket. My sister was the whole reason I'd transferred to this college, and I wasn't even sure if she would show up.

"Tiffany!" I screamed, running up to hug her as she came out of the airport doors.

"Lyssa!" We hugged each other and then I turned to open the trunk.

I could barely get her luggage off the ground. "Are you

moving here or just visiting for my graduation?" I asked.

She giggled and helped me lift the body bag into the car.

"I dunno, maybe. If I like it here."

Tiffany had super straight light brown hair, like Alicia Silverstone in that Aerosmith video. Tiffany was a couple inches shorter than me, which made it hard to swap jeans. When she got in the car, her black and white plaid skirt hiked up past her knees. Thankfully, my dad would not see us today. He gave me such grief when he did not approve of my friends' outfits. Tiffany adjusted the black purse strapped over her shoulder and turned the radio on as I pulled away from the airport.

"So, this is downtown San Diego," I said. "It's always sunny here." I loved being the tour guide when my friends came to visit. "Don't you just love how the water is right next to the streets and buildings here?"

"Yeah, when can we take some pictures? This place is gorgeous. I don't know how you ever studied."

"I didn't," I said, laughing.

I took Nimitz to Rosecrans so I could cut over to Hill Street and show her Ocean Beach. It was one of the dirtier beach towns, but there were some cool little surfer boutiques there I thought Tiffany would like.

"Is this where you live?" she asked.

"Ew, no. I live up the road, away from the skuzzy beach. My apartment is so cool. It is right next to a dog park where all these cute guys come and hang out."

"Awesome. We should go."

"I don't have a dog, Tiffany."

"So, we could borrow one. Just ask your neighbor or something. Tell them we'll bring the dog right back. Ha!"

"Oh, good idea."

I pulled up to the underground parking and opened the small rusty gate with my remote. I shared a bedroom with another girl from school. It was small, but so nice not to be living on campus. Crystal never got to live off campus. Our parents wouldn't let her. Our campus had strict curfews, so it had been just like living at home.

"How many people live in this apartment?" Tiffany asked as I lugged her baggage up the cement staircase to our back door.

"Four. You don't mind sleeping on the couch, do you?"

"No, I can pass out anywhere."

"That's the truth!"

I unlocked the back door and led Tiffany into the kitchen, which was barely big enough for one person at a time. Our puffy tan leather couch and recliner looked as if they had come out of a dumpster behind Dr. Jefe's.

"Where's Crystal going to sleep?" Tiffany asked.

I let her bags fall to the floor in a heap as she threw herself backward onto the couch and landed with as much force as her luggage.

"I don't even know if she's coming. She has not returned any of my emails or phone calls in months. If she does come, she'll probably get a hotel room with her husband."

"Isn't it weird that she's, like, married now?" Tiffany giggled as though she were immune to the aging process. "And now you're about to graduate from college. It's so great that all your credits from that other school transferred. I wish I had taken more AP classes. Gosh. We're all growing up so fast. So, do you have all your stuff packed to move outta here?"

"No. I think I am going to go to Arizona with my friend Cindy. She said she can get me a job at this really cool bar. So, we're just going to rent a truck and drive out there."

"Wow. That sounds so cool. Have you told your parents you're going to work at a bar? I bet they're thrilled," Tiffany giggled again. "They'll probably disown you."

"No," I said. "They only disown you if you if you have sex

before marriage."

Tiffany started laughing and said in a fake grown-up voice, "Now, Lyssa, you listen here. There are only two rules: No sex before marriage and finish college."

"Tiffany, I think you're ready to be a parent!" I replied.

The doorbell rang and we both jumped. Through the cheap curtains, I could see two figures standing on my front porch.

"Lyssa!" my mom cried and embraced me as I opened the door. "Our little graduate."

"Hey, Pumpkin!" Dad followed immediately. "How's it feel? Today's your big day. You're going to be a part of the first graduating class of the new millennium. That's exciting! Right?"

I just smiled. "I'm glad you're here."

"Hi, Tiffany," my mom said as she walked over to the couch. "Give me a hug, sweetheart. How are you? How was your flight?"

My mom treated all of my friends like they were extended family. Tiffany and I had known each other since middle school, and we called each other's parents Mom and Dad.

"It was good. I just can't believe Lyssa went to school here. This is so unfair. And so much nicer than Gainesville, Florida."

"Anything's nicer than Gainesville, Tiff." I shut the door and plopped down next to Tiffany on the couch. "Has anyone heard from Crystal?"

"I think she and Duncan are staying on Coronado Island," my dad said, cleaning his glasses.

I always thought he looked like a skinny version of Tom Selleck. Since my mom looked like Mary Tyler Moore, they made a funny couple. My dad always wore business suits and my mom always wore tight skirts. Crystal and I called her Tina Turner because of her great legs.

"Well, don't you think we need to know for sure? I mean how many seats do we have for dinner? Are they even coming, or are they just acting like they are on vacation here?" All the words came out before I took a moment to breathe.

"Now, Lyssa, your sister is married," said Mom. "You have to allow them some privacy. The two of you aren't roommates anymore. She doesn't have to ask permission to come and go."

"I know, but this is my graduation. She could at least return my phone calls. Do you have any idea how many messages I've left her and she hasn't returned a single one? I just think it's rude, that's all."

Of course, one of the reasons I hadn't seen her was because I avoided going back to Orlando this past Thanksgiving and Christmas. I spent Thanksgiving in Arizona with Cindy's parents in their huge mansion. And Christmas was depressing, since I was taking winter session classes and didn't know anyone.

"I'll give Crystal a call," my mom offered. "Go and get changed, Lyssa. You don't want to be late for the baccalaureate service. Your father wants to go."

"I don't even know what that word means," I said.

"I have some colleagues who are going to be there. Go get dressed," Dad ordered.

I had on jeans and a pink tank top. No event in San Diego requires much more dressing up than this. He just liked bossing me and Mom around.

When Crystal and I were in high school, we still had to go to bed by nine o'clock. We weren't allowed to watch R-rated movies, even after we turned seventeen. What he did not realize, and still might not know, was that Mom would let us sneak downstairs on Friday nights to watch *Miami Vice* and *Dallas* when we were little. Dad would have killed her if he'd ever found out.

"Why don't you go on ahead and we'll meet you there?" I suggested, with no intention of actually showing up. "Tiffany just got here and we both have to get ready."

He reluctantly agreed and they left.

The baccalaureate service was a snooze fest. The reason my

dad wanted to be there was because there were fewer people and he would get a chance to speak with the college's president, Dr. William Drake. By the time the actual graduation ceremony got started, I was ready for a nap. Dr. Drake droned on for almost an hour. The valedictorian only took fifteen minutes to tell us that we were the hope of the world and not just of our country.

I scanned the crowded bleachers behind me for a sign of Crystal. I was beginning to worry that something had happened to her. Then the president called my name, and I walked up to receive my diploma, passing by my history professor, Dr. Nolan.

Dr. Nolan was a big part of my decision to declare political science as my major. I could recall dates, names, and historical events at the drop of a hat, but history always bored me. Dr. Nolan suggested current events, and that changed my life. I took classes about how modern warfare and uprisings affected my friends overseas. It was the best academic move I could have made. I only wished I could have taken a year off before joining the business world. I still wasn't sure exactly what I would do with my degree.

When the ceremony ended, I went to look for Mom, Dad, and Tiffany and tried not to think about the possibility that Crystal and Duncan had missed it. Hundreds of black-robed graduates crammed together in the street behind the amphitheater. The school had award-winning landscaping year-round, so the smell of jasmine mixed with the ocean air blew across our campus.

Pink and white impatiens blooms lined the sidewalks where families were dabbing at tears and taking pictures. You could always tell which families were from Hawaii—they brought real-flower leis to drape around graduates' necks. That was another aspect of this college that I really liked: Even though it was about the size of Oviedo High School, I made friends with people from all over the world.

I was sad to say goodbye. The past few years had gone by so fast. I felt like I'd just gotten here. My parents made me take summer school, and with all my college-level courses transferring in, I was able to finish college in less than three years.

Later that night, my graduation dinner was at the restaurant at the Ramada on Shelter Island. We arranged a group of tables overlooking the bay. All the seats were filled with my friends and some of my dad's colleagues. I even invited my history professor. Crystal's and Duncan's chairs were empty. But before I could make my way over to ask Mom if she knew their whereabouts, they strolled in, arm in arm. I ran up to Crystal and gave her a hug.

"Where have you been?" I demanded.

"Hey, sis, I'm sorry. We haven't been able to catch up with you all day. Those crowds today were awful. There was nowhere to park. When did they start all that construction on Lomaland Drive?"

"Like a year ago," I answered.

Duncan leaned in to give me a hug and Crystal went to sit down. He did not notice that I cringed at his touch.

"Hey, Pumpkin," Duncan said in my ear.

"You can't call me that. That's for family only."

Duncan's hair was slicked back with too much gel. The first two buttons of his blue and white striped shirt were undone, and his chest hair was sticking out. I thought my sister hated chest hair as much as I did. How does she put up with that?

I took my seat next to Crystal and my dad stood up, chiming his spoon against his glass, indicating he was about to make a speech.

"I would like to thank you all for coming," Dad started.

Like a good speaker, he made eye contact with each member of his audience, but then stopped as he got to Crystal and Duncan. When she noticed he had made eye contact with her, she quickly looked away.

Dad paused for a moment, then continued. "This is a big day for our little girl. Her grades were never as good in college as they were in high school, but now that we've all seen it here, I'm sure you can understand why."

The crowd chuckled kindly. Dad never had a problem making his kids the butt of a public joke.

"But, seriously, we have known since Lyssa was a little girl that she would be successful. I knew it the day I took her with me to a booksellers' convention and she rounded up every business card on the floor. She was the first eight-year-old to ever ask me for a business-card holder."

"Now, since not everyone knows each other, let's go around the table, stand, and introduce ourselves. We'll start to my right, with Peter. Peter here is a longtime family friend. He's actually the British guy that we wanted our older daughter to marry. Peter?"

Dad sat down and Peter stood up, blushing from my father's introduction.

Peter and Crystal were the same age, and both our fathers had been attending Nazarene conventions since they were twelve years old. There were never any sparks between them, but when I looked over at Crystal, she was crying. Duncan's chair was empty, and she bolted after him.

The rounds of introductions continued, despite the dramatic scene. I leaned back in my chair and grabbed the handle of the French door behind me that led to the bar. Cracking it open, I could see Duncan slamming down a shot of what looked like tequila. Crystal pulled at his arm, trying to get him to come back. He did not look at her, shooing her away with his arm. The bartender put another shot glass down in front of him. Why was that jerk getting drunk at my graduation dinner?

They did not make it back to their seats in time for their

introductions, so I made a joke about newlyweds leaving their plates untouched. Crystal had not eaten a morsel, and my dad had spent all this money on a nice dinner.

After everyone had left, they came back and sat down. Duncan reeked of booze.

"Pardon me, sir, excuse me, waiter," Duncan slurred. "Terribly sorry, but could you possibly warm this plate up a bit? Oh, too kind, too kind."

The waiter took his plate and Crystal's. I had never been so embarrassed.

"So, right then," Duncan continued. "The se'cret out! Your father'd prefer it if you married someone else. Cheerio!" He slammed down another drink and droplets of sweat dotted his forehead.

Crystal turned to me and took my hands in hers.

"I'm sorry, Lyssa. We've been at the beach all day, and he's tired. He doesn't know how Dad jokes about stuff like that. Look, we had a really good time today. Our hotel is beautiful. You should go out with your friends tonight and have a great time. Just do me a favor and don't go down to Tijuana. It always sounds like a good idea when you're drunk, but trust me, it's not."

"Crys, this is such a cop out," I said. I wanted to stomp my foot on the ground. "Mom and Dad are not going out with us tonight, and by the way, how long has it been since you talked to Dad? Is this the first time you've even seen him since you got married? That's insane!" I argued. "Look, please come! I miss you."

"I can't," said Crystal. She looked like she was going to cry.

I gave my sister a hug and a kiss on the forehead as I got up to leave. She seemed so much older than the last time I saw her. The waiter brought their food, reheated, and I left.

12

CRYSTAL

July 31, 2001

IT'D BEEN THREE LONG YEARS SINCE MY DAD TOLD ME I COULDN'T COME HOME. He'd been true to his word, though Mom and I have met for lunch and shopping. She tried to intervene on my behalf, but Dad was incredibly stubborn. At this point, I was not going to beg him anymore. He was banned from my house, just as much as I was banned from his. He deserved to be in the dark about my life. You can't love someone only if certain conditions are met, as long as certain behaviors are followed. That's not love. At least, that's not what I wanted love to be. I wanted it to be unconditional. I wanted it to survive for better or worse. Right now, it was definitely worse.

I no longer cared about ever going on a cruise to the Bahamas, or traveling at all. I even stopped journaling. The house was dirty. The laundry was piling up. I needed more and more sleep, but I found a million reasons to stop dreaming. All the wind had gone out of my sails. My life felt like the moment right before a thunderstorm, when the soft, dark gray blanket would unroll itself over our heads and the afternoon breeze would disappear. When the air would get sucked up into the sky and all God's creatures got eerily quiet. Even the crickets stopped chirping.

A half-filled diary was all that remained of my former self, like a field half plowed because the farmer just decided to up and walk away. I sat in the middle of a small room inside my house surrounded by clean clothes that should have been put away and mail that needed sorting. I couldn't even move. My grades were hurting too. I barely made deadlines and couldn't concentrate in class.

Duncan wouldn't let me go back on Zoloft. He said antidepressants were for crazy people. Inside my head, I felt like I was losing a battle that was part of a war I could not see. Maybe I was crazy.

To not write, for me, was to not live. As I flipped through my journal, I could see all these empty pages, all these significant days that had flown by unrecorded. What happened in them? Where were all the days going? What would be left behind when I was gone?

Actually, I shouldn't have made such a big deal about it. Everyone was busy. Who cared if I wrote in my journal, really? What was important was that I finished the laundry, sorted through the mail, and got milk before Duncan got back from his business trip. All he asked of me, he said, was that I have fresh two percent milk in the fridge when he got home.

I was comfortable with the idea that I was alone most weeks, Monday through Thursday. Sometimes I felt like I wanted to talk to God, but I didn't. What was I going to say? I was too afraid it would come out as complaints, which would be rude, since I had so many blessings. I had my cat, Figment, to keep me company. I went to the gym after work. I cooked for one. I shouldn't fuss.

My life was kind of nice, actually. I felt like I had my own apartment. I felt sort of independent. I could go out with my friends and not catch any slack from Duncan. He said he would never prevent me from hanging out with my friends like his dad had with his mom. However, he'd systematically insulted all of my friends or found reasons not to trust them. He said most of my friends were ugly, like Jessica, with her horse teeth, who never stopped talking. Sure, I could hang out with them, but he wouldn't join in.

What's strange was that Duncan didn't have any friends outside of work, save Drew. Not that I minded—they were all very nice guys and funny. And they always took me out dancing when they went downtown, since Duncan hated dancing. Who wouldn't want to show up downtown with two boys on each arm?

Orange Ave was alive on Saturday nights. Throngs of stumbling partiers ebbed and flowed in and out of pulsating bars and night clubs. We always started out at Kate O'Brien's. The times when Duncan did come downtown, we parked in the five-dollar lot, even though I told Duncan it was cheaper across the street, but he said you couldn't back your car into those spaces. Only boys backed their cars in. After Kate's, we would go to Wall Street Cantina, where the music was much better. Then, we'd stumble into Slingapore's or One Eyed Jack's, where the floors were so beer-stained it sounded like you were walking on Velcro. You could feel the bottoms of your shoes become slightly harder to lift, like you had just stepped in honey. The entire street needed a good pressure washing. Slingapore's was more of a dance club than a bar, which I preferred. But the boys from Wisconsin and Penn State preferred the dive bars.

Duncan said he trusted them. He told them not to let me get

too drunk before they brought me home. The guys were cute, but my husband was gorgeous. I loved him so much; I would do anything for him. I couldn't let my dad be right about him. I had to make this marriage work. Maybe when he got home from this trip to New York, we could go out to a nice romantic dinner. We should go to that bistro on Park Avenue and order tiramisu. Maybe we could make it rain again.

One hot July afternoon, I stood at the kitchen table to sort through the mail. It was mostly junk and the occasional letter asking for donations to Point Loma. Duncan usually took care of all the bills, but he hadn't been home in so long, I thought it best to at least make sure we didn't miss something urgent.

Duncan set up most of the bills to be paid online; he was so organized. He had a brown leather checkbook cover with a black fountain pen clipped on the fold. I thought that was so cool. Nobody used real fountain pens anymore.

A white envelope from American Express caught my attention because of how thick it seemed. I pulled out a chair, folded my left leg underneath me, and sat down. My blue Victoria's Secret pajama pants wrinkled up around my legs. Figment jumped up on my lap and curled herself into a little black ball.

My dad had set me up with a gold card when I was eighteen years old; then, he put it away and wouldn't let me touch it. It was to help me build credit, he'd explained. I'd never understood the point of having a credit card I couldn't use.

When Duncan started to travel, he needed a credit card with a higher spending limit so he could book his flights and rental cars. The secretary could do that for him, he'd explained, but they never upgraded him to first class. That's when he started scheduling his own itineraries. I made him an additional signer on my AMEX account and got him his own card. I was happy to do it. I never used the card.

But when I opened the bill, I was horrified at what I found. More than $30,000 was due—and that was in addition to the $16,000 owed on my account number. My eyes scanned the pages in disbelief. I tried to find a charge or credit that made sense, but I didn't recognize any of it.

Just then, Duncan walked in the kitchen from the garage. He was on the phone, but I jumped up, grabbed it from his ear, and closed it shut. I was furious and out of patience. I scared my poor cat to death; she went scampering out the kitchen, her little feet slipping on the tile as she ran.

"What's wrong with you? That was a very important phone call!" Duncan yelled and dropped his briefcase to the floor.

I shoved the bill in his face. "What the heck is this? How do we owe American Express $46,000? Did we buy a car I don't know about?"

A bead of sweat formed on his hairline. Duncan grabbed the papers from me and looked down at them.

"And as long as we're on the subject, can you tell me why we live in this outdated townhouse but still drive really nice cars? Do you have something against living in a tract home like everyone else in this city?"

Duncan picked up the papers and looked through them.

"Well, this part here that says $6,000—my company owes me that much in expense reports. I already turned in most of them. Just haven't gotten them back yet."

"Okay, so what's the $40,000 balance?"

"Are you deaf? I just said I don't know what this is!" Duncan yelled back. His eyes grew wide with anger.

"Yes, you do! You just don't want to tell me!" I yelled.

Duncan threw the papers into the air and lunged at me. He

grabbed me by the neck and lifted me off the ground with one hand. I couldn't breathe. I grabbed his wrist with both hands.

He shoved me backwards into the living room. I was on my back on the floor, stunned. I gasped for one big breath of air and his hand was back on my throat before I knew it. He got down on his knees next to me and leaned over so all I could see were his fierce blue eyes. I tried to hold my breath, knowing I wouldn't get any air right now if I tried.

"You want to know why we live in this house? Because we could abandon it in the middle of the night if we had to. You can't take a house with you. Car titles are easier to change. Cars you can get into and drive away. I don't give two shits about this house."

He wasn't making any sense, but I couldn't concentrate on what he was saying. I focused all my effort on trying to get one quick breath in.

"This is your warning, lassie," said Duncan. "Keep out of it."

He released my neck and stood up. I sucked in air loudly and coughed.

"And don't ever take my phone from me again."

Duncan wiped sweat from his forehead and walked calmly back into the kitchen. I rolled over onto my stomach and curled up in a ball and started to cry. I heard Duncan collect the mail and his briefcase. I saw stars and struggled to breathe normally. I felt I needed to get out of his way before he came through the living room on his way upstairs.

My mind said move, yet my body remained in the same fetal position on the floor. Duncan stepped right over me.

"Go turn the air on," he said. "It's bloody hot in here."

His cell phone rang. He answered it.

"Hey, Kurt. What's up?" His voice sounded cheery, like we were having margaritas by the pool. "No way, man. Congratulations! That's great . . . Sure, we'd love to join you guys. I'm just home from New York, so let me get settled here and we'll meet you guys at Kate's. Yeah, buddy, again, congratulations."

Duncan hung up the phone and turned to me as he headed up the stairs. "Get dressed. We're going out with the boys. Wear something that hides how thick you're getting around the middle."

"No," I said, still on the floor in shock. "I'm not going anywhere with you."

"You'll go, or I'll snap your kitten's little neck," he said and kept walking up the stairs.

A couple hours later, Duncan and I were driving my car downtown. We would have left sooner, but Duncan made me change my outfit twice. Apparently, I had put on too much weight around my waist. I didn't want to wear jeans because it was too stinking hot.

Duncan said my jean skirt made my legs look fat and that working out so much made my quads look huge and my ankles too small. I reverted back to jeans and a black shirt. I wore my hair down to hide the red marks on my neck.

"You need to cheer up before we get there," said Duncan. "I don't want the guys to see you like this. You can be such a downer. Kurt just got engaged, so we are going to celebrate with him. You'll probably have to drive home, so don't drink too much."

"My sister's coming to town next week," I said, not caring about Kurt. It still hurt to talk. "I told her she could stay with us so she doesn't have to deal with Mom and Dad's curfew and rules. Plus, I can't go over there."

"I don't remember you asking me first."

"Well, you're out of town next week, aren't you?"

"No, that trip got cancelled. But your sister can stay with us, but only because I'm a nice guy."

"Sorry I didn't ask first."

"Alright," said Duncan, pulling in backward in his usual parking spot. "How's my hair look? Do you think it's thinning?"

"It looks fine," I said.

Duncan always walked ahead of me as we entered a bar or restaurant or house party. I walked a little slower than him, usually because I had heels on. Tonight, I let him walk into Kate's and disappear. I was walking in alone, and everything seemed to happen in slow motion.

I looked around the bar. I had been coming here for years, but tonight, it was strange to me, like I had never been there before. I felt as though I was having an out-of-body experience. The live music sounded like it was being played underwater and the murky orange lights coming from behind the liquor bottles hurt my head.

I was a girl walking. I was alive, but I was dead. I was physically here, but I was still mentally on the floor of the living room. A shell of myself walked past the live band and out to the patio area, where our friends were waiting for us.

"Crystal," Kurt said, hugging me. "You look great. Let me buy you a drink, hon."

"Thanks," I said. "Where's the bride-to-be?"

"She's outside having a smoke. You should go say hi."

I smiled and went to tell Duncan I was going outside. I tapped him on the shoulder, but he didn't turn around. He was talking to one of the owners of the firm about work. I tapped again. His boss saw me and smiled.

"Hello, Crystal." He gave me a hug. "You look great. Good to see you."

"You, too, sir," I said and turned to Duncan. "I'm going outside to find Jamie."

"Okay, sweetheart."

By midnight, Duncan was drunk. I sipped water by myself on a bar stool and checked my watch. I wanted to go home, but did not want to go home. A couple of drunk guys passed by me and whistled. One guy said a black T-shirt never looked so good on a girl. It didn't matter anymore. I couldn't care less how I looked.

The ride home that night was long. We didn't speak. I fought tears as I crawled into the loathed waterbed frame; our cats, Luscious and Figment, were curled up in their respective corners. My brain struggled to reconcile what had happened earlier. I had made him snap. I shouldn't have done that. He was probably under a lot of stress at work and I'd just made it worse.

I had just fallen asleep when a movement in my stomach forced me to sit straight up. My head was killing me. I crept into the bathroom and swallowed a couple of aspirin. When I tried to lie down, the room swelled.

I was going to throw up. Breathe, Crystal, just breathe.

I took a deep breath and a ball of liquid rose from the pit of my stomach into my mouth. Not wanting to wake Duncan, I raced for the toilet down the hall. I lifted the porcelain lid and hurled into the bowl. Little pieces of aspirin floated to the top and my head throbbed like my brain was suddenly too big for my skull. I flushed and collapsed onto the cold tile floor. My hand felt its way up the avocado wall to the window, trying to push it open. Air. I needed some air. My fingers found the ledge, but I was too weak to press against it.

I sat on the floor for a few minutes and decided to crawl back to bed. But when I tried to move, I threw up again. Maybe I'll just stay here for a bit.

I fluttered in and out of consciousness. My nostrils burned with acid and my tongue dissolved in my mouth like Pop Rocks in water. I vomited again and began to cry. Couldn't Duncan hear me? I wanted to scream, but I couldn't find my voice.

I took another deep breath and began to crawl slowly down the hallway. My cat met me halfway, licking my face. Go get Duncan. Go get Duncan. But Figment just kept licking. Cats.

I made it to the foot of the bed and fought the liquid ball rising in my esophagus. Unable to stand, I pulled the comforter down off the bed, exposing Duncan's naked body to the chilling breeze of the ceiling fan. He sat up and looked down.

"What the hell are you doing?"

"I'm sick," I barely whispered.

"Well, you shouldn't've drunk so much," he said and pulled the comforter back up over his head.

I'd only had two beers. This couldn't be alcohol poisoning. I spotted his car keys on the edge of the rolltop desk and pulled them down. That got his attention.

"Crystal, put my keys back," he said from the bed.

"Hospital," I said, swallowing bits of vomit.

"Are you serious?"

Duncan was pissed, but I didn't care. I felt like I was going to die.

"You're really pissing me off, you know that?"

Duncan got up and got dressed. He brought me a small bucket and I continued to throw up in it until we reached the ER. I couldn't wait to crawl into a hospital bed and pass out.

A doctor woke me up, flashing a light in my eyes. My feet were cold. Duncan tucked the blanket around my feet and my IV. It triggered the memory of the night my sister had been in this very hospital. Feelings of nostalgia mingled with nausea as the room spun wildly. Duncan put his hand on mine and leaned over.

"You know, if you wanted to celebrate our anniversary here, you could've just said so."

"I'm sorry about this," I said, fighting back tears.

"It's not your fault, Crystal. They tested your blood. There's not enough alcohol for it to be poisoned. The doctor thinks you have a migraine. A bad one. The nurse is going to give you a shot. If it works, you'll need to see Dr. Rosen as soon as possible."

"Why our family doctor?"

"Apparently you are likely to get this again. He can give you something to help." Duncan ran his fingers through my hair. "I'm so sorry I lost my temper with you. I love you, Crystal."

"I love you, too, Duncan."

The nurse gave me a shot and I fell back asleep. Less than twenty minutes later, my body convulsed, twitching in dramatic muscle spasms. The medicine was working its way through my body. Duncan rushed to my side to hold me and didn't let go until it stopped. When that passed, I felt much better–tired, but much better.

"When we get home, I'll darken the bedroom, just like the doctor said, and we can lie down and watch a movie. How's that sound?"

"Good," I said, relieved to have the sweet version of my Duncan back. "Can I get some of my kids' cereal too?"

"As much as you want," he said. "Captain Crunch, right?"

"Peanut Butter Captain Crunch," I replied.

I had introduced Duncan to kids' cereals when we got married. Apparently, they didn't have Kellogg's products in English boarding schools.

"Just don't make me drink your tea," I told him.

"We don't give any to you Americans," he said, his accent slipping out. "You idiots just toss it into the harbor." He laughed and kissed me on the forehead.

13

LYSSA

August 30, 2001

"So, D.C. is awesome, Crys," I said and sipped up the rest of my Vanilla Stoli and Diet Coke. "You should move there with me. At restaurants, you can hear all these different languages being spoken at the tables around you. It's just like being in Europe."

Crystal and I had decided to go out for a drink when Duncan got home. I was nice to him only because he was my brother-in-law. Crystal said she knew this restaurant in Winter Park Village that had great spinach dip. So, there we sat, two Nazarene college kids catching up on their lives over drinks in one of the most expensive places in Orlando. We sat at one of the small tables next to a window looking out at Park Ave. We'd gotten there early and had the place mostly to ourselves.

"Did you talk to Mom and Dad about what happened in

Arizona?" Crystal asked.

She was drinking a white wine I couldn't pronounce. Guess she got all fancy, being married now. She was still wearing her favorite black tank top, the one she'd bought from On the Contrary in Ocean Beach when I came out to visit her. I felt overdressed in my blue plaid shirt and khaki skirt.

"No," I said firmly.

"Have you even talked to Mom and Dad at all?"

She didn't respond. She lifted her wine glass to her lips and took a long sip. I didn't get to see her very much, so I dropped the subject. Didn't want to waste what little time we had together arguing about Dad's stupid temper.

"Crys, the guys there are so different," I said. "They have real jobs and went to Ivy League schools."

"Since when do you care about Ivy League schools?" she laughed.

Our waiter, a tall thin young man with dark hair, came by and asked to refill our drinks. We agreed in unison.

"Since the boys are preppy and cute."

"Oh yeah? Have you hooked up with any of these preppy boys?"

"Please don't go there," I begged.

"I can't go there? I'm your sister and I'm concerned. You've been through a lot, Lyssa. All I'm saying is, you loved Arizona, then you hated it. Now, you love D.C. . . . ."

"With Cindy, I think she wanted to move in with her boyfriend, but couldn't while I was still staying at her parents' house, so she booted me. I was only there like six weeks before moving to D.C."

"Did you sleep with her boyfriend, Lyssa?"

I threw her a look and gave her a solid "No." I don't know that she believed me.

"Do you find that you have trouble trusting guys?"

asked Crystal.

"You can't blame me for not trusting guys," I told her. "After one guy takes advantage of you, you don't trust any of them."

"Well, you'll eventually need to trust one. The right one. The perfect guy for you will be like an Alex P. Keaton—preppy, but not shallow. Smart, but not snobby. But the only way you're going to realize you've found him is if you leave your past here."

"Let's not talk about it right now, okay? Why don't we talk about you and Duncan? So, have you guys talked about having kids?" I asked her, not realizing I had surfaced a sensitive topic.

Crystal winced without pausing on the spinach dip.

"Kinda busy with school right now, Lyssa. Besides, have you ever known me to want kids?" said Crystal.

"No, but I just thought since you are not working right now that maybe you two were starting a family."

"Turns out I'm sort of allergic to birth control pills. They give me migraines so bad I end up in the hospital."

"So, what are you and Duncan using?" I asked.

"You don't need to use anything if you're not having sex," she muttered.

"Why aren't you having sex?" Not that I was surprised.

"I mean, sometimes . . . it's not all it's cracked up to be anyway. Sometimes it's downright painful."

"Crys, it's never supposed to be painful," I said.

"I could live with or without it, that's all I'm saying," she replied. "Besides, if we're not, I mean, if we were meant to get pregnant . . ."

I wanted to stop her right there. This did not sound like a relationship that would improve by bringing children into the picture. We knew girls in high school who would "forget" to take their birth control and end up pregnant so their boyfriends would not leave them. Today, those girls were single moms in trailer homes in Chuluota.

"Do you think you're ready to have kids? You're only twenty-five."

"Honestly, no. I have this long checklist of things I want to do before I have kids. I remember Mom getting her master's degree while trying to raise us, and how miserable she was. I'd like to get that out of the way first. I don't even have a master's degree yet. And there are still several countries I've never been to before."

"There's nothing stopping you from traveling, Crys. Just go."

"It's not that simple, Ms. 'My Passport Was Full Before I Graduated College.'"

She was right. I've been to more countries than she has. I kept traveling with Dad after she left for college. His trips only got better. Milan. Peru. She was so jealous.

"That tourism bureau where I used to intern in high school has an assistant position open. One of the directors is a former student of Mom's. He said he would put in a good word, but I didn't go for it."

"Why not?" I asked, truly surprised.

"Duncan says it doesn't pay enough."

The waiter could not bring our drinks fast enough. More tables filled up with beautiful young couples dressed to impress, but in a grown-up way, with sleek, off-the-shoulder black tops and expensive strappy purses.

"What about that company that publishes travel guides?" I asked. "The one by where Tiffany's dad works."

"Again, nothing in publishing is going to pay enough for what Duncan thinks we need to make." She sounded so defeated.

"My Lord, Crystal," I said and slammed my empty glass on the table. "What is up with you?"

Our drinks finally showed up, but I refused to break eye contact. "I've never heard you care about how much money you make. How much does Duncan make? It looks like he has new toys in the driveway, but you're still wearing the same clothes from college. You never even travel, anywhere, ever, which is so weird for you. You never went on a cruise for your honeymoon. I still don't understand why . . ."

"Honestly, what is up with all those nice cars when your house looks like something from a 1960s Sears catalogue?"

Crystal didn't reply. She took a swig of her wine and looked out the window. She was never this quiet. Even her small voice could silence the shouting at our family dinner table with one precisely interjected word.

One time, my dad was trying to explain to us why Nazarenes did not condone dancing. Crystal referenced a Bible verse where David danced before the Lord. Dad quipped back with how certain behavior was only appropriate at certain times, to which Crystal replied that she would have to ask God for grace. "For your spiritual walk?" my father asked. "No," replied Crystal. "On the dance floor. People who are not 'grace-full' . . . ha, ha."

But that version of Crystal wasn't here tonight. This girl just looked sad. Like she had given up.

"So, Lyssa," said Crystal as she came back to life, "I know you hate being back here in Orlando, so what are your plans for D.C.? What are you going to do there exactly?"

She was right. I hated Orlando. I had returned only a handful of times, even when I was in high school. During those times, I noticed how much had changed. Many of my favorite local haunts were gone, replaced with family-oriented restaurants or demolished to make way for new retirement housing.

Oviedo used to be nothing more than a couple of stoplights and dozens of chickens with right-of-way in front of the First Baptist Church by the Village Inn Diner. To my disbelief, a toll road now stretched over Red Bug Road all the way past Winter Springs Boulevard. Pretzels, the bar by Publix, had closed down, and the movie theater by UCF was abandoned.

But it was the things that hadn't changed that bothered me the most. The downtown bars and clubs were still playing the same techno mix of top forty songs, which were more like the top four songs over and over. And what retiree or recently married couple wouldn't want to live within forty minutes of Disney and the beach? They called them "newlyweds and nearly-deads" and they moved here in droves. Especially the Brits. I had read somewhere that thousands of people from the UK moved to Central Florida every year because of the weather and the exchange rate.

We both looked down and realized we had eaten all the chips. Crystal scooped up the rest of the spinach dip with a spoon. The room darkened as the afternoon clouds rolled in. A waiter came out from the kitchen and started to light each of the tea candles on the tables along the back wall, giving the place a warm orange glow. I was still hungry and wanted to order more food. I looked around for our waiter, but he was nowhere to be found.

"I think I'm going to quit my job," I said. The words fell out of my head and through my mouth before I had a chance to think about them. Once they were out, it felt right. It felt like I had just made a good decision.

"Do you have another job lined up? Do you have any money in the bank?" Crystal asked somewhat condescendingly.

"Remember Stacey from your World Civ class?"

Crystal shook her head. Crystal never remembered anyone. It's not that she was bad with names—she just wasn't good with people. Sometimes I wondered if she realized that others occupied the same planet she did.

"No? Hmm. Shocker," I teased. "Well, she's living in D.C. and can introduce me to some people at a think tank."

"What's a think tank?" Crystal asked.

"I don't know, but Dick Cheney's wife works there, so I know

I'll be in good company. Remember I told you about that old man I sat next to on the plane going to Arizona, the one who talked about missing nuclear missiles? Well, he gave me his business card, which had his name and an email address. It turns out he is good friends with the guy in D.C. who is going to interview me. Small world, huh?"

"But I wouldn't want to paint it," Crystal said, mocking a joke my dad always made. I don't think either of us ever understood it.

"Remember when we were in Switzerland and Mom and I were supposed to meet up with you and Dad in Zurich?"

Crystal's eyes widened as she remembered how ludicrous this meet-up turned out to be. "Yes! And we had like nine pieces of luggage each, and Dad and I had gotten on the train, trying to save seats, but we were on the wrong part of the train." Crystal was trying to talk, but started laughing so hard she could barely finish her sentence.

"But we didn't know! So Mom and I start, like, chucking our luggage up, but you were the only one strong enough to lift the last bag, so you got down on the platform and lifted it up to us . . ." I continued.

"And the train started moving . . ." Crystal said, all but in tears at this point.

"And I'm like run, Crystal, or we'll see you in Berlin!"

And with that, we were both in tears.

We lifted our heads and tried to draw breath between the guttural laughter as a waiter leaned over to light our candle. As the hand reached out for the candle on our table, I couldn't believe what I saw. Peeking out from under a white, rolled-up sleeve on the waiter's left wrist was the mirror image of Crystal's tattoo. I would recognize that unique dolphin outline anywhere. Mom screamed her head off when she saw it, and Crys had begged her not to tell Dad.

I looked up to see his face, warm tears of laughter still streaming down my cheeks. Instinctively, I grabbed my mouth with my hand as I gasped. The guy jumped back and stared at me, then Crystal. It was Sammy. The guy who'd swept her off her feet and then vanished without a reason. And now, he was our waiter. I gasped.

"Sammy?" Crystal asked in disbelief.

"What are you doing here?" Sammy asked, staring at her. "I thought you were in living in San Diego."

Crystal stared at him like she was looking at a ghost.

"I was. I moved. I'm here."

And she's married, dude.

"What are you doing here?" I piped in, but I might as well have been invisible.

"I'm going back to school at UCF to finish my degree," Sammy said.

He answered my question, but he didn't take his eyes off Crystal. I didn't see what was so attractive to Crystal about this guy. He had a beautiful wide smile, like a homecoming king, but he wore his dark hair super short and had brown eyes. He wasn't even that tall. Sammy just looked plain to me.

"Somebody once told me I had the potential to run my own business," he continued. "I believed her. So, I'm getting my business degree. I mean, you were about to graduate and I felt like I didn't deserve to be with someone like you. Actually, it's more like you deserved more than what I had to offer—and it looks like you got it." Sammy took her left hand and lifted it up to get a closer look at the two carats sitting on her ring finger. "Is that platinum?"

"You disappeared!" shouted Crystal. "I thought you were dead, Sam. Dead!"

"I'm sorry," he said. "I didn't have the guts to tell you I wanted to strike out on my own and let you graduate on your own."

"You were supposed to be my Secret Sharer!" Crystal's loud voice was now drawing attention. I needed to get her outside.

"Just tell me you are happy now, aren't you?" he asked, backing away from the table.

Good, I thought. Maybe if Sammy drills into her, he can get her to admit she's in a bad spot.

"I hate it when people tell me to be happy," she said. "Happiness was never my baseline."

"Just make sure he treats you right," said Sammy. "You deserve to be happy."

"I will be," said Crystal.

I looked down and noticed they were holding hands. Maybe there was hope.

Another waiter called to Sammy from the host stand. Sammy gave Crystal one last smile and walked away.

"Are you okay?" I asked.

"Peachy," said Crystal. She finished her wine and stood up, running her hand through her hair.

We paid the tab and headed out into the muggy night air.

"Sorry," I said. "At least you got some closure on that one." I didn't know what to say.

We got into her convertible and put the top down.

"No, you're right. I did," she said as she wiped tears from her cheeks. "You know, I don't think guys have any idea how much they can hurt us. Even when they don't mean to. It's what they don't say that stays with us. They don't say why they never called again. They don't tell you they don't love you anymore. Sometimes they don't even tell you when they've met somebody else."

"You're too pensive," I told her. "And melodramatic."

"Shut up."

"You shut up."

Crystal started up the car and the alto voice of Sheryl Crow's "Strong Enough" played faintly on the radio.

Crystal belted out as loudly as she could, the irony not lost on me. I joined in and we looked at each other and smiled. We sang in unison, and it was like all our problems were suddenly gone. We rolled down the windows and kept singing at the top of our lungs.

That's the great thing about having a sister. You could have the worst voice in the world, but when a good song came on, she encouraged singing out loud, even mid-conversation. For that brief two and a half minutes, nothing else mattered.

If you played it loud enough, the perfect song could help you transcend the moment, take you to a place devoid of time, a place without strict parents, a place where you don't run into ex-boyfriends, a place that suspended your heart and soul above the mess so you could be with your sister the way you remembered her.

For that short drive from Winter Park to Casselberry, there was just me, Crystal, and Sheryl Crow in the convertible on a dark and warm Florida evening.

14

DUNCAN

September 10, 2001

Since this last presidential election, Crystal hasn't shut up about my bloody U.S. citizenship. I know that was primarily why I needed her, but I was not in a rush to get the official paperwork done. At least, not yet. I'll admit, though, when the older gentleman came knocking about a U.S. census, it got me quite nervous. They said the information was anonymized, but I didn't trust them. Americans couldn't even figure out their own voting systems. And these Floridians, for Pete's sake, no wonder so many stupid Brits moved here. They felt right at home with these idiots who couldn't even count their own ballots.

This whole bloody country was bloody stupid. One minute, Gore won. Next minute, Bush won. Such a young nation— couldn't figure out what it wanted or how to get it. Parliaments worked much more efficiently. Not that I cared for this Blair fellow. Looked a bit like a wanker, if you asked me.

Of all the years I'd lived stateside, Florida had never been in such a national spotlight. Bloody idiots couldn't even figure out which boxes to check. I'd like to see the Queen give a rat's ass about punching chads. It upset Crystal, though. She'd stood in some line for more than an hour to vote for a loser.

I wondered what one of those ballots looked like. One thing was for sure—our firm shouldn't have been letting employees out to vote in the middle of the day. Affected productivity. Middle of the day, these blokes pushed back and shouted, "Heading to the polls to rock the vote." At one point, I was the only one at my desk signing off on blueprints. That's why America couldn't get ahead of China or become as rich as Saudi Arabia. Didn't see little chinks or towelheads up and leaving in the middle of the day to "rock the vote."

So, I'd let Crystal drag me into an immigration attorney's office "just to see what he said" about my situation. I wasn't sure how far to let her run with this. Far enough that she felt like she had explored all options, but not so far as to uncover the truth.

Crystal started her new job at a mega-church about two days ago after the magazine she had been working for was sold to a bigger publisher and laid everyone off. One of the missionaries for the church told her to use this particular immigration attorney. Bloody ridiculous job, helping missionaries and such. If God had wanted to help them, he would have had them born into a different country, if you ask me.

The office was in one of those desolate-looking two-level strip malls along the highway. "Immigration Attorney" read the black lettering on the Plexiglas door. A homely-looking secretary sat behind a tall dark brown desk with an oversized American flag hanging behind her.

Cheap furniture littered the small office. I assumed he

must not be a very good attorney, which was probably best. Four brown plastic chairs lined the wall back into the rear of the office. They looked terribly dingy in the fluorescent light. I didn't want to sit in them.

Crystal put in our name and handed the pudgy lady an envelope with a check to pay for the consultation. What a waste of money. We were told to take a seat. Rather stand, I would, than touch those chairs.

"You sure this guy's alright?" I asked Crystal.

"Yes, I overheard one of missionaries at the church. Said he helped several men from Sierra Leone get out during the war."

"What's Sierra Leone got to do with my situation?"

"They're both difficult situations."

"I don't see how that'll do me any good."

Moments later, a short, stout man in his early forties came 'round the corner. He was wearing a cheap brown suit, white shirt, no tie. Not very professional. He did have more hair than me, though. He led us back through a maze of gray-carpeted cubicles to a white door with a glass window and dusty mini blinds. At least his office was a decent size.

He introduced himself as Matt Simmons and motioned us to have a seat in the two shiny green chairs facing his wide wooden desk. Several diplomas hung on the wall behind him. Nothing Ivy League. Stacks of white paper lined the front of his desk. A gold nameplate faced us: Matt Simmons, Esq. The wall on the far side of the office was lined with bookshelves holding nice leather-bound collections.

Another bloody American flag stood on a tall bronze pole in the back corner. Crystal brought a satchel full of our wedding memorabilia, the marriage certificate and photos from the elopement. Her hair was pulled back and twisted into a clip. Her white shirt was wrinkled—she never ironed anything. Her ass looked good in those blue pants, though.

I checked my Seamaster. If we wrapped this up nice and quick, I could get back to the office for the 3 p.m. conference call with United Hospital Associates, our multi-million-dollar client, and then drinks with Tina on Park Ave.

I wore my favorite watch on days like today, when clients were in town. My boss, Rich, had a $20,000 Rolex, but he almost never wore it to the office, except when Danny was in town. Danny was president and CEO of UHA. Every year, they went sailing together on Danny's million-dollar yacht. Never been on it, but there were framed photos of it on Rich's desk that showed two levels below the main deck and a tower with satellite reception. One room even had a full-length dining hall. It was all a write-off, too.

They always hauled a ski boat on deck for Danny's wife, Marge. Danny took his wife, and my boss took whichever girl he was shagging at the time. They fished for days off the Atlantic Coast. Even if they didn't catch anything, Danny's little chef served up fresh fish for dinner each night. That was the life right there. I should have Crystal find out who he was dating, make them become friends. That was a sure way onboard.

"Well, then, what can I do for you folks?" Matt asked, folding his hands together on the desk. He probably did that to make us think he was sincerely interested in what we had to say.

I leaned back in my chair, toward the right. I needed to see Crystal out of the corner of my eye without letting her know I was checking her face for signals. She could not hide her emotions at all and overreacted to the stupidest things.

One day, she had planned on going to the beach, but it started raining. Weather Channel said beaches would be totally overcast for the day. One day, just one silly day, and she was all waterworks. Then she looked at me like I had to solve it. I had no control over the weather. What could I have done? I wasn't planning on going with her anyhow. I hated the beach.

When Crystal and I first got married, I used to take her to the beach on the back of my bike. We'd go, spur of the moment, just the two of us. She'd put all the goodies in her satchel on her back and we'd ride up there. Didn't like how the sand got all up in my engine, though. I knew I would only have to take her a handful of times to make her think I enjoyed the same things she did. After that, she could go with her mum if she wanted. Wasn't going to ruin my bike over it. Sea spray was not good for the engine.

"Well, Matt—I'm sorry, may I call you Matt?" I asked in my most polite accent.

"Of course, Duncan, of course," he said, smiling like a bloody idiot.

He didn't know what was about to hit him. I smiled and laughed.

"Well, Matt, long story short, I came over here on an E-2 investor's visa with my family. My father owned a construction company with another gentleman. It was doing quite well for some time. Then his partner ran the company into debt, stole all the money, and they had to shut down. I was already living here when it went belly up. Having graduated from school in England, I took a job with an engineering firm here in Orlando. That's where I've been ever since."

Nice delivery, I thought. Try to punch holes in that.

"When did you two get married?" Matt asked, looking at Crystal.

Why is he looking at Crystal? We are here for me.

"August 1, 1998. We eloped to St. Augustine. We stayed at this nice little bed and breakfast, which just happened to have a cancellation that morning for the honeymoon suite. So, we were able to get it for that weekend. Do you need the photos?"

"Not now, Crystal. But I'll mention those here in a bit because you will need them. Who witnessed the wedding?"

"The minister and my in-laws," she told the attorney.

"Anyone else? Anyone from your family?" he asked her.

Were my parents not valid witnesses? Why does this even matter?

"My sister was there, too," she said.

"No one else?" he was persistent about this.

"No," said Crystal, giving up.

The attorney paused for a moment and jotted down a few notes. He paused for a moment and then started up again with the questions.

"When was the last time the E-2 visa was renewed?" he asked, looking in my direction.

"Not sure," I said.

"Do you have a British passport?" he inquired.

"See, that's a funny story," I said and gave a chuckle. This guy was getting on my nerves. "When our plane landed at the airport, we had our dogs with us and all our luggage. My mother was in charge of the trolley. Our dog Bobby, he was one of those long-haired dogs, you know, where you can't see their eyes. Right cute, he was. Mom loved that dog, but I think my Pop could have done without it, you know? Well, Bobby got loose and we were all distracted. When we turned back round the trolley, my mom's purse had been robbed. Including all of our passports. I have a copy of the police report somewhere."

"Do you remember what airline you took coming over here?" Matt took out a pen and began writing something down.

Going to have to be more careful.

"No, I don't remember. It was so long ago."

"When exactly was it? That flight I mean."

"I'm not sure." I leaned further back in my chair.

"That's amazing, because you seem to have almost completely lost your accent."

Crystal shot me a glance and then looked down at her hands.

"You know, most of my clients are so excited to get to America that they never forget the first time they set foot on U.S. soil. And they rarely ever forget what airline they took." Matt sat back.

"Well, that wasn't the first time I'd been to the United States."

"Really? When did you first come here?"

Beads of sweat began to tickle my forehead. I ran my hand through what was left of my thinning hair.

"I was twelve when I came to Orlando for the first time. But I had to return because I wasn't finished with my O levels. You know what those are, right?"

"It's the British equivalent to high school. Am I correct?"

"Yes, you really know your stuff." I gave another forced laugh.

"Duncan, are your parents still living here?" Matt asked.

"No," I said, never losing eye contact. "They live back in England."

Crystal's eyes were burning a hole through my shirt. She'd best keep her yap shut till we left here. She began cracking each of her knuckles. I was done with this.

"Well, Duncan, Crystal, to proceed with getting permanent residency, we're going to need that investor's visa. Without a way to show that Duncan entered the country legally, it's going to be very difficult . . ."

"But we're married," said Crystal. "Doesn't that count for anything?"

"I'm afraid not," said Matt. "At least, not now. It will help when Duncan has to return to England, then asks for a green card to get back into the country. Even if we got him permanent residency, that doesn't allow him to work in the United States."

"What do you mean, return to England?" I asked at full attention.

"It's more than likely that during the process of filing the paperwork, you'll have to return to England for a brief time. From there, you can apply for a green card. We'll send in your marriage certificate and wedding photos. Since you have an engineering degree, that will help too, showing that you're qualified to work here."

"How long would he have to stay in England?" Crystal asked.

"Not long. Two months. A year at most. But I honestly don't think this case will take that long. I'm going to have my secretary give you a folder that will have a receipt for today's meeting and an I-90 form. Once you fill that out and sign it, send it back to me. Just curious, Duncan, when you were hired by the engineering firm, did you check the box that said you were a U.S. citizen?"

"Yes. I have a Social Security card."

"Really? I'd like to see it if you have it with you."

"No," I started to say, but then Crystal shot off her big mouth.

"Yes, I have a copy right here." She handed it to Matt.

"How did you get this?" he asked me.

"My father got it for me."

"Do you know where he got it from?"

"No, I've had it since I was about fifteen."

"Interesting," Matt said, staring at the photocopy. "What year did you say you started with your company?"

"Around 1992, I think."

"That's good. Because if you checked that little box after 1996, I'd have to tell you that you committed a felony," Matt said matter-of-factly.

"Excuse me?" I asked. "What did you just say?"

"In 1996, President Clinton made it illegal to falsely claim citizenship. Duncan, you've never committed a felony, have you? No criminal records here or in England or anything like that, right?"

"No, sir," I replied convincingly.

"Good. Well, then, as soon as you get that form back to me, we can get started."

"Matt, I'm sorry to ask this, but how much is it going to cost to file that form?" Crystal asked.

"That form is only $150 if it gets processed with no problems. If the INS decides, for whatever reason, that Duncan needs to return to the UK and apply for a green card from there, that will cost around $2,500, which will include permanent residency."

"But you don't foresee any major problems with getting him citizenship?"

"It might take a year, but, no, I don't see any problems with this case."

Crystal stood to shake Matt's hand. "Great, well, thank you so much, Matt. I really appreciate you getting us in on short notice."

"No problem," Matt said and rose from his chair. "That pastor of yours is a good friend of mine. Tell him I said hello, will you?"

"I will." Crystal went to the door to leave.

I smiled and shook Matt's hand with the firmest grip possible.

"And try to find that investor's visa, if you can. I'm sure the British Embassy has a copy. It'll be a huge help."

"Will do, Matt," I assured him and followed Crystal out the door.

As we walked back to our respective cars, my head was swimming with details.

"Well, that's some good news, isn't it?" Crystal asked. "I'll contact the British Embassy and start looking for that investor's visa. Are you sure your dad doesn't have a copy of it somewhere?"

She unlocked and opened her car door, but I came up behind her and slammed it shut.

"Let's get one thing set straightaway," I said. I pushed her body up against the car and leaned in so I could whisper. "I'm not going back to fucking England."

"But Duncan—" Crystal started.

"Drop it! This is your last warning," I said and headed to my truck.

Crystal chased after me like old Bobby and put her hands on my arm.

"Duncan, listen to me. I know you hate England. I know you think it's rainy and cold and miserable. But we need to do this now. I just have this feeling in the pit of my stomach that if we don't do this soon, something catastrophic is going to happen and things won't be this easy any more. Don't you feel like time is running out?"

I noticed the small scar on Crystal's face that flared when she was emotional. Several strands of her brown hair had escaped from the clip and the wind was blowing them mercilessly across her face. Crystal didn't always dry her hair for work. She would rather sleep in an extra twenty minutes than fix herself up right. Sounded lazy to me, but the girl looked beautiful either way.

"Duncan, we can do this. We can face anything together. Look, I can't explain it, I just know that if we don't do this now, it's going to be too late."

"We are done with talking to Matt-fucking-esquire, or anyone else. I am not getting any visas and we are not filling out any paperwork. Do you understand me?"

I stared into her eyes, making her fear me. Needed to know I got my message across.

"This ends now. I'm not going to tell you again," I growled.

I grabbed her arm just above the elbow and squeezed it until I felt her veins throb in the palm of my hand. I imagined the flow of blood insider her body slowing, getting choked off. All I could see was red. The thought of that color made me even more angry.

"You have no idea what you're talking about. Go back to your car. I'm late for work." I shoved her hands off me and climbed into my new truck.

"Duncan, wait. How long are you going to be at work?" Crystal asked. She looked like a pathetic little pup.

"Late," I shouted back at her as I peeled away.

She'd learn. She'd learn soon, or she'd be sorry. As I drove away, I could see her in my side mirror. She stood there with that blue folder in her hand. Did she really plan to call the British Embassy? Got to at least admire her ambition. Didn't know about the felony bit. Damn Clinton. Knew I didn't like that lying bastard.

That settled things for sure at the firm. Couldn't just be an employee. Needed to be indispensable. If I could work my way to partner, then they definitely wouldn't fire me. Each partner was now the head of his own division. I'd need my own division. Mechanical, fire protection, plumbing, even electrical had already been taken.

If I could combine my computer engineering knowledge with what I knew about my clients' electrical systems, I could create a systems design unit within the firm. I already had two guys on my team who were interested in telecom. If I could recruit a couple more and sell up my Y2K successes, I'd be indispensable. A security specialist. God, I was a bloody genius.

15

CRYSTAL

September 15, 2001

IT'S SAD HOW MARRIED LIFE BECOMES NOTHING BUT A SERIES OF OBLI-
GATIONS. My parents had always controlled every move I made
growing up, so adulthood should have been the freedom I
longed for. Instead, I was locked down again, only this time
there was no end in sight, so I had nothing to look forward
to—just being dragged from one dinner party to the next, one
friend's wedding to the next, and so on.

Now that it looked like our country would be going to war, I
knew I couldn't pursue legal immigration for Duncan anymore.
The government would be looking for anyone who wasn't in the
country legally and deporting them, even if they weren't Muslim
or from the Middle East. Everything was going to shift now. Our
country had been too open. We had been too welcoming. We'd

let in these criminals. We'd fed them. We'd housed them. We'd trained them. Now, they were killing us from the inside out. No one could be trusted. Not even neighbors.

This was probably why Duncan's parents never left their apartment anymore. They were becoming paranoid. Gail had invited me over for dinner while Duncan was in Boston for work again. She seemed to be smoking more, if that was even possible. The night I was at their apartment, she would smoke and cook at the same time, her eyes glued to the news on TV. She jumped every time the phone rang.

I didn't want to be there. I hated the smell of their cigarettes and listening to their stories of England and Scotland over and over again. It was like they were talking about other people's lives. They repeated what their families said to them, but they could never remember real life dates or events from those stories. They began to give me the creeps.

Every other girl my age was out with her friends, laughing and drinking margaritas. But Duncan slowly choked off all communication with my friends. He never forbade me to see them outright. He'd said his father did that to his mother and he would never do that to me, but he did do it, in his own way. Duncan would tell me my friends were so "brainy and unattractive."

I never wanted to spend time with my parents before I was married. Perhaps I took for granted that the option to do so would always be there. My parents lived only twenty minutes away, but they may as well have been on the other side of the world. My dad never even tried to apologize to me. I stopped trying to play the mediator. It was easier to be Duncan's wife than be my parents' daughter. Trying to be both would kill me.

It didn't help that Mom kept bugging me about grandchildren. For some reason, I felt it wasn't wise for Duncan and me to have kids. I was haunted by fears of leaving my child alone with his parents. At first, I'd thought their teasing was cute, but there was a scary unpredictability in his mother, even when she wasn't drunk in the middle of the day.

Howard was converting our back porch into a sunroom. We moved the sliding glass door back and filled in the screen with a wall. The next step was laying the tile—the same tile we had in the kitchen. We were paying Howard to do the job, mostly in cash, partly in beer.

He would come over and crack open a can of Natural Light at nine o'clock in the morning. The biggest drinkers I knew didn't start that early. I felt uneasy about having him in our house while Duncan was out of town, but nobody cared what I thought. My job at the church was only two miles down the road, but I refused to come home for lunch, in case Howard was there.

Our neighbors said he sat on an upside-down paint bucket for hours in our garage and smoked. I told them he was doing construction work on our porch. They didn't seem to believe me.

For a man who used to own a small hotel in England, Howard seemed really rough around the edges. Howard's many lively anecdotes were filled with beatings, pain, coldness, and poverty. His father was a whaler and his mother had to pick the fish bones from his clothes before washing them. Howard had nine brothers and sisters, all of whom still lived in Edinburgh. Duncan hoped I would never meet them.

They called us on Christmas and New Year's Eve. I tried to talk to them, but their dialect was so thick, I had no idea what they were saying. Howard's mom joked about drinking her whiskey through a straw—that was the most I ever understood.

Duncan showed me pictures of the estate, with its helipad and horse stables. Must have been hard losing all that. I often wondered why they hadn't returned to the UK, where the country's health-care system would take care of them. I worried that if one of them got sick here, we wouldn't have the money to pay the hospital bill. I especially felt sorry for Gale. Her mom died just before New Year's Eve and she never got to say goodbye.

Duncan's best friend, Drew, threw a party at his house, and invited everyone over to meet his new girlfriend, Jenny. She was beautiful—tall and thin with a flat stomach and straight dark hair. She was a paralegal downtown and had a gorgeous singing voice. She reminded me of the wives at the firm. She knew how to cook and clean and dreamed of being a wife and mother. I felt like a failure around her.

Duncan and I left the party shortly after midnight. Their house in Sanford wasn't far from our townhouse in Fern Park, but we didn't want to be on the road with all the crazy drunks. Drew begged us to stay over. His girlfriend had worked her magic estrogen wand, transforming Drew's two-bedroom house into a coordinated, candle-filled home. She had a real knack for interior design on a budget. I didn't think I would ever be that domestic.

A few minutes after Duncan fell asleep, we got a call from Gale. She needed a ride home because Howard left her at a bar after they got into a fight. I was still wide awake, eating ice cream on the couch, so I offered to go get her. I knew kids in high school who did this to each other, but never a couple who had been married for thirty years.

I volunteered to pick her up at the restaurant where she had been left, which was my first mistake. Gale was wasted. With a sincere look of pity, the waiter handed me my drunk mother-in-law like a rag doll. The transaction felt even more bizarre since I was still wearing the silver halter top I'd had on for Drew's party. I was a young woman all dressed up suddenly made old by having to care for a wrinkled crone more than twice my age.

I buckled Gale in the car, tucking her rose-patterned dress under her legs so it wouldn't get stuck in the door. Poor Gale. The last time she had seen her mom was when she left England with Howard more than twenty years before, vowing never to return to such a dreary place. I did not want to end up like this, never having seen my dad or my home again.

Then, Gale said something very strange: If she had flown back to England to bury her mother, she would not have been able to return to the United States. Maybe part of what Duncan had told the attorney was true after all. That's the best way to get people to believe what you tell them. Mix some truth in with the lies.

So, there she sat, slumped over in my car, a petite old woman at sixty-two, crying. When we stopped at the light before getting on I-4, I looked hard at the lines on her face. During that suspended moment in time, my subconscious imposed my own visage beneath her wrinkles. Duncan would become his father and I would become this faded drunken woman, aged before her time. I looked at Gale, watching the reflection of red from the street light change to green on the patterns of her dress. This would be me in twenty years if I didn't do something soon.

"Gale," I said. I nudged her slightly. "Gale, are you alright? Did you have a bit too much to drink?"

"Oh, Crystal, I'm terribly sorry."

"It's okay. I've had my fair share of passing out on the way home. Everyone has."

"Here I am, your own mother-in-law, and you're having to cart me 'round like a bloody child."

"Gale, please. Don't worry about it."

"That Howard's a bastard," she said, tugging on her safety belt. "His temper is simply inexcusable."

She straightened out her skirt, pretending to have manners in the midst of a mess.

"This isn't the first time he's left me, you know."

I didn't say anything for fear I'd say too much.

"One time, he left me alone for three months on a supposed

business trip. That's when I started having an affair with a nice young Frenchman."

I nearly slammed on the brakes. Why was she telling me this?

"Gale, does that explain Duncan's brother? The one who died . . ."

"I think Howard knew, but he never asked me about it," she continued as if she couldn't hear me. "It's not like I didn't know about his little indiscretions."

Okay, that was more than enough information for one night. Starting off the day in a drunken confessional with Duncan's mother talking about cheating on his father was not my idea of a good time.

"Gale, I don't need to know . . ." I said.

But she wasn't listening.

"It only went on for about three years. I never thought I would do such a thing. But for some reason, the next time Howard lost his temper and hit me in the face, it didn't hurt as much."

I wanted to run my car off the road.

"No, after that, he never hurt me as much."

I dropped Gale off at their apartment and made sure she got in. As I watched her walk through the door, I realized how much Gale and I had in common. I thought about the day she went with Duncan and me to sign our marriage license at the courthouse. She was supposed to be a witness, but when it came time to sign the paperwork, she refused to come in. Duncan looked down at the certificate; sweat dripped from his forehead. There was a blank line beneath the place for his signature: "Birth City/State/Country." He hesitated. He put the pen to the paper, then pulled away again.

"Why doesn't your mother want to sign?"

"She's just nervous," Duncan whispered.

Duncan looked down and penned the words "Yorkshire, England," on the line. The old lady behind the counter took the paper, signed it, stamped it, made a photocopy, and handed us the original.

"That's it?" Duncan asked.

"That's it," she replied. "Just make sure you get the minister to sign it at the bottom and mail us a copy once that's done."

Duncan took in a deep breath.

"Brilliant, thank you very much," he'd said, and we'd hurried out to the parking lot.

Gale and I had both married men our parents didn't like—and we stayed married to them because we had made our beds, and now we had to lie in them. Some days, they were beds of nails. Some days, they were beds of luxury. But they were beds we had chosen and we could not look back.

As I walked up my stairs to go to my actual bed, I thought about how Duncan had no idea of his mom's affair. I thought about what he might do if he found out. It was not my place to tell him. He had already suffered enough because of his parents' dysfunctional marriage.

When I passed by our spare bathroom upstairs, I noticed there was still a hole in the door from Duncan's fist. A few nights ago, he was aiming for my face, but said he missed on purpose. He had promised to replace the door when we started building in the porch. Part of me wondered if he was proud of the damage his wrath had caused. He probably left it there as a reminder that I was not to make him angry again.

I had yelled at him about something trivial; I don't even remember what it was, but he was furious. He drew his arm back, and I'd ducked behind the bathroom door just in time for him to nail it with his fist.

My eyes were closed, but I heard the crunch of bone against wood. Then the gold door knob came flying back at me, hitting me in the eye as I crouched behind the flying bits of the door.

Technically, that was the second door he had destroyed in

this house. The first was the metal bi-fold in our bedroom. He left the bloodstain from his knuckles on the door for two weeks as a reminder to not make him angry again. I made him "see red," he told me. I cleaned it off while he was out of town.

He brought home flowers for me after that. Promised never to do it again. He was just stressed from work, he said. The firm was giving him his own division, and he had a lot more responsibilities. I shouldn't have added to his stress.

At least I was able to get a job. Thank goodness the church where I was volunteering was able to hire me on full-time. I loved helping them coordinate international travel for their missionaries and group trips. At least I could help some nice people see the world, even if I couldn't. Heck, I couldn't even leave the state to visit my sister in D.C. I swore Duncan was erasing her calls.

Without a creative outlet, I wasn't motivated to do much of anything. I sat on our ugly green couch in a living room that reminded me of a cave. I ate popcorn while watching Buffy the Vampire Slayer alone with our two black cats. Any other show with normal relationships in it was too hard for me to watch. I tried to stick to horror movies, because romantic comedies were too depressing for me. It was hard to watch anyone, in person or in movies, getting attention like that from someone.

Duncan rarely wanted to have sex with me anymore and when he did, my obligation was to "please him." I hated doing it, but he made me feel so guilty if I didn't—like it was my fault that I was allergic to birth control pills and I was actively trying not to get pregnant now.

It was around this time that the dreams started. I was drowning, but instead of trying to save myself, because I could still feel a sandy floor beneath my toes, I let my arms float and I just let go. Sometimes I opened my mouth and let the water rush in; other times I would change my mind at the last minute and swim for the shore.

16

DUNCAN

September 29, 2001

WILLIAM FINALLY INVITED ME OUT TO DINNER WITH HIS WIFE AND DAUGH-
TER. This was just the opportunity I needed to get chummy with
the owners of the firm. I suggested Indian food, since his lovely
wife, Sharon, grew up in the UK, and she would like that.

William was the only partner-owner without a field of exper-
tise, so to speak. Mechanical engineering was his background
and he did have his professional engineering license, but I
didn't see him as deserving as the other blokes. If the firm was
willing to sell him shares, they'd certainly do the same for me.
Soon as I got my security department up and running, maybe
I'd get a few certificates of my own, not to mention I would get
control of purchasing equipment. Our clients didn't question
what got purchased for them, or at what price.

Besides, with more than 100 employees and new recruits all the time, I couldn't just tread water. Like a shark, I had to keep moving or I might lose my job, and I knew I'd never get another one, at least not without committing an outright felony.

These new recruits were coming out of schools like Penn State and the Milwaukee School of Engineering with better and better training. Experience was my best weapon right now. They might have been smart, but they weren't learning systems engineering yet. And now that William had me on salary, I had to get more bonus cash out of them.

I knew what the other guys were making because I could hack into our payroll system, and it was more than what I was making. Some idiot left a backdoor open. I went in and found all the bloody salaries and bonuses just sitting there. I wanted at least a $30,000 bonus this year. Damn credit card bills were stressing me out beyond belief. I'd earned at least that amount, all the overtime I'd put in.

I had traded in my Alfa for a Range Rover and I still owed Drew for the new paint job. Owed my pa for finishing off the porch. And I was going to need a new suit for the grand opening of the Cheshire Medical Center in New York next week. Our latest score from Sanford hadn't paid off yet. That cash might not show up for weeks. Waiting for it stressed me out, which was causing my hair to fall out.

That reminded me. Needed to get more Rogaine tomorrow. I wondered if my hair loss was noticeable in the dark like this.

"I got great feedback on my photography portfolio at school," said Crystal.

"Good for you. Does my hair look alright?" I asked, leaning over to the rearview mirror, running my hands through the thinning black threads.

"It's hard to tell," said Crystal. "It's kinda dark out."

"No shit, Crys. Turn the schtupid light on then."

"I don't know where it is, Duncan! This isn't my car."

I clicked the light above the mirror.

"Yeah, it looks fine," she said.

"You didn't even look," I protested.

"Yes, I did look at your hair. I have a brush if you want to use it."

"Never mind. You're worthless," I murmured under my breath.

I got out of the car and checked for my phone and my wallet. I always put my cell phone on the same clip in the car. Sometimes I forgot to transfer it back to my belt when I got out.

"How can we afford this car anyway?" Crystal asked.

She got out of the car and pulled down her skirt so it sat lower on her hips. She adjusted her shirt so her left shoulder was exposed. She had put on so much weight, I didn't even want to be seen with her.

"I'm going to get a big bonus this year."

We began walking up to the Indian Spice restaurant, and I didn't see any other Range Rovers in the parking lot. I loved that.

"How do you know?"

"Because this dinner with William is going to go really well. Just try to be friendly instead of your usual self, okay?"

"What is that supposed to mean?" she asked.

I didn't answer.

"Well, do I look okay? I never know how to dress for these dinners with the partners. All my work clothes are too business-like, and all my go-out clothes are too skimpy."

"You need to get back to the gym. Stomach's hanging out a little," I said, putting my index finger on her abs right below her belly button. "You should find out what Drew's girlfriend does to work out. She always looks great."

"She only works part-time and—"

"See," I said, opening the door and breathing in the smell of curry. "That's what you should do."

"I thought I explained to you how important—"

"Crystal, stop talking," I said, shooting her a glance. "William might already be here."

I spotted William across the restaurant. He stood up from a round table where his wife and daughter were seated next to two empty chairs. William Vertige was in his early forties and married to a gorgeous white South African woman about the same age. With as much money as he had, he should have married younger, but in this case, he found a dame who was petite and beautiful, so I guess she was an exception. His stepdaughter Whitney was stunning as well. She was just a couple years younger than my wife.

"Hey, man, how's it goin'?" William gave my hand a firm shake.

I smiled and shook his hand just as hard.

"Hey, good to see you." I replied.

"Duncan, you know my wife, Sharon," William said, gesturing toward her.

"Hello, Duncan," Sharon smiled.

"Yes, always a pleasure to see you. You look lovely," I said.

"And this is my daughter, Whitney."

I took Whitney's hand and kissed it. "Clearly you're going to be just as beautiful as your mother," I laughed.

She had dark brown hair and tempting eyes. Her black pants and white top made her look super skinny. Like Crystal used to be.

Crystal quickly took a seat next to Whitney and I sat next to Sharon.

The place was packed for a Friday night. Gaudy gold ornaments hung along the peach walls that glowed in the candlelight. A row of serving tables laden with silver buffet trays was pushed up against the far wall of the main dining area of the restaurant.

"So, Sharon," Crystal said, looking over the top of her menu. "What's South Africa like? Duncan tells me that's where you were born."

"Just like every other British colony, I s'pose," I said, reminding them that my roots were of superior origin.

"Yes, Duncan, it was a colony, many, many years ago," said Sharon. "It's beautiful, Crystal. There are these stunning Victorian buildings along the waterfront near Cape Town. And the further north you go, you come across these vineyards that stretch for dozens of kilometers."

"Oh, really? So, they have good wine there?" Crystal asked.

"Oh, excellent wines," said Sharon.

Sharon held her fork and knife the proper way, with her index fingers extended long against the stems. I noticed Whitney did the same.

"The French actually noticed the soil was perfect, um, Napoleon, I think it was. They planted their grapevines in African soil and created amazing pinot noirs and sauvignon blancs."

"Speaking of alcohol," I said, getting bored of their conversation, "should we order some wine?"

"Yes," William agreed. "Let's share a white. What goes well with curry, Sharon?"

"Any pinot grigio will be fine, dear," said Sharon.

"Whitney, I hear you went to college in California," I said.

Whitney had on a strapless top that made her quite the looker. There was something sultry about the way she subtly pulled her hair around toward her right shoulder and let it drape down over her chest.

"So did my wife."

"Oh, where at?" Whitney asked Crystal.

"In San Diego," replied Crystal. "A small private school that no one's ever heard of called Point Loma Nazarene University. Where did you go?"

"UCLA. I got a pre-law degree. I'm an assistant at a law firm downtown."

"That's amazing. How do you like being back in Orlando?"

"I don't," Whitney laughed.

"Me neither," said Crystal, smiling.

The waiter came to take our order and I gave him specific instructions on how I liked my curry. I let the women talk about female stuff, and William and I got down to business. After a few drinks, he let slip that the firm was moving into a new building across the street from its current location. I offered to pre-wire the first floor with CAT6 cable. I explained how I could even get some for free. William knew I was good for it.

I never offered to hook people up without knowing I could deliver. When the office wanted to get Nextel phones, I worked a deal with the sales guy and got everyone in my department a free phone. They loved me for it. I was the guy who knew someone. Guys in other departments came to me for their PDAs, installing speakers in their homes, and re-keying their locks. The keying set I had from when I worked at a door manufacturer had come in handy on more than one occasion.

"Duncan," Sharon called to me from across the table, "you simply must take this beautiful wife of yours on a cruise."

I shot a look at Crystal. Crikey! Was she bringing this up already?

"I was just telling her about how the three of us went to Greece this past summer," said Sharon. "It was the most gorgeous trip I've ever taken. Someone as well-traveled as your wife would truly enjoy it."

I refused to look at Crystal. I didn't want to deal with the daggers that were probably coming out of her eyes.

"That's a lovely idea, Sharon, except I put in more than sixty hours a week on a regular basis. And if I want to pass my certifications later this year, I need to study."

"William, you're not being a slave driver at the office, are you?" Sharon asked.

"Who, me? Never. Actually, this guy right here clocked in more overtime hours than any other employee at the firm," William said, placing his hand firmly on my shoulder.

"I could've told you that," Crystal murmured, sipping her glass of wine.

After getting a little tipsy, the small talk seemed like it dribbled on forever. Surely it must have been getting time for dessert.

"Will there be anything else?" The waiter came up behind me, his white napkin folded perfectly over his left arm.

"Yes," I said. "I'll have some rice pudding. Room temperature, if you can."

"I'm not sure if we have any, but I'll check, sir. Anyone else?" Everyone shook his or her head.

"This is an Indian restaurant, is it not?" I asked. "I know there's rice pudding back there somewhere. Mum used to make the best rice pudding."

The waiter brought out a small bowl several minutes later. It was a bit cold, but felt good after all that curry.

"Well, thanks for meeting us for dinner," said William. "This was great."

"Yes, we should do this again," I said.

After the bill was paid, we all stood up to leave. I offered to pay it without really wanting to, so when William refused to let me, I was relieved.

On our way out, Whitney grabbed Crystal's arm. I wasn't sure I wanted the two of them becoming chums, but I did want to get more facetime with William.

"Hey, I'm going downtown later tonight with some friends if you want to meet up," Whitney said to Crystal.

"I'd love to!" Crystal replied, but then looked over at me. "I'll call you if I can make it."

"Great," said Whitney. "If you can't tonight, call me later anyway. We should go out."

"Definitely," said Crystal.

As we headed toward the car, I strategized around Whitney's interest in Crystal. I'd rather Crystal spend time with my boss's girlfriend, or maybe Sharon.

When we were almost home, I told Crystal she couldn't meet Whitney downtown. At least not tonight.

"Why don't you hang out with Amanda?" I asked.

"She scares me. She's so fit. She only works three days a week and spends the rest of her time at the gym or shopping. I don't want to hang out with her. We don't have anything in common."

"You're both with engineers," I explained. "You're both at every firm event."

"Duncan, she said she doesn't watch the news because it's too depressing. She's never left the country and can't wait to be a mom. What could I possibly have in common with someone like that?"

"I don't know. Why don't you try not being such a snob?"

"None of the guys at the firm think I'm a snob."

"I know, trust me," I said.

I didn't tell her that the other week, one of the good-looking new recruits named Justin owed me money from lunch. When he wrote the check out, he wrote in the memo line "for a date with your wife." Arrogant asshole.

"It's not like I can become real friends with any of these women anyway," said Crystal. "When they ask me why you and I haven't been on a cruise together, I have to lie to them. I don't like lying."

"You get used to it," I said. "Just don't get that close to anyone."

"What do you mean, don't get that close to anyone? I'm not

like you, Duncan. When I become friends with someone, I try to be as open with them as they are with me. You don't like any of my friends. You don't like any of my family . . . and if I didn't know any better, I'd say you're the reason my sister never leaves a message when she calls. You probably erase it."

"Your sister's a slut," I told her.

I couldn't drive fast enough. We kept hitting every red light along 17-92. It was agonizing.

"Don't call her that!" Crystal shouted.

"What? You know she's slept around and your parents still treat her like an angel and you always get the shaft," I said. "Your dad was only going to spend a couple grand on a wedding for you. Meanwhile, he's paying to fly your sister all over the world."

"Stop it," Crystal protested. "Do you realize I almost lost her? I thought she was dead for an entire day on September 11th and I felt horrible because you have driven a wedge between us.

"When that plane flew into the Pentagon, I thought she was in that building. I had to stand in front of the TV and watch, not knowing if my dad was safe in New York, not knowing if my sister was still alive in D.C. Did you do anything to help me try to find them? No! Tiffany actually reached Lyssa before any of us. How pathetic is that? Thank God we got ahold of my dad, who had actually missed his flight that morning." Crystal stopped for a moment to catch her breath and get ready to have another go at me.

"All you care about is your job, because you know if you lose it, you'll have to go back to England or take up contract construction work like your dad. You eat, sleep, and breathe the firm. You only hang out with guys from the firm, who we are lying to all the time."

I pulled into our driveway and threw the Range Rover into park.

"Get out," I said without looking at her.

"What?" Crystal asked.

"Get out of the car, you schtupid girl, and go inside the house."

"Aren't you coming in?" she asked naïvely.

"No," I said. "You're going in. I'm going out downtown with everyone else."

"But I wanted to meet up with Whitney," said Crystal.

She had opened her door and stepped out. She was standing there, holding the door and staring at me.

"Then maybe you shouldn't act like such an annoying bitch."

I threw the car into reverse, nearly tearing the passenger door from Crystal's arm. As I slammed on the gas and turned to head out, the door swung itself closed. I thought I heard Crystal give out a yell and saw her clutch her arm as I drove away. Served her right.

17

LYSSA

January 30, 2002

I HAD BEEN WORKING FOR RON TYSON FOR TWO MONTHS. He showed every bit of confidence in me, yet I still got nervous before our meetings. Who wouldn't, I suppose. He stole me from the top think tank in D.C. Four of the six people attending this meeting were former agency employees—nobody who actually worked for the CIA calls it that. They all say "the agency." One of them had citizenship in four countries and spoke ten languages. Even that guy was not as intimidating as my boss, the sixth and final attendee seated at the head of the oblong table in our small, nondescript conference room.

Tyson International Consulting was doing some amazing work in Europe, and I was so fortunate to work here. I just never felt like my report summaries provided sufficient information.

My colleagues were some of the sharpest minds I had ever met. I finally felt like I was a part of something worth working around the clock for.

"What we have found, sir, is that there is a sharp increase in activity throughout Turkey prior to these Muslim holidays," I said. I stood, spoke loudly, and kept my chin raised. "Our sources, however, found no communication between the previously mentioned imams in France and the popular mosques in the southern region."

The soundproof room we were in started to feel more like it was vacuum-sealed. My voice sounded soft and weak as it landed firm against the white walls. A flash of heat went across my forehead and I remembered that this narrow conference room tended to get warm quickly when the door was closed.

"Based on this information," I continued, "I would like to recommend an additional four weeks to monitor the chat rooms from our watchlist, sir." My stomach growled from beneath my navy-blue Ann Taylor suit.

"Sounds great, Lyssa," Ron replied. He had shaggy dark blond hair and wore his button-down shirts untucked around our office. Like most men in D.C., he had a belly like he was slightly pregnant. "Good work. Also, if you don't mind, please add Egypt and Iraq to your list."

"But I have Egypt, sir," Jodie Seamens added. She was a Middle East researcher like me, but her dad had been in the military, so she knew more acronyms than I did. She also dressed like a Slavic hospital worker.

"Yes, but you no longer have any agency ties there, and I'd like to hear what our prodigy finds out. Lyssa, you've got two weeks to bring me that information. Meeting adjourned."

Two weeks? Is he joking? I collected my notes and headed back to my desk to grab my purse. If I wanted to leave before nightfall, lunch would have to be scarfed down in front of my laptop.

There were no individual desks in our office. Ron preferred to be as mobile as possible. With a moment's notice, we could have everything in boxes and be working two floors above this one and nobody would be the wiser. He even kept a "go" bag in the closet with a bottle of water, first aid kit, and change of clothes. Some people thought he was paranoid. I just thought he knew more than the rest of us.

"What is this?" I asked, knowing no one would even look up. A small red rose with a white envelope tied around the stem lay on my keyboard. Next to it was a brown envelope, obviously government related.

"I assume somebody already checked this for anthrax?" I asked with a laugh.

Those kinds of jokes were not funny in Ron's office, but occasionally he laughed at them anyway.

"Dinner tomorrow night," the note read. "The Willard Hotel. No press."

Graham and I got engaged at that hotel. A long red carpet ran from the main entrance of the ornate lobby past the restaurant. Black marble walls held up a cream-colored ceiling crowded with ornate floral crests and crystal chandeliers.

I'll never forget leaving through the front doors, hand in hand, having accepted his proposal, the faint smell of cigars wafting past us from the Round Robin entrance.

The Pentagon was where I met Graham. I thought he was so handsome and mature looking with his thick, short blond hair and blue eyes. He was working on Capitol Hill at the time and had one of his friends from the White House "detain me for questioning" after a briefing. Once his friend thought I was qualified after some intense and odd questioning, he gave Graham my phone number. Dating here seemed to follow some sort of obligatory vetting procedure. It was weird. I had never heard people use the word "pedigree" when talking about dating and marriage until I moved here.

The brown envelope was probably my security clearance application. That was going to have to hit the backburner for a while. I opened the seal and pulled out an inch-thick stack of papers and a lanyard with the generic temporary White House pass Ron had hooked me up with for the time being. It didn't have my name on it, but at least it would get me in the same room with Graham for events.

"What's the matter?" asked Jodie. She stared at the envelope.

"Nothing. I'm fine," I managed to say. "I'm leaving early today. I'll see you tomorrow."

"Don't forget about our lunch meeting at the White House," Jodie said.

"Wouldn't miss it," I replied and darted toward the door.

I fumbled for my keys to let myself out. Our office locked from the inside and the outside. Terrorists were plotting against the U.S. government at all hours, so our office was never closed. No matter what time our researchers found something, Ron had to be the first to know. With news breaking online ahead of the TV stations lately, we had to post updates every minute of the day. I imagined Ron slept with his eyes open, like a fish.

I turned and locked the plain brown door behind me. There were no markings to indicate which office was ours. The first week I worked here, I mistakenly tried to unlock the janitor's closet.

As I sat on the Key Bridge on my way home, I tried to think of how I would break the news to Graham that we were going to have a baby. Should I stop somewhere and buy a tiny rattle, or maybe a pair of infant-sized shoes? No, he'd think I'd picked them up off the sidewalk. I'd just pour him a glass of wine and tell him to guess why I was not drinking.

I walked into our brownstone on the block behind M Street and hung my keychain on the mail holder by the front door.

"Graham! Are you home?" I yelled unnecessarily loudly into our small, two-bedroom home. We hadn't had any snow yet this year, yet it was bitterly cold. Mom and Dad had come to stay with us for Christmas and didn't bring enough layers, so we'd taken them shopping at Tyson's Corner on December 24. What a nightmare that was.

"Hey, my wife is home," said Graham and then he kissed my cheek. I could tell he loved the sound of that.

"Hello, honey, how are you?" I asked. "Thank you so much for my rose. I love it."

"Getting a flower inside your office is harder than getting an agent inside Kabul," said Graham as he pulled the burgundy tie off from around his neck.

"I know. Ron's paranoid. Probably for good reason."

"For very good reason," said Graham. "What he's doing in South Africa is borderline illegal."

"Oh, come on. When our country does it, it's called leader-ship," I retorted.

I took Graham's hand in mine. The blue polo shirt he was wearing made his eyes stand out. "So, let's sit on the couch and chat."

"Uh-oh," Graham said hesitantly. "Am I in trouble?"

I shook my head and led him by the hand into the living room with its 100-year-old fireplace and creaky wooden floors. We sat down on the beige three-seater sofa my mom had found at a garage sale.

I looked Graham straight in the eyes and just blurted it out: "I'm pregnant!" I was smiling from ear to ear. "We're going to have a baby!"

Graham was shocked, probably as much as I was when the doctor told me why I had missed my period. I'd honestly thought it was stress from work. We hadn't even been trying.

"That's great! Wow! That's great!" Graham said and gave me

a big hug. "How far along are we? When did you find out? Have you told your parents?"

"Whoa with the questions," I said. "I'm not that far along and no, I haven't told my parents. We can probably tell our folks, but I don't want to tell anyone else until I'm at least twelve weeks. That's what the doctor suggested."

I went through a list of people I wanted to tell and my thoughts fell on my sister.

"What's wrong?" Graham asked, having seen the cloud come over my face.

"Crystal . . . I want to tell her."

"So, call her."

"Duncan blocked my number from her cell phone."

"Are you serious?"

Graham got up and went upstairs to our bedroom. When he came back down, he had a huge brick of a phone in his hand.

"What is that?" I asked.

"It's a government-issued sat phone," he said. "Can't block this number."

I laughed so hard I almost peed myself.

"Is this what they call counterintelligence?"

Graham laughed. "No," he said. "Here, I'll show you how to use it."

I did what he showed me, pressing down very hard on the thick plastic covering each of the numbers. Crystal didn't answer, so I left her a message. It was a clever trick with the phone, but I didn't want to spend the next nine months figuring out ways around Duncan. I wished she would just wake up and leave him.

18

CRYSTAL

June 7, 2002

I HAD BEEN TELLING MYSELF THAT MOST TWENTY-SIX-YEAR-OLD WOMEN IN AMERICA WOULD HAVE GIVEN THEIR RIGHT ARMS FOR WHAT I HAD: a beautiful house, a gorgeous husband who made a lot of money, and a job that I loved. Yet I could not shake the feeling that it meant nothing because it was all a giant façade. The fact that love was missing from this picture made it all worthless, like fool's gold. Duncan and I were more like roommates than husband and wife. There was no room left in my brain for dreaming. My thoughts were completely occupied with ways to avoid making the beast angry.

I had no idea what went on at his job other than what his coworkers told me. Duncan had no idea how I spent my free time. It was like the string connecting us had snapped. I'd thought that if I went through the motions of loving him, I could tie the loose ends back together again. But I came to realize that was impossible. He terrified me—even if he was my husband. So, sex was the only defense I had to prevent his wrath. And even then, he never looked at me anymore.

I tried to pursue my own personal goals, getting my MFA, and volunteering for the church, but I hid most of my dreams from him. One time, I was helping a friend with her thesis at Duncan's company beach retreat. I was editing her manuscript by the pool when Duncan snatched the marked-up papers from my hands and tossed them into the water; the pages fell like crisp leaves and dissolved. He scolded me for not being social. It was the weekend before she needed my final changes, and now they were lost. He said I was being rude by not joining in with the other owners' wives at the bar. I had to redo all my edits by flashlight at night while he slept.

So, by the time my graduation ceremony rolled around, it would reveal cracks in the House of Douglas. Having received an A+ on my portfolio, I proudly went forward with my classmates to accept my diploma on that harshly bright morning in late June. After pushing through this degree on my own, this day meant a great deal to me. And, of course, my husband had not yet arrived.

During the commencement speech, my eyes scanned the bleachers for his white button-down shirt and dark pants. He had been asleep when I left the house, but there was a ninety percent chance that was exactly what he would be wearing.

When the ceremony concluded, I found my family members outside. Still no Duncan. The sun was bright and the parking lot was packed. Jessica brought our friend Norm to my graduation. The plan was to all go to lunch afterwards to congratulate me on my achievement. I was foolish to think I could have a day to celebrate me.

When my phone rang, I knew who it was. I didn't want to answer it.

"Look, don't be mad, but I can't make it," Duncan said.

"What?" I was furious. "This is my graduation day! Are you crazy? You've been completely unsupportive this entire time and now you're just going to . . ."

"Mum tried to kill herself this morning. She took a bunch of pills and is lying on her bed, not moving. Pa just called and asked me to come over."

"Well, that would explain why they are not here," I said callously.

"I don't want your family to know, so just tell them I had to go into work. It's an emergency."

"No, Duncan. We can lie to your boss. We can lie to our friends. But we are done lying to my family."

Duncan's tone changed.

"You'll do what I tell you to do."

I couldn't see him in front of me, but I knew he had that look in his eyes. The soulless blue trying to physically pierce me with its stare.

A voice seemed to come from outside of me and whispered gently to my mind: This is not the life I had planned for you. It was so clear; I looked around to see if anyone else had heard it.

"No, Duncan," I said firmly. "No."

"Crystal, don't do this to me. Not today."

I stood there, silent and resolute.

"I'll deal with you later," Duncan said and hung up.

I wondered if Gail had purposely chosen my graduation day to pull her stunt, if it had even happened at all.

"Hey Belle, I got you some flowers," I heard my dad's voice call out my old nickname.

I turned around and there he was, standing in front of me with a bouquet of stargazer lilies. He was wearing a blue, long-sleeve button down shirt and khaki pants. Casual for him, but he looked nice.

"I was so proud seeing you today. I wanted to make sure I told you that in person."

My dad handed me the flowers and I took them willingly. I had several speeches rehearsed in my head that I wanted to tell him. Like how he'd hurt our whole family, not just me. And how spending Christmases at restaurants and church services would never be as good as spending them on the floor of his living room. But I didn't say any of these things. Despite all my anger towards him, I was so happy to see him at my graduation.

"Thank you," I said. "I didn't realize you were coming."

Mom walked up and stood next to Dad in her bright, knee-length Lilly Pulitzer dress. She looked at us and smiled. She'd probably been working on making this moment happen for three years. Her persistence and prayers finally paid off.

"We're so proud of you, sweetheart," my mom said. "We wouldn't miss it for the world."

"Do you want to grab dinner?" My dad asked. "I promise it won't be Chinese food."

"I would, really, but, um, Duncan's mom is sick," I said.

It was an excuse. I could have gone to eat with them. Going out for Chinese food was my dad's favorite. None of us had the heart to tell him people order Chinese food to take out. We were always the only ones in the restaurant. While I wasn't ready to break bread with my dad again just yet, I was touched that they came today.

"Thank you so much for the flowers," I said. "Stargazers are my favorite."

"Well, we hope your mother-in-law feels better soon," my mom said and gave me a hug.

I waved good-bye and headed towards my car. My dad was always terrible at apologies. I don't think I've ever heard him say "I'm sorry" to anyone, so this was as close as I was going to get. I looked at the flowers in the passenger seat and took them as a peace offering–a beautiful, long overdue peace offering.

When I got home that night, I learned it was true. Gail had swallowed a fistful of sleeping pills and a jug of white zin.

I stepped into the kitchen and hung my keys on the rack. Duncan was sitting on the couch, watching TV. I took a deep breath and walked over to him like death descending mercifully upon its prey. He didn't look at me. The sting of my invisibility was gone.

"Hey, you have a good time?" he asked, still looking at the screen.

"Yes. How is your mother?"

I looked at him and he looked at the TV. It had been the same routine for years, but I was done with this type of performance.

"Rough," he replied. "I don't want to talk about it. Are we finally done with this grad school nonsense?"

"Yes," I said coldly, suddenly realizing how little I cared whether he wanted to talk about it. "By the way, I got a call from Whitney on the way home. She said she got a call from Steve something about her cheating on him. You didn't tell Steve what I told you, did you?"

"Oh, yeah," Duncan said, still not turning toward me.

"Did you know Whitney and Steve were dating?"

"Steve is my top engineer," said Duncan. "Of course I knew they were dating. Guys talk at the office. Steve and Dana broke up almost a year ago. I warned Steve about Whitney, but he started dating her anyway. I don't want my guy getting hurt."

"So, you told him what I told you in private? What my best

friend told me in confidence? You weren't supposed to tell anyone. It's none of your business."

"It's my business when it involves my guys," Duncan said. Now he was looking at me. "Who cares what Whitney thinks? She's a slut."

I couldn't believe the words that were coming out of his mouth. "So, you don't care that you've ruined my friendship with Whitney, much less her mother, Sharon? The only women I've been able to become real friends with at the firm? Sharon once told me that you used to be a gossipmonger."

"Sharon has no right to judge me. What else did she say about me? You call her up right now. I want to talk to her. I'll give her a piece of my mind, talking about me behind my back!"

Duncan stood up and went for the phone. I was fuming, but didn't want this to spiral out of control. With any luck, I could use this argument to sleep upstairs tonight and not next to him.

"No!" I shouted. "You've done enough damage. I'll take the blame for this. Just forget about it, alright?" I stood up and headed for the bedroom.

"Where are you going?" Duncan shouted.

"The bedroom. Is that okay with you? I'd like to get ready for bed."

"No, wait," he said, putting down the cordless phone. "Come here, sweetie. I'm sorry."

I didn't move. I just stood beside the couch. Duncan came up behind me and wrapped his arms around me. He kissed the side of my face and it almost stung. He had no loyalty to me. I was a fool for being so loyal to him.

"Look, finish watching this movie with me. We'll have some Cadbury Flakes and milk and just chill out."

He took my hand and led me back to the couch. I didn't know why I was being so complacent. It really didn't matter anymore. I was more worried about Whitney hating me than I was about

Duncan suspecting something was wrong.

"You know what, Duncan, I'm not hungry. Thank you for the offer, but I'm going to bed." I got up and walked toward the bedroom.

"Fine. Suit yourself, bitch."

That last word made me stop in my tracks. It was like calling Marty McFly a chicken. I hoped he enjoyed that. That was his last potshot.

I walked into the room and shut the door behind me. I prayed I could get ready for bed before he came in. I put on my purple silk nightgown and sat down on the edge of the bed.

Afraid I would not be able to sleep, I popped a couple of Tylenol PMs. The last thing I needed was to wake up with a migraine. I swallowed the little blue pills using a bottle of water I always kept on my nightstand. I took a good look around the bedroom. I said goodbye to the plum walls, the white comforter, and the nine-foot ceiling. I said goodbye to all of it because it was no longer real.

19

DUNCAN

June 8, 2002

PA AND I LEFT CRYSTAL WITH MUM AT THE APARTMENT. Crystal would keep Mum from hurting herself and Mum would prevent Crystal from following us or finding out where we were going.

We headed for the Dragon Pub on International Drive. More Scots hung out at this place than any other Brit-owned pub in Central Florida. Apparently, more than a hundred of these pubs existed in the state. From the outside, it looked like any other chain restaurant. Inside, the place looked like a run-down boat. Wood beams stretched across the ceiling, coming down to the floor in four main pillars. It had a small fireplace on one end and a dingy bar with four bar stools at the other. Two dart boards were crammed into the corner, and Off Kilter's bagpipe music played low over the hum of families arguing and eating.

The American-owned pubs that tried to look British came off more like rides at Disney—American impressions of what they thought England felt like. But this place was damn near close to authentic. Family crests from real clans decorated the posts and walls.

A sash from a real family tartan hung above the fireplace. Names like McDougal, Wallace, and Taylor hung like war medals, each with a horse, sword, or helmet representing its history. Names like those had been around for centuries; they deserved respect. I had chosen the name Douglas for our new identities in the U.S. because it was such a common sounding name, yet still had UK roots.

"Pa, do we still have the Douglas crest?" I asked, grabbing a table in the corner by the fireplace.

"Och aye," he said, looking down. He hadn't spoken more than two words on the way here.

"Do you think maybe I could have it? I'd like to hang it up somewhere prominent in the house."

"Ahe, 'course you can," Pa said, smoothing his thin gray hair across the top of his head.

Pa used to have a full head of auburn hair with a dark orange beard. I always thought it strange that my stubble grew in orange, even though my hair was black. He never used to wear glasses either. Together, the bifocals and gray wisps on his forehead made him seem old and weak.

"Can I take your order, love?"

A fat young Scottish woman with one long braid in her hair stood at our table. She was the reason I found American women so attractive. Her roundish face and beady eyes gave me the willies.

"I'll have a shandy," I said, looking back down at the menu to avoid the sight of her.

"Guinness," said Pa, "in the largest glass you've got."

"I'll get right on that and be back in a minute to take your orders."

She waddled off, and I watched a family of Scots bustle through the front door. Short, loud and pale. Two of the children headed for the dartboards straightaway. The women headed for the can and the men plopped themselves down at the table. Scots never did have small families. That's why I always thought of us as being more British than Scottish.

The fat lass brought our drinks in tall glass mugs. Pa and I ordered some fish and chips. We drank, but barely talked.

"You wankers usually meet in the open like this?" I asked.

"Son, nobody in here's got ears for what we're sayin'—lest they find themselves in need of our help and can't get it," said Pa.

"Does Uncle Pete know who's comin'?"

"Nah, those lazy sons o' bitches. They don't wanna be bothered with details. They ain't got the brains neither. All muscle, they are."

"I'm smarter than Uncle Pete. I could run jobs like this from over here."

"It's not like that, son," Pa said, signaling to the waitress for another beer. "You've got a nice legitimate day job. Don't lose it. Don't do nothin' to risk losin' it. When we finish getting the rest of our clan out safely, we won't have this money coming in. You'll need an income. That's all."

"But we could sell this opportunity to others—" I said.

"Son, I said no. Those days are over, and there's no' a damn thing we can do to change that. We had our run of it. Just work directly with him on this last run and be done with it."

A tall man with a potbelly and dishcloth hanging from his belt brought out our dishes. He had terrible teeth. Must have been British. The smell of the beer batter made me realize how hungry I was. Finding good fish and chips in the States was damn near impossible. You found good fish, they had soggy batter. You found good batter, they had bad fish. And the chips, the chips were almost always undercooked. Then nobody thought to put any bloody vinegar on the table.

"Has Crystal noticed the safe?" asked Pa.

"Not at all," I said confidently. "And she dropped the whole citizenship thing after the towers were hit. Something about immigration laws changing."

"Shit," said Pa. "Might have to up our prices."

"I've already added more encryption to the files," I boasted.

"Sounds like your boarding school education is finally paying off," said Pa, downing the rest of his beer. "Remember when I had to come get you out of school for blowing out that boy's kneecaps with a pipe? That was Bruce's boy you got! I were pissed off with you that day. I paid cash, up front, for that bloody boarding school, so I could take care of business at the house without a young lad running around. And what do you do? One year before your A-Levels, you go and blow out that boy's kneecaps. Ha."

"Nothing you and Pete didn't teach me."

"I taught yer bugger all, son! You couldn't even get into that school without me taking your entrance exam for you."

"I never did figure out how you got the headmaster to leave the room."

"In those days, son, our clan never had to ask twice for nothing," Pa said, finishing off his beer and signaling for another round.

"How come all that's different now? I never hear any new stories."

"Things are different now. After the big fall out between the two clans, the money we got was never enough. Bruce's clan bought the insurance on the hotel. I was supposed to make it look like an accident, but the investigation labeled it arson and they lost it all. Millions. I sold the loot we had stolen before setting the fire–jewelry, artwork, everything. Hundreds of thousands of dollars. They came after us. I tried to give them most of the cash to leave us be, but that didn't settle it. They wanted blood. That's why we are here. That's why we had to get the others out. Don't get greedy and keep doing this for anyone else."

"When did Mum find out about you and Bonnie?"

As soon as the name came out of my mouth, I wished it hadn't, but as long as Pa was in the mood to talk, I thought I'd ask about it. That was a mistake. Pa pointed his fork at me, pushing down on it with his pointer finger like he could put it straight through my eye before I could blink. Pa had an affair with Mum's best friend. Mum thought Bonnie stayed behind in England, but she'd actually followed us to Orlando. We had Nanna tell Mum Bonnie died of cancer.

"I told you never to mention that name in front of me." He stabbed his fork back into his fish and looked 'round the room. "I still remember that day the bobbies came to our front door after you hacked into Scotland Yard," he said, completely changing the subject.

"I'll never forget the look on your face, Pa."

"You were just a lad of fifteen, and when they came in and saw your room. Och. I've never seen two people pick up so much computer equipment in my life."

"Took me longer to explain to you what I'd done," I said, laughing.

"I still don't understand it. Something about our phone lines and the two computers . . ."

"Come on, Pa. I thought you'd be proud of me, hacking before I could drive." I smiled and Pa kept chortling.

"Those were the good ol' days," Pa said, lifting his finger in the air for another beer. "Now look at us, two saps with balls and chains attached to our asses."

"At least I have good-looking one," I said. "I'll still trade her in for two twenty-year-olds when she turns forty though."

That tickled Pa. We finished up our food and I paid the bill.

"So, you don't think you'll ever go back?"

"No, son. We can't go back. You have to get us one final big sum. And soon."

Just then, a short, square-chested man came through the front door and looked both ways around the restaurant. He was a Scot alright. Terse facial expression. Glowing blue eyes, and disproportionately large fists hanging down out of his wrinkled white button-down shirt. Pa saw him too. They both meandered up to the bar. I started to rise, but Pa put his right hand out, fingers splayed, and lowered it in my direction. I sat back down and looked around to see if anyone else noticed what was going on. Nobody gave two shits. Pa was right.

The two angry men sat on adjacent bar stools and kept their gazes forward. I could barely make out what they were saying. I pushed my chair backward toward the bar so I could hear them better.

"Why are you here?" asked the square-chested man.

"It's a bar. I'm ordering a beer. What's it look like?" said Pa. "Why are you here?"

"I'm looking for Uncle Pete's kin," he replied. "Didn't expect him to be an old fart."

"Ya, well, this is my last meet," said Pa. "Got to show the youngster how it's done."

"Not thinkin' of any funny business, are ya?" said the man.

"Too long in the tooth for that, aye," said Pa.

Both men gave a chuckle.

The man pushed a small envelope over to Pa. Pa felt it, picked it up, and weighed in his hand. It seemed to meet his satisfaction, because Pa then slipped the Social Security cards I'd given him out of his back jeans pocket and put them on the bar.

The man looked down at them and put his grizzly paw on top of the cards. He slid the cards toward his chest and got up from his bar stool. For the first time, he looked Pa in the eyes.

"Don't return to Scotland," he said. "Uncle Pete's turned on ya."

With that, he walked right back out the front door.

20

LYSSA

July 3, 2002

"How's my mommy-to-be?" Mom cooed.

Graham and I entered the foyer of their townhouse and the screen door slammed behind us. I jumped, even though I knew the sound was coming. They could have fixed that years ago. I think they left it so they could hear when someone was coming or going.

It felt good to hear my mom's voice. I smelled her amazing chocolate chip cookies and headed straight for the kitchen.

"I'm doing fine. The baby is doing fine . . ." I said.

Mom greeted Graham with a hug and pointed him in the direction of the upstairs bedroom where we would be staying this weekend. We could only come down for a few days. Mom insisted on hosting my baby shower in Orlando instead of D.C.

It was also likely the only way to get Crystal there, so I accepted.

"Do you need some new clothes?" Mom asked as she followed me to the cookie jar. "There's a new maternity store that just opened here . . ."

"No, Mom, I don't need any clothes. Thank you, though."

I bit into one of the cookies and my eyes rolled into the back of my head. She'd jam packed those piles of dough with more semi-sweet morsels than any cookie should rightly contain. Graham came around the corner and I shoved one in his face.

"You must eat one," I said.

He accepted and was probably thankful to have anything to eat. Our flight out of Reagan had been delayed almost two hours due to weather, and he spent the time on his cell phone instead of chowing down like I had.

Dad came in from his home office off the garage and greeted us with his traditional formal handshake. He was afraid to hug me and my big belly, so he gave me a kiss on the cheek, which was rare.

"Sit down, guys," said Dad. "We are so glad to have you here with us. Are you excited about the shower? Your mom's been hovering like a bumble bee planning everything."

Graham and I took a seat at the kitchen table and continued to nosh on cookies. I suddenly wanted milk.

"I'm sure it will all be great," said Graham. "Thanks for having us here."

"Oh, our pleasure," said Dad. "And don't you worry, Graham. You and I will go golfing at the Tuskawilla Country Club during the shower. Weather's supposed to be beautiful."

"That sounds wonderful, Anthony, thank you," said Graham. He looked genuinely relieved.

"How many people are coming?" I asked Mom.

"About fifteen or so, including one of your friends from D.C.— Blair, I think," she said. Then she paused and began to fidget with her hair and the nape of her neck.

"What is it?" I said bluntly.

"Crystal isn't sure if she can come," Mom said. She couldn't even look at me.

"She has to come!" I shouted. "She's the main reason we are having this shower here. Graham's mom is flying in from Maryland."

I tried to stop and take a breath. Getting upset like this was not going to help anything. I would go over and get her myself if I had to. She wasn't in prison.

Things really felt like they were getting to be over the top. I looked at Graham in a way that silently asked him if we should bring it up now. Graham looked back at me, then down at his cookie. He put his cookie down on his napkin and I took that to mean I should bring it up now. My mom came over and joined us at the kitchen table.

"Mom, Dad, for my job in D.C., you know how I have to have a certain level of security clearance?" I started.

They nodded.

"Well, my application a couple of months ago came back as denied."

Mom and Dad stared blank-faced at me. I wasn't sure how much detail to go into. Graham, as always, came to the rescue.

"It could be for any reason," said Graham. "Sometimes if they can't reach a relative or source after a certain number of attempts, they will fail it and you have to run it through again later. So, it might be nothing."

"Or, it might be Duncan," I blurted out.

"What?" said Mom.

"Now, don't jump to conclusions, Lyssa," said Graham. "We'll know more when—"

"When what?" said Mom. "When will you know more?"

Graham and I exchanged looks again. In a split second,

without thinking, I just decided to tell her everything.

"Graham and I want to hire a private investigator to look into Duncan and his family. Graham knows someone really good, someone he used to work with. He's got connections all over the place, and has done this for years."

My parent's mouths were now agape.

"I just think it's about time we all knew the truth about Duncan," I continued my rant. "Even if Crystal decides not to leave him, at least she'll know who or what she's living with."

That felt good. If they decided not to do anything at this point, I was okay with my decision to move forward anyway. There was one time I got between Crystal's relationship with my parents when we were in high school. Crystal had stayed home while I went out to dinner with my parents. I was sure she had stayed home so she could meet up with her boyfriend, Michael, who my parents had forbidden her from seeing once he left for college. They did not want her dating a college guy. He was super smart, but he had long hair, so my parents hated him. When we got back from the restaurant, I picked up the phone and dialed *69, which called back the last number dialed from that phone. Sure enough, it was Michael's phone number. I was so proud of my sleuthing, I immediately told Mom and Dad. Crystal didn't give me a ride to school after that. She was so mad. This time, my sleuthing really was for her benefit, not mine.

"Donna and I have been praying for her," said Dad as he took Mom's hand. She looked at Dad and pursed her lips.

"That's great," I said. "But I think it's about time we do more than pray."

"I don't even see her for lunch anymore," said Mom. She was starting to cry. "And when I do, she just doesn't seem to be herself. Did I tell you that we went shopping together for window treatments and she wouldn't buy the ones she liked because Duncan would have hated the color? They were perfect for her living room and a total bargain. She wouldn't even take them home to try them out."

"I remember when Crystal didn't care about what other people thought," I said. "Especially if it was something as trivial as curtains."

"She said she was tired of arguing," Mom continued. "I know it seems like a silly example, but I think it's a small sign of a bigger picture we're not seeing. I can hear him cuss her out when he calls her on her cell phone. He talks to her like she's a child. The Crystal I raised would never put up with that."

I did not want to hear any more. I was surprised my mom hadn't confronted Duncan in her own way, like directly in his face.

"He's manipulative, Mom. What do you expect? He has to control her because he has no control over his own life. She's just a beautiful mantelpiece in his fake showroom."

"Is there anything we can do?" Dad asked. "Can we help pay for the investigator?"

"No, but thanks for offering. It's probably best that we don't discuss any of this with Crystal," said Graham. "I'll set up a meeting with him later this month when I get back from Turkey."

There was a long pause at the Vargas kitchen table. I wondered if we all felt partially responsible for how Crystal ended up in this situation—not so much me (clearly, I could not control my appendix rupturing), but I did think about where she might be if that had never happened. Or if I had never had a party that night.

I looked up at Dad and imagined he must feel somewhat culpable here. He threw her out of the house for no good reason. And that didn't even begin to sum up the stiff-arm fatherhood he put us through. I didn't think my parents would ever have any idea how their constant focus on my sister's looks, above all else, actually hurt any chance Crystal had at true happiness. We never discussed what Crystal wanted, only what guys wanted from her.

"I've got my entire Bible study praying for her, too," Mom said. "We've been praying that God would send someone into her life to help wake her up from the lie she's been living."

"Why hasn't God sent you?" I asked. "Why haven't you helped her wake up?"

I felt a kick and put my hand on my very round stomach near the movement. Graham noticed and put his hand right above mine.

"Is the baby moving?" Mom asked and put her hand where mine was.

I looked down at all our hands covering my belly. I was so fortunate to be surrounded by so much love and support.

"Mom," I said, "why don't we just help her leave him? At least, let her know that we would support her and love her no matter what. And if she chose to leave him, we would be there for her."

This was a radical idea in the Vargas household, where Scripture came first, unconditional love second. But it was about time we flipped those around. If we didn't, I might lose a sister and a best friend.

"Besides, if she leaves him because of something we find out in this report, she could just run right into another bad relationship. Whereas, if she leaves him because she realizes she deserves better, well, nothing like this will happen to her again."

Everyone looked at each other. No one seemed to want to be the first one to speak.

"When did you get to be so wise?" said Dad, breaking the silence.

"I don't feel very wise," I said. "I feel angry with myself for watching my sister get gaslighted and not doing anything to help her. The least we can do is offer to help her if she wants out. I think that's the least any loving family member would do."

21

CRYSTAL

July 5, 2002

"OH MY GOD, WHAT THE HECK HAPPENED HERE?"

Whitney stood in the kitchen of my new home, gasping at the horrific mess before her. I warned her not to come any further into the kitchen. She was only wearing flip-flops. Her long skinny legs stuck out from her terrycloth mini skirt. Her wide-necked shirt draped off her right shoulder. She put her car keys into her Gucci bag and stepped backward into the family room.

"Don't go in there, either," I said.

Glass was everywhere. I had dropped a jar of spaghetti sauce on the floor in the kitchen. Shards and marinara sauce carpeted the sand-colored tile like chunky blood with sparkles in it. The wire-mesh garbage can lay on its side, dented from where Duncan had kicked it against the wall repeatedly while I ran for cover.

Whitney had been cooking dinner with me every Tuesday since Duncan and I moved into our new home across town from where we used to live. Duncan actually chose a nice four-bedroom home with a three-car garage. He had to have enough room for his Range Rover, his Cutlass, his brand-new motorcycle, and his workbench. It was non-negotiable. I wanted him to be happy. The house was beautiful, all 2,500 square feet of it. Best of all, the neighborhood was gated, so his parents couldn't drop by unexpectedly. Though, I still was not sure why we moved.

"The jar slipped out of my hands when I was trying to open it," I explained. "I'm sorry. I'll have it cleaned up in a second."

"And what about this?" Whitney asked. She pointed to the coffee table in the family room. "Were you trying to open your glass coffee table with a pickaxe?"

Duncan had put his fist through it before he left to go over to Tina's house. I opened my mouth to explain the mess, but the enormity of everything in my life overwhelmed me. No words came out. I couldn't lie to Whitney. But I couldn't tell her the truth, either. Since I'd started going back to church again, the lying was more difficult. I replaced the lying with vacant stares and silence.

"Crystal, come here," Whitney put her arms up and motioned me toward her.

I tiptoed through the sea of broken glass and accepted her embrace, passively at first. Then I started to sob and hugged her as tightly as humanly possible. She stroked my hair and kissed my cheek.

"Shhh, hon, it's okay," she whispered. "We'll clean it up."

Whitney's soft hazel eyes were barely visible from under her shaggy black bangs. Her voice was a little scratchy.

"But that's just it, Whitney," I said. I threw the dishcloth down to the floor. "It's not okay. It's not okay anymore."

She let me go and folded her arms across her chest.

"Duncan is not out of town tonight, is he, sweetie?" she asked.

I shook my head.

"We got into a fight. He's mad I went to my parent's house for my sister's baby shower. He left here about an hour ago. He took a bottle of wine over to Tina's house."

"Tina's! That slut?" Whitney hated her.

"He said I'm miserable to be around. I depress him. He said Tina is more fun to hang out with, so he left and said not to call him."

"What an asshole," said Whitney.

"Please don't tell your dad," I begged.

"What? Why?" Whitney asked.

"I don't want to get him in trouble at work," I said. "That would make him so mad at me."

Whitney seemed frustrated, but I couldn't tell at which part exactly.

"OK, just stop right there," she said.

Whitney put her hand on her forehead and scanned the room as she formulated a plan of action.

"I'm going to change into some of your jeans and sneakers. Then I'm going to find bags that can hold this glass. Then I'm going to open your most expensive bottle of wine, and you and I are going to drink the whole thing."

I couldn't stop crying. Whitney looked at her watch.

"Crystal, look at me. Is it safe for you to stay here tonight? Maybe you should stay at my place?"

"Oh, I can't stay at your place. Duncan would kill me if he even knew I invited you over tonight. I mean, if your dad finds out, he could . . ."

Whitney put her hand on my shoulder. "My dad's not going to know about any of this, I promise."

Whitney grabbed a bottle from the wine rack without setting foot in the kitchen. She leaned over and grabbed the opener, but could reach only one long-stemmed wine glass.

"Got any straws?"

We both laughed. I grabbed another glass.

We sat on the floor in the family room, our backs against the wall furthest from the shattered coffee table, sharing the wine. Duncan and I had gotten this bottle of wine as a gift from the Hotel Del Coronado at my sister's graduation—a burgundy, chocolatey with a cherry aftertaste. I downed my glass and held it out for another. We smiled, and she filled my glass.

Whitney and I could drink a lot of wine when we were together. Every time we hung out was like a celebration. She was the most selfless person I'd ever met. Despite our differences in faith, we never fought about religion. She believed in numerology and she knew that I was a Christian. She shared her horoscopes with me and I shared my Bible verses with her.

"Whitney," I said, "I'm tired of being afraid of him, but I don't know how to make it stop. I don't know how to explain it. He tells me every day he loves me. But sometimes he gets this look, and the blue in his eyes turns to ice and there's no soul inside of them. It's chilling."

I stopped crying and took a deep breath. "And the lies . . ."

There. It was out of my mouth. That was all I could find the courage to say. I hoped she would take the thread and pull at it until it all unraveled.

Whitney took a deep breath, measuring her words. "Do you want to tell me about the lies?"

"I don't know what to tell you, actually," I started, but then paused.

Here was my big moment of disclosure and suddenly, the amount of information I had seemed so insignificant. The wine must have hit me pretty hard. My restraints were gone.

"When Duncan and I got married, he told me he had dual citizenship in the U.S. and England. Turns out he only had a

British passport. I knew his parents were illegal immigrants. Well, they came over legally but never renewed their visas. I thought that once we were married, he would apply for permanent residency, but he has refused to file the paperwork."

The words slipped from my mouth like that jar of pasta sauce from my hands. I couldn't believe I had just told one of the owners' daughters about my husband's biggest secret. The one person I should never have told anything.

"Why not?" Now Whitney was sitting on her heels, leaning in, hanging on every word.

"I don't know. The possibility that he might have to return to England has him horrified and I have no idea why."

"Maybe he doesn't really have British citizenship either. Have you seen his passport?" she asked. "Didn't you have to show your birth certificate when you got married?"

Her questions were embarrassingly obvious, yet I could not answer them.

"Would you believe I've never seen either one?"

"You might want to ask him if you can just see them. You can make up some reason . . ."

"He has a small safe," I said, shrugging my shoulders.

"Where?" she asked.

"When we moved, I saw him put it in his giant toolbox outside," I said.

"Do you have the combination? Have you seen what's inside?" Whitney asked and stood to her feet.

"No, but I could guess. The toolbox has a lock on it, though," I said.

"Crys," Whitney shivered as she spoke, and goosebumps ran down her arms, "you need to find out. You go look for the key. I'm going to start cleaning up here, okay?"

I nodded and stood up slowly, trying to gain my balance and fathom what was happening. Why did I open my mouth? What if

Duncan comes home while Whitney is inside cleaning? I almost didn't care anymore. Sometimes I wished he would have hit me straight on instead of the grabbing and throwing and squeezing until it hurt. That was the hardest part about dealing with his temper. I felt like I ought to be as black and blue on the outside as I was on the inside.

It was like being the only witness to a miracle—no one would have believed me if I had told them. The closest he came to leaving a mark was the one time the door knob hit me, but that was because of where I was standing. That wasn't him hitting me directly. No, actually, there was the one time he grabbed my arm just above the elbow and pushed me into the closet wall. The nail where I hung my necklaces was perfectly positioned to ramrod my spine. I prayed that there would be a bruise there the next morning, but when I woke up, there was nothing. Not even a red mark. Just a sore back. Nothing to prove he had hurt me. Just the reliable skip in my heart rate whenever he got upset.

I couldn't believe I wanted to be hit to show other people how much pain I was in. Everyone at church thought he was a saint. So friendly. So outgoing. No one knew he was a monster. They all thought Duncan was a good person and I was just imagining things. He didn't mean to hurt me.

I walked past the bookcases his father had made for me at the old house. I felt bad for hating his parents. I wished Harold and Gale would just go back to the UK. They were a huge factor in the amount of stress Duncan carried around with him all the time.

I flicked on the light to the garage and surveyed the vehicles. Duncan loved these things more than life itself. More than me as well. If there was a key to the toolbox around, it would be in here. The only vehicle missing was the Range Rover he had taken to Tina's house. I grabbed a cloth from the workbench and used it to grab the metal handle of the passenger's side door to the Cutlass. He would see a fingerprint on the shiny handle because he polished this thing with a spit cloth. It was unlocked. I leaned in and carefully squeezed the button on the glove compartment and tried to give it a pull. It wouldn't open. I bet it was locked.

I stood back up and gently closed the door. Every compartment of every vehicle was probably locked. The bike, however, had a secret compartment in the seat. I know he was missing the keys to lock it because he'd accused me of taking them a few days ago. I didn't know what he was talking about until I saw Figment playing with something silver under the couch.

I ran back into the family room and kneeled down by the sofa. Before Whitney could throw a warning my way, my knee cap landed right on a piece of glass.

I let out a scream. I pulled my leg up to see the blood running down my shin. I pulled the glass out and tried to stay on task. Whitney had given me the courage to do something I should have done a long time ago. Maybe it was the wine, but I didn't want to lose the momentum of the moment. More carefully this time, I lowered my head to peer under the couch. There it was. A silver key ring with one small key on it. I grabbed it and ran back to the garage.

The small silver key worked. The seat of the bike lifted to reveal a small compartment with a Master Lock key inside. Sure enough, that key opened the toolbox. Inside the tall red and silver toolbox was a black, fire-proof safe.

I stared at the numbers. It wouldn't be our anniversary. It certainly would not be my birthday. What did he love more than anything? The answer was right in front of me. Or rather, behind me. It was either the year these vehicles were made, or a sequence from their license plates. I tried the Cutlass first. The most important one. 69. Then to the right. The Rover. 1. Click.

That was it! Oh God, please help me remember what year the R1 came out. 98. Click.

The door swung open just then as Whitney came out to the garage.

"What'd you find?" she asked.

"I don't know." I blindly pulled papers and photographs out of the safe.

"I'm sorry, but I can't believe you've been married to him for almost four years and you've never looked inside your own safe."

"How many people live their whole lives and never really look inside themselves?" I asked without looking up.

"What's this?" Whitney held up a picture of the Haworth Hotel. A partial address and phone number were scrawled across the back in blue ink.

"That's the hotel he said his parents used to own in England."

"That's not England, sweetheart," Whitney said, flipping over the photograph. "See that postal code on the back? That's Scotland."

"How do you know?" I asked.

"My real dad sends me postcards every year from the Scottish Highland games."

I looked down at the computer-engineering diploma I held in my hands.

"Whitney, take this into my office over there. Open up my laptop and try to find this university on the Internet."

"You think it's fake?" she asked.

"I don't know what to think anymore," I replied.

Whitney went back into the house and I closed my eyes. Dear God, please help me to know what to do with what I find here.

I pulled out Duncan's passport and a police report dated July 18, 1986. I thought he said it was 1989 when his stuff was stolen. The passport was issued by the British Embassy. It didn't have a date. There were no stamps in it. I reached into the back of the safe. My hand pulled out four Social Security cards, all with different numbers. None of them were Duncan's.

"Well, I have bad news and more bad news," Whitney said, coming over to stand next to me. "I can't find this school anywhere online. I found the city where the college is supposed to be, but there's only a tech school there. Something like ITT Tech, but for Brits."

"Okay, and what's the more bad news?" I asked.

"Honey, when's the last time you and Duncan had sex?" Whitney said and looked me straight in the eyes.

"Why?" I was beginning to get nauseated.

"There's porn all over that laptop," she explained.

Suddenly, a loud cell phone ring made us jump.

It was mine.

It was Duncan.

It rang again.

It was so loud.

It rang again.

"Answer it," Whitney whispered, as if his ominous presence was somehow in the room with us.

I slowly picked up the phone and took a deep breath. "Hello."

"Hey, sweetheart." His voice sounded distant. "I wanted to call and apologize for the way I left things. I'm just really stressed out right now from work."

"I know," I said robotically. "It's okay."

"Listen, I'm gonna come home and we can just cuddle, okay? I'll be home in like thirty minutes."

"Sounds good. I'll see you then," I said and hung up the phone. I turned to Whitney. "He's going to be here in half an hour. Help me put everything back and then you've got to go!"

I began throwing things back in the safe, but then I froze. I realized that if didn't replace everything exactly as it was, there would be hell to pay. I took a deep breath and closed my eyes. I saw where things had been and started to place them back there.

I pushed the Social Security cards to the back of the safe, and my hand hit the hard corners of a rectangular box. It was too big to be one of his watch cases. I ran my fingers along it and felt a small keypad. There wasn't enough time to pull it out and examine it. I closed the safe and put the key back into the bike seat. I even tossed the small silver key back under the couch where Figment had left it.

Whitney had finished cleaning up and left a few moments before I heard Duncan pull his Range Rover in to the garage. I sat in front of the wall-mounted 52-inch plasma TV, flipping the channels, taking deep breaths, trying to slow my heart rate. Duncan came in and sat down on the couch next to me.

"Hey, you," he said. "You're not still mad at me, are you?"

I tried not to look at him. "No. Hey, listen. I was watching this documentary about British schools. It said they didn't have two-year degrees for technical programs like the one you have." I glanced over at him, but he didn't look back at me.

"Well, in England, our two years is like four years in the States," he said, taking the remote from my hand. "And computer engineering and computer science are the same thing. I just told the firm my degree was in computer engineering so I wouldn't have to explain how the programs are the same thing."

"Oh," I said, watching him flip through the same stations I had just screened.

He was lying and I didn't have the guts to call him on it. Just like I didn't have the guts to say anything in New York last year when he lied to me at the hotel. Our floor came with a concierge breakfast in a room on the twelfth floor. The day we checked in, the concierge room was closed for renovations. To compensate us, the hotel manager provided vouchers we could use to get breakfast in the lobby restaurant. We ate there the first two days, enjoying the white linen tablecloths and eggs cooked to order. But on the last day of our visit, the restaurant manager told us he could not seat us because there was a long wait for other customers and the concierge floor was open again. Our vouchers could not be used. Duncan threw a fit. Raising his voice at the manager, he threatened to file a complaint if we weren't seated immediately.

"But, sir," the restaurant manager said politely, "the concierge on the twelfth floor is open."

"Duncan," I'd said, pulling at his shirt sleeve, "What are you doing? If the other floor is open, let's just go up there."

"Quiet," he told me.

"I was just up there," Duncan said firmly to the manager. "It's not open."

The manager radioed up to the concierge room. We heard on the radio, loud and clear, that it was indeed open. Duncan cursed him and stormed toward the elevators. I ran to catch up with him. As the elevator doors closed, I asked him if he really knew the twelfth floor was open.

"Yeah," he said nonchalantly. "I just didn't want to eat up there."

I was shocked he would cause such a scene over something as stupid as breakfast. But I didn't scold him for it. What was the point? If I had said something then, I should have said something when I found the wetsuit he stole from SeaWorld or the fiber-optic cables he took from his office. After four years of pointing out his wrongdoings, his behavior had never changed. I saw no point in continuing my defense for integrity.

"Nothing on the telly," he said, after he flipped through over a hundred channels. "What do you say we hit the sack?"

"Sure, I'm really tired," I said.

I was lying. My veins still pulsed with the fight or flight response set off by the discoveries in the safe. Who was I going to bed with?

"Listen, about tonight," he started, but I didn't want the instant replay of it in my mind.

"Don't worry about it," I said.

"No, let me apologize. We'll go to Scan Design tomorrow and you can pick out any coffee table you want, OK?"

All of our furniture was from Scan Design. The sleek, modern Danish look was one of the few things Duncan and I agreed on. He really liked the meticulous look of those clean lines. Even his shirts hung exactly one inch apart on his side of the closet. His pants were perfectly folded on the crease and lined up with the lightest shades first. The vanity on his side of the bathroom was always spotless. He even dried his toothbrush with a special cloth before placing it back in the chrome stand that held his razor.

"Promise?" I said.

"I promise," Duncan said, kissing my forehead. "I promise."

22

DUNCAN

July 6, 2002

MAINTAINING APPEARANCES COULD BE BLOODY INCONVENIENT AT TIMES. Sharing a space this intimately on a constant basis while keeping my family's side hustle secret was fun at first. Lately, it had become annoying. Crystal was asking strange questions. I had a feeling she had found the safe. I went to see if anything looked out of place.

Pa didn't want any of the passports kept at his place. Only good for a one-way ticket, these were. Irreplaceable. Once I gave him these back, he and Mum could leave whenever they wanted to without mixing me up in any of it. All four Social Security cards lay on the top shelf. I grabbed two from the top and felt the metal box behind them. I removed the box and held it. I bet Pa didn't even know I had this. I smiled and put it back in the safe.

If Crystal knew I actually had a passport I could have used to leave the country, she would have been so pissed. It was fake, of course, but I didn't think I could use it in front of her. I had no interest in following up on the citizenship thing, no interest in leaving the States. But all Crystal wanted to do was go places with me. So, I made her hate spending time with me. The less she enjoyed my company, the less likely she would be to drag this out. She could travel on her own. She could even travel with other men. She just couldn't leave me. She wouldn't dare. That's what made this so perfect. I could treat her like dirt and her religious beliefs would prevent her from divorcing me.

I heard a small noise in the hallway outside the garage door and leapt to my toes. I heard a small meow. Figment slinked her black body in between my legs.

"Hey, you schtupid little cat," I said, kneeling down to pet her. "You didn't wake Crystal, did you?"

Figment purred and brushed the side of my leg.

I went back to the safe and straightened out my diploma and the brown envelope where I kept the emergency cash. Now everything was nice and neat. Life was much more pleasant when there was a place for everything and everything was in its place. Stability. Predictability. Control. Words to live by.

Figment brushed against my side, really starting to piss me off. I pushed the box to the back and closed the door, spinning the knob several cycles. That should do it. I picked up the cat and headed back inside through the door to the kitchen.

Buying this house stressed me out at first, but I was smart enough to use one of the IDs I found a few cycles ago. Buying the new furniture was great. I liked clean lines. No clutter. The couch, in particular, was my favorite. It had headrests like my Alfa did; the tan color was nice and neutral, too. Even the lever for the footrests was hidden between the armrest and the seat cushion.

Behind drywall in the family room, I paid the electrician forty dollars to look the other way while Kurt and I strung fiber through the conduit. It went behind the wall, up to the attic, then down into the linen closet. Crystal was upset that she lost two shelves for towels, but the idea was brilliant. I put the cable box, the jack and the wireless router in the closet. When you look around the family room, there were no wires, no mess. But Crystal couldn't stand having a mess in the closet. She had to go in and organize the wires and cable boxes. We weren't paying for cable—I'd found a way to get that for free, too.

This house was nice. The community looked like a pleasant, family-oriented place. It would make a great impression in front of my boss. We wanted to have him over for dinner so he could get a good look at it, see how stable and reliable I was.

People were so gullible. They wanted to believe other people were nice. It took time and attention to detail to win that many people over, but it was so simple to do. Like driving in the car. If a taxi needed in your lane, you could let them in, smile and wave—meanwhile, you were wishing the damn towelheads would go back to their own country. Most of the people at this church were pleasant, which made it even easier. And there weren't too many blacks, you know, the really dark kind. The ones that were there came from England, South Africa or West Africa, which was always better than the ones from the U.S. Couldn't understand a damn word they were saying.

I put Figment down on the bed and she curled up in her space on the left side of Crystal. They both look so peaceful. The bed creaked a bit, but Crystal didn't wake.

I really missed my old fake waterbed. I tried to tell Crystal that bed had seen a lot of good times for more than ten years. She didn't seem too interested, though. I had let her choose this bed since she had cash to pay for it. Some guy paid her to edit his novel. Gave her some extra spending money. Didn't really like this four-poster piece of crap she bought, though. Didn't like her down-filled comforter, either.

The next morning, I woke up craving Weetabix. A nice cold bowl of cereal with sugar on top. And a cup of Red Rose tea.

Crystal was still asleep. That girl could sleep through a hurricane. I nudged her and she blinked her eyes open. She rolled over and looked at me with those gorgeous green eyes.

"Morning, Duncan," she said.

I brushed the hair gently from her face.

"You look so peaceful when you're asleep," I told her. "In fact, you look the most beautiful when you are not talking."

"What?" she said, barely awake.

"Well, you know, you look beautiful when your mouth isn't moving. Usually when you are awake, you're always on some mission to change the world. But when you're asleep, you look much more relaxed."

I got out of bed and turned the shower on. If I timed it right, the water warmed up exactly when I finished brushing my teeth. After I showered, I usually had approximately twenty minutes to reach the office and start my second cup of tea.

I selected one of the white shirts hanging on white wire frames in the walk-in closet and headed into the kitchen. I was adding fresh water to the kettle when I noticed the stains on the black stovetop. Crystal's domestic skills were not up to par, so we had hired a maid to come in once a month and clean. Crystal was a strange female. She didn't know how to clean properly and she didn't like to cook. I grabbed the Weetabix from the walk-in pantry. Two bricks left. Perfect. But when I went to open our new black refrigerator, there was no new milk, just the jug that had expired two days ago.

"Crystal!" I shouted back to the bedroom on the other side of the family room. "There's no bloody milk."

Damn. That also meant no tea.

"Crystal, how many times do I have to tell you? I don't ask you to do anything around the house. I never have. Just get me fresh two percent milk and a new loaf of bread. Is that too much for your little brain to handle? Should we ask the maid to do those things as well?"

"I'm sorry." Crystal poked her head around the corner, toothbrush in hand. "I'll get some on my way home from work today."

"That doesn't help me with my tea this morning, darling."

"I don't know what to tell you, we don't have any cows." She turned and went back into the bedroom.

"You're never going to make it to work on time," I shouted. "It's already a quarter till. You would think when we moved closer to your office, you might actually arrive there before nine."

I grabbed my silver mug and emptied some water into it about halfway. Had to leave plenty of room for sugar. The cream would have to come from my office, which meant it wouldn't be two percent. This was not a good way to start my day.

"Oh, and Crystal, don't forget to book us a hotel room for the annual beach retreat. I want a nice suite. Try to get a room near the other guys."

I ran into my closet to grab a tie. Crystal stood like a zombie, staring at her clothes.

"Why don't we get a room away from the guys? A little more privacy."

"Why would we want to be farther from the action? We go to these company events to be with other people. We spend enough time alone. Do we still have that $300 voucher from last year? You should use that to pay for the room."

"No, Duncan, I spend enough time alone. Besides, I was

saving that voucher for a weekend when we could go away together. A sexy beach retreat, just the two of us." Crystal turned around to face me.

"Don't start with me. I'll buy you anything you want, but you know I hate the sand. I refuse to go to the beach any more than absolutely necessary." I kissed her on the forehead.

"I wasn't thinking we would leave the room," she said, but I wasn't paying attention. I was running late, so I dashed out the door.

"Don't forget my milk," I yelled before shutting the door to the garage.

After everything I provided for her, she was so ungrateful. I was under too much stress. Leading my own division at the firm was taking a lot out of me. They gave me eight guys. I was able to negotiate my own office after wiring the entire building. If only my house stayed as clean and cold as my office. I kept the thermostat at a comfortable sixty-three degrees. Most people didn't realize that computers run like well-oiled machines in lower temperatures. Not too cold, of course.

We had two jobs going out this week. One in New York. I couldn't wait to get back to the Hotel Grande. The receptionist there, Stacey, was so nice. Perky, big knockers. She was always glad to see me. Being in charge of a department wasn't easy. I deserved to give myself upgrades whenever possible. Speaking of which, the new model of my motorbike was coming out next month. Maybe I could stop before going home and see about trading mine in. I wanted to get one before Drew did. He always had a better bike than me, even though I made more money.

When I got to the office, the guys were huddled by my desk.

"Hey, guys, what's up?" I asked, setting down my briefcase and moving my Oakleys down around my neck. I didn't like to fold them too often. Wore on the hinges.

Kurt was leaning against the dry erase board. Justin sat

halfway on my desk, his sleeves rolled up to his forearms. He still had a full head of hair. Justin was a good-looking kid—tall, blond, tan, blue eyes, lean. I didn't want any fat kids on my team.

"We were just trying to figure out if you had anything planned for Crystal's birthday this weekend," Justin asked, taking a sip of coffee.

"Shit. I forgot," I said, taking a seat behind my desk and turning on my monitor.

"We thought you might have," said Kurt.

"What do you guys want to do for her?" I asked, not really caring.

"We were thinking of getting a bunch of tables at Book Ends, you know, that restaurant she likes with all the shelves of books around the place."

"Yeah, man. That's a good idea," I said as Tina walked by in a blue dress and heels. Crystal never wore heels anymore.

"Hey, Tina," I shouted. The guys all turned to check out her curves. "Listen, I need a huge favor. Call Book Ends for me and get some tables for this Friday night. Is Friday night better for you or Saturday?"

"Friday night," she said. "My daughter has a ballet performance on Saturday."

"Great then, that's lovely," I said. "Tell them it's a birthday and tell them to put up balloons or something."

"Sure thing," Tina said, winking at me as she turned and left, the guys' eyes following her.

"Did you just ask your ex-girlfriend to plan your wife's birthday?" Kurt asked.

"Yeah, why? Is that bad?" I joked.

The guys laughed. They thought I was funny.

"Just a little," said Justin. "What are you getting her, by the way?"

"I don't know," I replied. "Wanna take care of that for me?

It'll look good on your annual review. Get her something from Tiffany's. Here's my credit card."

"Crystal hates Tiffany's," Justin said, picking up my card.

"Get her whatever you think she would like," I said; the topic was starting to irritate me. "Now, you guys get to work."

The team slowly filed out of my room. I called Justin back.

"Hey, Justin, just don't sleep with my wife," I said. "But seriously, though, buy her whatever you think she would want. You know her tastes better than I do."

"Sure thing, boss."

Justin turned and left, closing my door behind him.

My office wasn't big enough. When my whole team came in here, there was hardly room to walk. I didn't want to give up my additional desk, though. I needed a separate desk for signing blueprints. The other offices were painted tan or cream to match the camel-and-black color palette of the building. I'd left my walls white. I liked it better that way.

23

CRYSTAL

July 14, 2002

YESTERDAY, A CATEGORY 3 HURRICANE MADE A LAST MINUTE SHARP LEFT TURN, COMING ASHORE UP THE COAST FROM WHERE THE FIRM WAS HOSTING ITS ANNUAL BEACH RETREAT. We initially thought it would miss us, so we all came down for the weekend, but Florida is really good at ruining vacations. Once it blew over (and luckily it did so very quickly), it followed the path of an existing freeway that led it up through Central Florida and out into the Gulf. About a dozen of us were huddled up in our hotel suites through the night. It was one of Marriott's largest hotels on the East Coast, so we felt safe inside the compound-like structure.

With a cooler full of vodka-soaked fruit and enough snack food to last a lifetime, many of the engineers and their girlfriends decided to ride out the storm (or "hunker down," as newscasters liked to say) rather than get stuck on I-4. We brought all the booze we had up to the party suite on the top floor. One of the partners rented out one room each year for the post-dinner soiree that always ended with the guys passed out on couches and chairs like drunken sailors. I tiptoed silently through the expansive hotel suite that was littered with bottles and plastic red cups as early morning sunshine pierced the room like a sword of light through the heavy curtains.

Taking stock of the hot mess around me, I spotted a tri-fin shortboard leaning up against the armoire. There was a leash wrapped around its base and enough wax to lock my feet in. I hadn't been surfing since I left Point Loma. With the storm gone, there might be a few good waves out there. Suddenly, I wanted nothing more than to be on the ocean. I wanted to be anywhere but here. I grabbed the board as stealthily as I could and snuck out the door.

I was so at peace with myself when I was surfing. This was the first time in years I had been on a board, alone in the water. Paddling out was extremely difficult, but the waves crashing down on me felt like baptismal redemption. The foamy saltwater stung my eyes as I pushed through the washing machine of swirling white caps. I had not felt this good in a long, long time. Surfing was like the great equalizer. You couldn't pretend to be someone else. The ocean would never let you lie about who you were. It would take you under, regardless. Mother Nature had a funny way of treating everyone with an equally unconditional indifference.

After enjoying several short yet intense rides, I was exhausted. I rode the last wave of a set in and found my way back to our hotel, as the current had carried me far from where I had entered the water.

But when I got to our room, Duncan was gone. I gently laid the board down on the floor by the window and looked across the parking lot for the Range Rover. It was gone too. Looking around the room, I noticed Duncan's luggage was missing. I checked the bathroom for his toiletries. They were all gone too. I threw some clothes on and walked across the hall to Opal's room.

"Does anybody know where Duncan went . . . with our car?" I asked the crowd of engineers.

They all gave me bleary-eyed blank stares. Opal's boyfriend came out of the bathroom in a towel. He stepped slightly backward when he saw me, a little caught off guard that I was in his room so early.

"Oh, hey Crystal," he said. "Everything alright?"

"I'm looking for Duncan," I said. "I went surfing this morning and when I got back to our room, he was gone."

"Oh, he came by earlier and offered to take a few guys from his crew down to start repairs immediately, in case they lost their back-up generators," Opal's boyfriend uttered. "We thought he told you."

"Nope," I replied.

"Well, you're welcome to hitch a ride home with us," Opal said with a wink. "If you promise to return my boyfriend's surfboard."

"Oh, sorry," I said. "It was in the party room and everyone was still asleep."

"No worries," said Opal. "He doesn't actually know how to use it."

We laughed and he threw a towel at both of us sitting on the bed.

On the ride home, we stared in silence as we passed by the devastation left behind by the storm. There were downed trees and power lines everywhere. The intersection of Highway 50 and Mills Avenue was completely underwater. We turned off to a side road, hoping to cut through to 17-92. Suddenly, we came up against a giant oak tree, standing eerily upright in the middle of the road. Most of its top roots were still intact, like it had walked itself there, and there were telephone wires wrapped around it like Christmas tree lights.

We tried to stay off I-4, since reports on the radio said that crews were still trying to clear away the billboards that were scattered down the road like a deck of cards. When we pulled up to my house, it looked completely unscathed. Doug and Opal waited while I checked to see if it had power. Not a drop of water had made its way inside, not a single tree branch had scratched the house, and we had power. We had been spared.

Later that afternoon, after police had warned drivers to stay off the unsafe roads, I went out with the digital camera the church had loaned me to take pictures of the damage by Lake Eola and the city's oldest movie theater downtown. The marquee had been completely snapped off by a palm tree. Behind me were a row of small pine trees that were all broken, snapped like toothpicks near their tops. It amazed me that an element like wind, naked to the human eye, could break what appeared to be strong trees. I wondered how something as intangible as air could take credit for the surrounding maelstrom. Harsh words, too, were like those winds. You couldn't see them or predict the damage they would leave behind.

I wished I could leave Duncan, but I couldn't leave him any easier than Florida could dodge a hurricane. I'm a Christian, and Christians didn't get divorced. We're not allowed to unless it's for very clear cut reasons, like adultery. Duncan had never cheated on me. I had tried separating from Duncan on a couple of occasions. He promised he would go to counseling with me, but then he lied about his citizenship, which was what I felt to be at the root of the problem. How a man could lie to a pastor, I could not comprehend. But this was the same man who lied to immigration lawyers—and was lying to me. I couldn't even tell anyone how Duncan treated me, because no one would believe me. I needed someone to take my side, someone who knew I wasn't exaggerating or making this up. Otherwise, I would resign myself to my fate—the mistake I had made.

I could feel tears mounting under my eyelids, so I tried to look up, which sometimes made them go away. As started to raise my eyes, I saw a familiar figure across the street, also taking pictures of the theater. His hair was a light chestnut color and still fell down around his shoulders, straight and shiny, just like it had in high school. He lowered his camera and turned around toward the street. I could see the press pass lanyard around his neck. He was wearing light blue jeans, even on this steamy day.

I met Michael when we were just fifteen years old. For an entire semester in school, unbeknownst to each other, he had been watching me at diving practice and I had been watching him in school plays. It wasn't until his best friend Norman introduced us that we became inseparable. Right up until he left for college. He was so smart and so funny. I felt honored that someone so intelligent would want to spend their time hanging out with me.

Before I could move, Michael glanced over and saw me standing across the street. The post-storm clouds reflect lighted with a rosy orange apocalyptic glow across the sky. Watching Michael cross the street to me was like being in a sepia-toned dream, one I didn't want to wake up from.

"Crystal Vargas. What the hell are you doing out here?" he said. He smiled at me and put his hands in his back pockets.

"I could ask you the same thing," I said. "Police are keeping everyone off the main roads."

"I know," said Michael, holding up his press pass. "I'm the reporter telling the cops what to say."

Of course he was. Now I felt like an idiot.

"I thought you would be off traveling the world," he said. "What are you doing in downtown Orlando? Right after a major hurricane, no less."

"I didn't want to be alone in my house," I said, surprised at my own transparency.

"Maybe I can help you find some shots where there aren't live power lines to jump over."

"Where's the fun in that?" I asked.

We stared at each other for a beat. This town was too small. How did I keep running into ex-boyfriends in the most random places and times? It would be impossible for a mermaid like me to make a clean start in such a tiny fishbowl.

"Come on, let me give you a ride home in the company car," he said.

We walked over and got into his white news van. It reminded me of interning at WESH Channel 2. We would have made a great team. I would have been the pretty little reporter. He would have been my videographer. Actually, he would have died before he took that role. He was way too talented to spend his days focusing his lens on my stupid face. He lit a cigarette and rolled down his window before driving away.

"I think it's great that you're doing photography now," he said, blowing a puff of smoke out the window. "But you were always such a great writer."

Brutal honesty was one of Michael's traits that I admired the most. He didn't always tell me what I wanted to hear. He always told me the truth. I knew I wasn't mature enough to hear the things he told me when we were younger. But he was never wrong. Eventually, I grew to hate him for his consistent articulation of my life's axioms.

Michael wasn't married. He was living with his girlfriend near College Park.

"Crystal," Michael said.

He stared through me at a stop light, as if he had X-ray vision and would know if I was lying when I answered him. Michael had these killer eyebrows that naturally arched in an angled way that made every look he gave seem more intense.

"Are you happy?"

The question was completely uninvited and, knowing Michael, was not a question at all. He knew I was smart enough to catch on, but polite enough to lie. I remembered Sammy asking me the same freaking thing. What was it with guys who felt like they had to ask this? Did it make them feel less bad about how they treated us when we were together? Did it alleviate some guilt of how they screwed things up or ended the relationship badly? Well, at least she is happy now. That's all that matters. Maybe they are sincere when they say such things, but it sure feels like a complete cop-out on the receiving end.

"Yes," I answered, not looking into his wide-set brown eyes. "I have everything that every girl could possibly want."

I met his gaze with equal intensity. He smiled his beautiful wry smile and threw his cigarette butt out the window.

"Save your Avon-lady pitch for your Stepford-wife friends, Crys," Michael said and smiled at me again.

I shifted my weight nervously in my seat and pulled the black rubber band from my right wrist. The humidity grew worse, and I pulled my hair back into a loose bun.

"Get all shifty and nervous if you want," said Michael. "It's your life. I'm just curious because the Crystal I knew wanted to travel around the world and be in love. . . So, I'm dying to know how the heck having what every girl wants could possibly make you happy. You are the farthest thing from every girl."

I felt a lump rise in my throat. I swallowed to keep it down. Other than my family, I didn't really hang out with friends who knew me before my marriage. I spent six days a week with people who had only known me a couple of years, so no one could hold me accountable for not becoming who I was meant to be.

When I eloped, I had to siphon off my closest friendships. Even some of my good friends who had moved out of Orlando and came back occasionally to visit were distant memories. Life got so busy and friends' lives took such different paths in adulthood. I was too ignorant to appreciate the importance of childhood friends. Michael refused to allow me to remain in hiding from my true self.

"Has your husband read any of your writing?" he asked, knowing it would be the sword in my side, the last test to see the blood split from the water.

"No." I laughed as I said it in order to hide the tears that were forming beneath my eyelids.

"So, he has no idea how talented you are?" Another state-ment in the form of a question.

"No," I said, punctuated by another shadow laugh. "You're very kind to say that though."

"I'm not kind, Belle. I'm honest."

He took one last puff from his cigarette and flicked it a mile away with his thumb and forefinger. It had been ages since he had called me that. Michael and my father were the only ones who called me by that nickname.

"Well, what about you? You've got to be happy. You're like freaking Peter Parker."

We both laughed.

"Yeah, I'm doing great. My family's doing great. I can't complain. Wish I made more money, but who doesn't, right? What I'm really looking forward to, though, is traveling to Europe and Africa, maybe doing a documentary on Rwanda. That's the stuff I'm passionate about and want to share with the woman I love."

I bit my lip so hard I thought it was going to bleed. That was it. That was what I wanted for my life. It wasn't that I wanted it with Michael, necessarily. It was that Michael wanted it—a guy who once had affection for me and maybe still did. He'd just conjured up a dream of mine and laid it out in front of me like the golden apple. Things I wanted for my life were totally possible with the right partner. They existed outside the realm of possibilities between Duncan and me, but they did exist. In less than twenty minutes, Michael had excavated my heart, my aspirations, my North Star.

"You are so beautiful, Crystal. It's like your outsides finally caught up with your insides. I mean, you were always beautiful, but now you are a stunning woman. It just makes me sad to see you walking around feeling like you're invisible. You're not invisible, Crystal. And if you are not writing these days it's a loss, not just for you, but for all of us who still care about you and feel closer to you through your narrator's voice."

We pulled up outside my house and he parked the van. He walked around to my door and opened it, just like he had when we were dating in high school. I got out and stood in front of him with my arms folded across my chest.

Michael closed the passenger door and leaned up against it. He crossed one black Converse shoe over the other and stared at me with those arched eyebrows. He was not going to let me go without a confession. He knew I was all buttoned up and it was probably driving him nuts. He used to pride himself on getting people to fess up to things and then getting them to go on the record about it.

"No!" I cried, feeling the tears fill up at the bottom of my eyes. "I'm sorry, but you can't do this to me right now!"

If Michael had surmised all that by our unspoken communication, imagine what he would do if he knew about Duncan's immigration status, or his treatment of me.

"Do what, exactly?" he asked.

"You can't just ask all the right questions and be right about everything, as always!" I exclaimed.

"It's kinda my job to ask people questions," he said.

"You have no idea what my life is like. I'm doing the best I can with what I've got, okay?!" Tears now streamed down my cheeks. I couldn't wipe them away fast enough. "I'll figure it out. I always do, don't I?"

I turned on my heels and practically ran for my front door in a huff. Michael ran up behind me, caught my arm, spun me around toward him and cupped my jaw with his hands. I didn't look away. He brought my face right up to his and kissed me hard on the lips. I didn't push back. Oh, God, the memories this brought back—really, really good memories. We finished kissing, but he held my face close to his and whispered in my ear.

"Crystal, I know I probably won't see you again after this, so I want you to do me a favor."

"Oh yeah," I choked, still wiping tears from my eyes, "What's that?"

"Do not go gentle into that good night. Rage, rage against the dying of the light."

He pulled the rubber band slowly out of my hair, and put it around his wrist. Then he hugged me tightly while I stood. I was almost too shocked to hug him back. A few moments later, he backed out of the driveway and was gone. Once again, I was a shell of a girl standing in my own front yard, watching my life happen to me.

Why hadn't my husband told me any of this? Why hadn't he made me feel this way? Why was I getting this support and acknowledgement from an ex-boyfriend in the middle of a

storm? His words made my insides hurt so much, but I medi-
tated on them as if they were Communion: *You're not invisible,
Crystal . . . Your lack of writing is a loss.*

The voices in my head were so loud, I couldn't stand them
anymore. They had a lot to say and they were saying it so quickly I
could barely understand them. Rage, rage against the dying of the
light. Rage. The girl I truly was inside had died within the prison
bars of my marriage, a prison I had entered willingly, like a fool.

I didn't know what to do with all of these emotions. I was
utterly confused. I knew that Michael was not the answer. His
words became the key that unlocked a door I had to walk through.
I thought about the lighter I had discovered in the coffee shop
in San Diego. The universe had found a way to remind me of the
storms I deeply missed. And now the universe had found a way
to remind me of the girl I used to be, and all that God originally
intended for me, plans to give me hope and a future.

As I sat in church that following Sunday, I struggled with
how to reconcile my present reality with God's unfulfilled
purpose for my life. I couldn't continue to live with this dichot-
omy for much longer, but I didn't see a way out. Pastor Isaac
spoke about the book of Micah and how it was better to know
the truth than to live a lie.

To drive home the point, he relayed an anecdote about how
he was with his wife in a rental car, venturing out across the
moors of Ireland, enjoying the adventure. But after several
wrong turns, many minutes had passed since they had seen any
buildings or even human beings. Despite his wife's protests, the
pastor refused to turn the car around. He had already dedicated
so much time and effort to the direction he was heading; he
felt it would be too great a loss to turn around. But, he said, as
his wife so gracefully pointed out, it was better to turn around
now and cut their losses while they still had enough gas to find
their way again.

24

CRYSTAL

July 19, 2002

I COULDN'T SLEEP. Duncan stayed at his parents' apartment, and I was alone in the house. Figment got so frustrated with my tossing and turning, she curled up on Duncan's empty pillow next to me. She was getting her hair all over his pillow. I let her sleep there anyway. It was so nice to have my little cat for company. I had taken to having full-on conversations with her, since I didn't really have anyone else to talk to.

My conversation with Michael played over and over in my mind. Then the pastor's sermon came back to me. They were like pieces of a puzzle where none of the edges lined up.

I used to love solving riddles and doing puzzles, but right now I needed someone from the outside to help me see what I could not (or would not). My life, my house, my room, it all appeared to be "normal," even though I knew it wasn't. I almost felt like I was in that scene from *Labyrinth,* where Sarah was in a bedroom exactly like her own in every way, except the room was inside the labyrinth. For a moment, she was relieved to be in her own room. But as she realized that none of it was real, the walls began to buckle and her friends reached down from outside to pull her up out of the crumbling façade.

I sat up in bed and turned on the lamp next to me. It was 4 a.m. I grabbed my notes from Isaac's sermon. I had written "Jeremiah 33" in the margin. I reached over and dug through the deep drawer of my nightstand and pulled out an old Bible I had from college. The verse read: "While Jeremiah was still confined in the courtyard, the word of the Lord came to him: Call to me and I will answer you and tell you great and unsearchable things you do not know . . . I will bring Judah and Israel back from captivity and will rebuild them as they were before."

I wanted to know the unsearchable things. I wanted to be rebuilt as I was before.

When I was in high school, prayer was an obligation. When I was in college, it was rhetorical. I didn't expect anyone to hear me. But now, I needed my faith to be real, despite the fact that I might have let it put me here in the first place. I needed out of a room where there were no real windows and no real doors. I needed these walls to crumble and my friends to lift me out.

Suddenly, I felt my heart tighten in my chest. I could barely breathe and a terrible twinge of fear took root in my stomach, as if my life was in danger. I tried to breathe slowly in through my nose and out through my mouth, but a strange rush of energy rose up from my toes and I didn't know what to do with it. I was having a 'fight or flight' adrenaline rush brought on by nothing. I panicked. I wanted to get out of the house.

I threw on a shirt and a pair of jeans and ran out the door.

It was now closer to 5 a.m., and the only people on the planet who would be up this early were my parents, so I drove to their house. I walked into the garage because someone had left the door open, but then realized I had put my t-shirt on backwards. Before I walked inside to the kitchen, I pulled my arms into the shirt and began to turn it around without taking it off. When the shirt was twisted halfway around my torso and my arms were still tucked inside, my dad opened the door to the garage and stepped outside.

"Well, Crys' either lost her arms or lost her mind," he said with a bit of a laugh. "What are you doing here so early?"

"I'm stuck," I said, looking at my dad and noticing his gray hairs were taking over his head. He was wearing his glasses and still had his pajamas on. He looked old.

"I can see that. I'm not sure what I'm more confused about. Why you're stuck inside your shirt or why you drove here at this hour."

"Can you just help me, please?" I asked.

Dad grabbed the corners of my dark blue Abercrombie shirt and twisted it into place. My arms popped out the sides and then I wrapped them around his neck. My mom opened the door and saw me standing there as I hugged my dad, his arms hung at his side.

"Donna, I think there's something wrong with our daughter."

My mom came up to me. I released my father and hugged my mom.

"Aw, sweetheart, what's wrong? Come inside and have some coffee with me."

"I need to talk to you guys. I . . . I think I might be having a panic attack."

Mom escorted me into the kitchen, which always smelled of cookies in the summer, and my father followed.

"Mom will get you some coffee and everything will be alright," said Dad.

"Tony, if she's having a panic attack, I can't give her coffee," Mom said, pulling two mugs down from the white country-style white cabinets.

Dad pulled out two chairs for us at the wooden table. We sat down and I took a deep breath.

"She's not having a panic attack," said Dad.

"I'm going out of my mind," I started. "I couldn't sleep last night. All this crazy stuff has been going on in my life. I was trying to make some sense of it all this morning. I was reading this Bible verse and then my heart seemed to stop beating."

Mom put a mug down in front of me with a small napkin. She placed some honey and crackers on the table and sat down next to me.

"I know this is going to sound crazy, but I feel like my life might be in danger. I don't know why, but I think it might have something to do with Duncan."

I expected to get strange stares from my parents, but when I looked up, they were sharing a knowing look of grave concern.

"Oh, no," I said. "What . . .?"

There was a moment of silence, but then the phone rang and we all jumped. Dad answered it and took it outside of the room. I assumed it was work related. Then I heard him talking about an apartment.

"Yes, actually, we found a one bedroom with a garage in Lake Nona. It's right near her new office."

I could barely make out what he was saying and I didn't understand why he was whispering.

"I can't get a moving truck that quickly," he said. "Now look, sweetheart, just calm down. You're pregnant. Don't get all upset. We're doing the best we can. Crystal is over here right now. I have to call you back."

As all good heartfelt confessions happen, my dad sat down at the kitchen table and started to say something to me, but no words came out. He took my mom's hand in his and began to cry, for what I'm pretty sure was the first time in his life. No, that was the second time. The first time was when his parents died within eight days of each other.

"Dad," I said, and I moved my hand from clasping the warm cup in front me to grabbing his wrist. "Were you talking with Lyssa? Was that phone call about me?" Now my eyes were watering. "Were you getting me an apartment . . . away from Duncan?"

"Yes, sweetheart," he confessed.

He looked defeated, as if someone had caught him cheating. He had the look of failure on his face, which he was trying to hide with his other hand. I saw it though. He looked ashamed. His oldest daughter's marriage was about to crumble. This would be hard to explain to his colleagues in the church.

Lots of girls go through life with daddy issues—some because their dads are not around, and some examples are much worse and more violent. Mine were none of these. I don't know what brought out the worst in me when I went for the wrong guys. I really didn't see them as such in the beginning, ever. Maybe that was my dad's fault. Maybe it wasn't. Either way, something in me grinned when he cried. Something in me felt satisfaction to see him shrink in shame.

Now you know how I felt, I thought, every time I did something wrong in your eyes, and you let me know it.

25

LYSSA

July 20, 2002

I LEFT WORK EARLY THAT EVENING TO MEET GRAHAM AND THE PRIVATE INVESTIGATOR FOR DINNER AT THE WATERGATE HOTEL. If only my sister had known, she would have truly appreciated the irony of it. Glass doors spanned the front of the round building. The entrance to the hotel restaurant was hidden from the street. Graham had chosen it for its "least likely to be seen in" quality. It was old, outdated, and nobody went there anymore.

In the foyer stood a thin gold marquee greeting the International Barista Club. If there was one thing this city had taught me, it was that every possible affiliation had its own club—and that club was headquartered here. The room reminded me of the dinner halls on cruise ships, with its low ceiling and porthole-shaped mirrors on the wall opposite the windows. Since I'd beaten everyone else there, I asked for a table overlooking the Potomac.

I had been anxiously awaiting this appointment for over a month. It was hard to believe only a few weeks ago, I had given Graham the bad news about my clearance. I had been terrified of moments like that one since moving here. I felt like it was an opportunity for my peers to find out that I was an imposter from Orlando who didn't even know anyone with connections to the Mayflower Society.

I sat by myself and glanced around the mostly empty restaurant. These people looked like they belonged in D.C., whereas I felt like I did not. Granted, I was younger than them by about twenty-five years; I also thought that I paid more attention to my appearance and accessorized with something other than pearls.

I thought back to the night I told Graham about my clearance. When I showed him the email stating it had been denied, he was truly surprised.

"This is not good, Lyssa," Graham said, looking down at the email. He still had on his dark suit and red tie. He loosened his tie as he read on.

"Are you sure you filled out the SF-86 correctly?" he had asked me.

He had been at the State Department for almost ten years, working with government organizations throughout the Middle East and Asia, and now his wife could not even get a basic level clearance.

Some of his stories were incredible. Graham's friends were all at Langley now. He was the only one who wanted to set policy, not break it, he said. When he traveled, foreign press treated him like a celebrity. He even had his profile put on a huge banner that flew over the consulate in Thailand during Embassy Row Week.

"Yes!" I snapped. I was never this harsh with Graham. I was frustrated.

We sat facing each other at our small dining room table. The townhomes in Georgetown didn't allow for big pieces of furniture, with their compartmentalized layouts. There were walls between every room in the house, not like the open concept houses that were being built in Orlando. Our walls were painted a bright red when we moved in. I guess I could have repainted them, but we were only going to live there for a year or two. We decided on just renting until Graham went into private practice.

Our china cabinet was packed with artifacts from his travels. It was an old, pine-colored cabinet with a glass display on top. Whoever lived here before us had left it, so I kept it, cleaned it up, and used it to store gifts he received from friends overseas. The Epcot-like display reminded me of how much Crystal and I loved to travel together.

Graham said he had a friend who could help us look into it if we didn't want to wait for a second application cycle. I told him I would really appreciate it if he could and then stood up to clear the dinner plates.

Even though I was the one having a bad day, my thoughts stayed on Crystal. I couldn't help but feel sorry about all the nights she'd had to eat dinner alone since she'd been married. I pictured Duncan standing in front of the minister at their elopement, his hair slicked back and that gold chain around his neck. His smile seemed so sinister in my memories of that day.

When I returned from the kitchen, I could not stop the tears from rolling down my face. Graham stood up and held me. I wanted to tell him it was just my hormones.

"Lyssa, I love you," he said, holding me tighter.

"I know. I love you, too."

He held me by the shoulders and looked me in the eyes. "Lyssa, why are you crying? I'm sure you'll get your clearance."

"I was thinking about Crystal," I cried. "The stuff in the china cabinet and travel and eating dinner alone all the time."

"The china cabinet? You lost me."

"Those friends of yours, can they also look into Duncan? I mean, can they just check and see if there's anything weird about him?"

"Of course. I mean, what's the point of being networked in D.C. if you can't call in a few favors?"

I started crying again. Graham hugged me tightly. He smelled like dry cleaning and aftershave.

"Alright, shh. It's okay. It's okay. Look, there's a guy we use strictly for international work. He's the best. My boss uses him all the time. He may even give me a discount."

"Thank you. Thank you."

"You're welcome. It's your sister. She's your best friend. I'm happy to do it."

Graham kissed my forehead and I prayed silently that I had been wrong about Duncan all these years.

Still, even if the investigator found something about him, there was no guarantee that Crystal would acknowledge it. Duncan had successfully controlled her mind for so long. Most women this unhappy in their marriages would have gotten divorces by now. But not Crystal. She was such a loyal person; she never even considered divorce a viable option.

I trusted Graham. And if he believed she was in danger, he would go down to Florida and bring her up here himself. I prayed to God it wouldn't come to that.

I took Graham's hands in mine and looked up at him.

"I want Crystal to be in our lives," I said. I put his hands on my belly. "We're going to need her as an auntie."

"Hey, sweetheart," Graham said as he approached the table, waking me from my daydream. "The guy called and said he would be a few minutes late. Got stuck behind a motorcade."

Graham had several blue ties, but this one with the small white specks on it was my favorite because it reminded me of the painting *The Starry Night*. He usually took his suit jacket off for dinner, but tonight he had left it on.

"How's our little guy doing in there?" Graham asked. "Is it getting hard to stand up or sit down?"

"Ha, ha. Yes, I do feel like I'm carrying around a watermelon in my shirt, like I'm stealing it in some Jane's Addiction video."

"Jane who?" he asked.

I couldn't tell if he was joking.

"Never mind." Sometimes I forgot there was a twelve-year age difference between us, not to mention the cultural music difference. "Besides, who says it's a little guy? Maybe it's a little girl."

I put my hand on my stomach and felt the muscles stretched hard, as if it could not possibly grow any larger. Often, I thought about how to express the joy of having a child inside me, but I did not think Graham would understand. I just kept telling him how exciting it was and what an enormous responsibility I felt.

I had become conscious of everything I ate, drank, or breathed, not to mention smelled. For several weeks, the mere mention of alfredo sauce sent me spinning. Eating out became too much of a gamble with my olfactory senses in hyperdrive. We cooked dinner at home most nights. Making food for two was a nice change. I loved surprising Graham with new dishes.

"How soon can we find out the gender?" Graham asked, filling my eight-ounce wine glass from the bottle of Evian on the table. He never drank anything other than water, coffee, or wine.

"We could have found out weeks ago, but I haven't had time to make my appointments."

"Do you think that's wise? Aren't those kind of important?"

"Yes, but Ron wanted several reports finished before he left for the Middle East. There are fewer people in our office working on Iraq than I think there should be. Ron keeps wanting to take on these other countries with conflicting ethnicities. It worries me."

I knew that was not a good excuse. It was hard to reprioritize my time after thinking a certain way for so long.

"Well, it's not like you have cocktail parties where you invite all your clients."

"That would be one awkward happy hour," I said. "It is just strange to think our office might have more extremist intel than the CIA."

"Doesn't everybody?" A deep voice came from behind me.

My heart jumped. I should have known better than to use certain words in public in this town. This pregnancy was sucking my brain cells.

I turned to see a tall gray-haired man in his mid-fifties carrying a black backpack. For a split second, I wondered if he might have ridden a bicycle here. He had a large hooked nose and very bushy eyebrows. Deep crow's feet accented the corners of his eyes, which were dark brown. His face looked as if it had seen more events in its lifetime than it had wanted to.

Graham stood and introduced himself, shaking the man's hand.

"Please, miss, don't get up. It's always harder to stand up for two people than it is for just one," said the tall man.

I smiled and shook his hand.

"I'm Dennis Yonday. It's a pleasure to make your acquaintance."

He pulled back on the upholstered dining chair and sat down. His voice reminded me of the Swiss-Germans who took their late lunches in downtown Zurich. He had the grace of a restaurateur. I had never met a private investigator before, but he is exactly what I would have anticipated. The three small glass centerpiece candles threw his face into a sharp contrasting light, deepening the appearance of his wrinkles as he smiled.

"So, tell me, Graham, how is the old goat?"

Dennis had worked with Graham's boss several adminis-trations ago.

"He's doing just fine," said Graham. "A few more clients and a few more rare wines in his collection. He's not complaining during this administration."

Dennis laughed from the bottom of his stomach, a raspy sound emerging from his throat.

"How's your work these days? Are you pretty busy?" Graham asked, looking at Dennis and unconsciously moving his silver-ware back and forth on the table.

"Actually, Graham, you would think, with this emphasis on Homeland Security, whatever that means, I would have less work. But because the government dollars are being allocated domestically, the private dollars are being used for more, um, foreign research. And I think we both know how lucrative private business can be."

Graham smiled and the waiter came up to take our orders.

We had offered to meet Dennis at his office, but he said he didn't have one. It was hard to imagine he worked out of his home. That just didn't seem safe. Though his home was probably just as secure and twice as discreet as Ron's office.

"But let's chat about how I can assist you," said Dennis, leaning into the left side of his chair. "I understand this is a family matter, an international one, which, as you know, is my specialty."

"Yes," I said, pulling my Burberry handbag up from under my chair. "This is about my sister, Crystal."

"How close in age are you and your sister?" asked Dennis.

Without looking up, I shuffled through my bag, pulling out a small, white envelope.

"She is two and a half years older than I am."

I took out a photo of Crystal and Duncan she sent me last Christmas. I placed it on the white tablecloth.

"That's her with her husband, Duncan Douglas."

Dennis pulled a pair of bifocals from the left breast pocket of his jacket and held the picture up in the candlelight.

"She's lovely. Duncan Douglas, you say? That's a solid Scottish name, isn't it?"

He looked down over the brown frames of his glasses at me. For a moment, I felt that I was the one being investigated. Thankfully, the waiter came and took our orders.

"Well, that's part of what we would like you to figure out," said Graham. "Lyssa's application for her security clearance was recently denied. We are not saying the two things are connected. We wanted to ask for your assistance with both. There shouldn't have been any reason for her clearance to get denied, but you know how they are. Could be just a mistake, what with the backlog in the last year and everything. It's sort of what prompted me to contact you sooner rather than later. Lyssa needs that clearance for her job right now, and will need it for any job in her line of work."

"I see," said Dennis. "That might be an easy place for me to start, actually. And where do Crystal and Duncan live now, or is that all in this neatly prepared envelope?"

"Crystal and Duncan live in Orlando, Florida. Duncan's parents were living with him until he married my sister. Now they are living in an apartment in Altamonte Springs, but yes, I put those details in there for you," I said, placing my hand gently on the envelope.

"So, what makes you want me to look into Duncan?" Dennis asked. He made eye contact with Graham and folded his hands together in a prayer position.

"About a year after they got married, Duncan told Crystal that he wasn't a U.S. citizen. He doesn't have a green card or anything. I'm pretty sure his parents are here illegally," Graham explained.

"Do you know how they came into the U.S. in the first place?" asked Dennis.

"We're not sure," I said. "Duncan says his dad came here on an E-2 investor's visa in the late 1980s. They never left, and they never filed for permanent residency. They've just been blending in with all the other Brits who move to Florida."

"So, you want me to find out how they got here and why they haven't gone back. Is that what you're saying?" Dennis asked, still looking at Graham.

"We don't trust anything at this point, Dennis," Graham stated, looking down at his silverware and then up at Dennis. "Their names, their birthplaces. All of it is up for grabs, in my opinion. Duncan is lying. I can't tell which parts, if any, are true. My sister-in-law has taken him to an immigration lawyer in Orlando. She said Duncan lied to the attorney about his story. A few weeks ago, Crystal wanted to go to England for a week to do an independent study to close out her master's degree coursework. She asked to stay with his mother's family while she was there, but he told her she couldn't because they were all away on holiday."

"That was probably true," Dennis said with a courteous smile. "Brits are always on holiday."

"Duncan refuses to return to England to file for permanent residency," I added. "He says he doesn't want to be deported because he hates England. My sister is an American citizen. It's not like he's from Iraq. There should not be this big of a problem. He's hiding something. He's been hiding it for four years. I want to know—we want to know—what it is."

"You two are close—" said Dennis.

"Were close," I corrected.

"Lyssa, I've been doing international private investigating for more than twenty years. Only some of those cases have been personal, but all of them leave us more questions than answers," said Dennis. He leaned over the table and lowered his voice. "I want to be clear. Even if we find out Duncan is a bad guy, there is no guarantee your sister is going to leave her husband. If that's what you're after here and you present her with our findings, it could upset her. You should think ahead about how you will handle the information I uncover. I take it she does not know you have hired me."

"No, she doesn't know," I confessed.

"Good. Let's keep it that way for now," said Dennis. "Since we have that settled, do you have any photographs of Duncan's parents?"

"Yes," I said, placing my hand on the envelope. "Everything is in here. You can have this. There is also a photo of a hotel they said they used to own in England. I've also included Duncan's Social Security Number."

"He has a Social?" Dennis sounded surprised. "How did he get it?"

"I don't know. It looks just like my card. He said his father got it for him while they were in Florida. His mom and dad have them, too, but I don't know those numbers."

The waiter brought out our food. Dennis lifted the envelope from the table and slipped it into his jacket. Luckily, none of the present aromas at the table nauseated me. Graham's steak actually smelled better than my lemon chicken.

We finished our meals as Dennis shared some nail-biting anecdotes. I was impressed with the manner in which he provided information without revealing significant details.

"Dennis," I started to explain, "my sister and I come from a pretty conservative family. Our father does consulting work. Our mother is a schoolteacher. We grew up in suburbia. Crystal was even on the varsity cheerleading team. The worst thing we did growing up was break curfew. All this international intrigue is so far outside our scope of reality. We cannot even begin to imagine what might be going on here. If you do find out something, well, I am not sure I would even know what to do."

Warm tears fell down my cheeks and onto my chicken. Graham grabbed my left hand and squeezed it. I looked at him for reassurance.

"It's alright, sweetheart," Graham said. "We know enough people who do know what to do."

Graham's father had been in Congress many years ago, representing Vermont. His mother, after the divorce, married an attorney.

"You don't need to imagine what is really happening," said Dennis. "I have contacts in Scotland. You have actually provided me with a good deal of information. If there is anything for you to be worried about, I will get to the root of it."

"How long do you think it will be before we can find out anything?" Graham asked.

"Something like this," Dennis said, pursing his lips together in a frown, "could take anywhere from four weeks to four months. I suspect I'll have something for you in a month." He scribbled something down on a cocktail napkin in what looked like doctor's handwriting. "I will give you an encrypted username and password. Don't lose them. The first two reports will have weekly updates from me and any supplemental contacts I use in the field. The final report will include my personal evaluation of the situation based on the information I've collected. There's also one condition: if I feel myself or my contacts are in any personal danger at any time, the investigation will be suspended until further notice."

My stomach tightened. I could not tell if it was the baby or the part about being in personal danger.

"What if my sister is in danger?" I asked.

"I will certainly let you know," said Dennis.

We finished our meals, and our plates were cleared. I could

tell Dennis needed to leave, but I felt like I had more to tell him.

"Dennis, my sister Crystal, she's a great person." I felt the tears coming back. "And, well, she's my best friend in the whole world. I would literally do anything for her."

I clutched my stomach and the importance of family relationships seized me intensely at that moment. The new life growing inside my body, the life of my sister thousands of miles away—nothing was more important than these two things.

"I'm sorry. I just—I fear we've left her alone in this situation for too long."

"Your compassion for your sister is extremely moving. I want you to know that you have hired the best man for the job. Now, if you'll excuse me." Dennis stood to leave.

"Thank you again," Graham said as he stood and shook Dennis's hand.

"My pleasure, Graham," Dennis replied. "By the way, Duncan Douglas . . . that's an interesting name."

"Why's that?" Graham asked.

"Well, black is a relatively uncommon color for a horse. I used to have a Friesian horse named Duncan, which means dark hair, and Douglas means dark water. So, the dark horse from the dark water—it's very mysterious, no?"

Dennis bowed to me as I blotted the corners of my eyes with my white napkin. I nodded to him in return and managed a weak smile. Graham took care of the check and we kissed before parting for our separately parked vehicles. The cool night air was refreshing to my tear-stained face. I should have blamed it on the hormones.

26

DUNCAN

July 30, 2002

I sat on the floor of our server room at the office and per-formed the mundane task of removing the motherboards from the laptops I'd scored. The new shipment arrived late yester-day and I wanted to get through this quickly. Our clients had no idea how long it took to order, format, install, secure and deliver something as simple as a desktop computer for a nurse's station, much less reformat a backup hard drive. It allowed me the time to build my own machine out of other parts no one would ever know were missing. Nevertheless, I didn't want to take too long delivering it to them, just in case.

My bum began to ache from sitting on the cold, hard tile for so long. Pa didn't appreciate the fact that I left no trace of my presence in the physical or digital worlds, even when working in the server room in my own office. And yet, I was risking my own job for his last one. I crawled over to the tall gray tower that held the processing power I needed and delicately pinched the cord's clear cap and pulled it out of the server. I slid the cable into my laptop and heard the plastic click with an echo that bounced across the dark room.

I needed to give it point three seconds to launch, then hack in the back door and watch the files open, more or less. It helped having a contact on the inside feed me the right names to fish for, and he was cheap, too. What amazed me, once I got in, was how unprotected the cards themselves were. Everyone was so paranoid about the eight-digit sequence, it's like they forgot about the two and a half inch by three and three quarter inch card image.

As easy and simple as this process was, it did take a bit of time. Finding file matches took so bloody long. I could feel the beads of sweat forming on my forehead even though the room was a steady sixty-two degrees Fahrenheit. I should know, since I programmed it.

I needed twenty-five males and thirty-three females, and then I could grab a bloody drink. I was already late to meet Drew. Normally, I just pulled a few of each gender and it only took a few minutes. Pulling down and sorting these by the dozen seemed to be taking much longer. I thought I had calculated for that in the USB I chose, so the duration was making me nervous. I also should not have been in these files or this room for so long.

Lydia B. Owen 967-98-0193

Patrick G. Brenan 584-34-2453

Oden R. Ratifer 458-01-9781

...

I should win awards for the things I could do with a laptop and a cable.

The next thing to be done, once the files were pulled, was leave a gap of time sufficient enough to prevent any idiotic moves on the buyer's side—not that anyone could move that quickly. Generally, these were delivered overseas and not drawn down on for several weeks after delivery. I didn't trust Pa's contact though. And if our uncle knew Pa was retiring, he couldn't be trusted. I added a layer of encryption to my files that would need to be unlocked before opening. Not until I knew we had the money would I give them the code. Now all I had to do was kill a couple of hours by not acting out of sorts.

Speaking of which, Crystal was acting strangely lately, but I had already moved on, so I didn't much care. When I traveled for work, I stayed at the same hotel and got to know the same women who worked there. It was so easy to tell who'd shag a bloke just because he had an accent. Used to be I could walk into Dexter's any Tuesday during happy hour and cherry pick the first three ladies who were ripe for the choosing. That was before my hairline started receding. Now, I had to get them outside, show them the Cutlass, maybe take them for a spin. It was a ton more effort, and not always worth it.

If I were to break down the "carrots" I used to get a woman in bed, the main three would be my hair, my accent, and my charm. To support those, however, especially in Orlando, I had to have the Omega Seamaster watch, the Cutlass, and the bike. It wasn't that any one of them was particularly impressive. I had to have all three working together to show that I was a sophisticated rebel who liked to have fun. That's what set me apart from the other guys in Winter Park, who had Rolex watches and yachts, but were all graying at the temples and had bellies that stuck out over their belts. Money goes pretty far, but being fun will come in a healthy second every time. Besides, I wasn't trying to land one of them. Just wanted to take them for a spin, was all.

Drew wasn't nearly as good at this as I was, but he made the girls laugh, and so he was good to have around. He loved cars as much as I did and had his own auto body shop in Oviedo. We spent every weekend working on different projects. We would buy a couple of $500 Oldsmobiles, take them out to Chuluota, do doughnuts, spin them out, and crash them. One year, Drew bought a camcorder and taped us setting a car on fire. One of the guys we rode with owned the land, so we just left the burning heaps of metal where they lay. Didn't have to clear anything away when we were done having our fun.

Drew owned a red 1967 Mustang in mint condition. We also bought our R1s at the same time, but then bought regular cars for driving to work and out on dates. He was also good for an alibi once in a while. When I rolled into Millie's off Orlando Avenue around ten o'clock, he was already chatting up a couple of D-cups at the bar and didn't even notice I was over an hour late to meet him.

"Duncan, my man," Drew called out when he saw me. He was wearing the same dumb three-button blue polo shirt he had on at the office earlier. Drew sported a middle-part 80s haircut and light blue denim jeans that only attracted women who graduated high school two decades ago.

"Drew, what is up, my friend," I said and put my motorcycle helmet on the bar.

That was my first cue to the two girls seated at the far right side, not currently talking with us. It was hard to see them clearly, since Millie's was cheap on lighting and mixed drinks, but their high cheekbones and tight skin around their arms clearly meant they were younger.

"Ladies, this is Duncan, and he is the only motorcycle-riding, cyber-coding specialist who looks that good on a bar stool," said Drew.

Drew was laying it on a bit thick. He was likely already hammered, which was perfect. He wouldn't remember what time I arrived here or what time I left. My work was only half completed. I still needed to make the drop.

"Hey there, handsome," said one of the blonde women in Drew's collection at the bar. "What kind of motorcycle do you ride?"

She tilted her hips on the vinyl bar stool when she turned toward me, and the skin on her legs stuck slightly to the cheap plastic. I hated cheap plastic, and the thought of her thighs on it nauseated me.

"One that probably goes too fast for you, sweetheart," I said.

I looked at Drew and tapped my finger on my Omega watch. Drew nodded and gave me the thumbs up just as one of the D-cups started running her hands through his hair. I would have been happy for him, but it only reminded me that my hair was thinning.

"See you beautiful people later," I yelled over the tops of their heads and headed out the back door. Most of the bars along 17-92 didn't have much parking out front, so the lots out back were bigger, darker. But as I slid my Arai helmet over my head, I caught a glimpse of a black sedan with tinted windows in the back of the lot. I didn't recognize the grill on the front, arched similar to a Cadillac, but with thin metallic lines, more like a Mercedes. Either way, it was much too posh of a motorcar to be parked in this lot. I paused for a second to stare hard into the driver's seat, but it was just a black hole.

I revved the engine and slowly pulled around front, making a right onto Orlando Ave. Nobody was on the roads this late on a weeknight. I could make it to Sanford in less than twenty minutes. I checked around for cops before turning right onto Orange Ave. There were no other cars on the road. My hands prepared to open the throttle and pop the clutch when I caught a flash of lights in my right mirror. I sped up and the car went faster as well. I couldn't take any chances. I hooked a right down Michigan Ave. There was a narrow entryway into Mead Garden hidden in the back. I would lose him in there.

I pulled around to the back, shut off the engine and walked the bike backwards into the gap of the garden gates. Not even two minutes passed before the same black sedan rolled down the street right in front of me. Damn. It was too dark to see the plates, but they were probably fake anyway. I would have to finish my work later and get Pa to help me figure out who this was.

27

CRYSTAL

August 1, 2002

I HAVE HELD MY BREATH FOR THE LAST SEVERAL DAYS. Like a secret agent trying desperately not to reveal my identity, I kept my escape plan to myself. Even at work, I refused to share my personal problems or even engage in small talk. At lunch yesterday, I took $1,000 out of the savings account I opened several years ago in my name only. I hid the cash in the trunk of my car and removed the valet key from the hook in the kitchen. I prayed Duncan would not notice its sudden absence.

I called Jessica and Norm yesterday and asked them to take the day off from work, dress in scrubby clothes, and come to the house as early as possible. I didn't tell Whitney so she would have plausible deniability. Norm was single, so I was pretty sure he could make the time, but Jessica was newly married with a kid. She might not have any vacation days left after flu season. I told them not to ask me any questions. Just show up. I felt so lucky to have them, yet so guilty for not spending more time with them in the last few years. Duncan didn't like them, so they'd gotten whatever time was left after work, family, and everything else. Thankfully, that would all be changing.

When I pulled my convertible into the garage after work, Duncan's Range Rover was already there. I parked my car in the middle, between the Rover and the R1 motorcycle. There was enough room for me to get out on the driver's side, but Duncan had installed a laser pointer to shine on my dashboard so I could always pull into the exact same location each time, never too close or too far from any of his vehicles.

I walked inside and hung up my keys, aware that the charade was about to begin. Technically, it had all been a charade, but it was reaching the point where I knew I was merely a player and this house would stage my final performance. I surprised myself with how nonchalant I could be around him. Maybe I had learned from him how to keep secrets, how to pretend like everything was fine and normal. Filling the dead space between us with meaningless chatter helped stave off questions that would have been elicited from my silence. Droning on about blockbuster movies and which car to buy next was a deterrent from topics like immigration reform and why we hadn't had children. It's really what couples don't say to each other that was so revealing.

Less than twenty-four hours before I was about to leave my husband, I was still telling him that I loved him. I was still emailing him about paying the homeowners' association fee. For a few moments, on the eve of my separation, it almost felt like it wasn't going to happen at all. Other than the churning in my stomach, it felt like just another weekday.

But the next morning, the day's exit plan felt very real. Adrenaline shot up from my feet, but my lungs seemed buried under a heavy blanket of sand. I had to tell myself I could do this. I am doing this. I woke up and got ready as if I were going to work, while Duncan did the same. I tried to follow my normal morning routine as closely as possible. Fed the cats. Made the coffee. Got dressed in work clothes. Barely spoke to husband.

Thankfully, he always left before I did, so when I saw his car pull around the side of the house and head up the street, I ran back to my room and changed into jeans, a shirt and sneakers. I had exactly three hours to get the keys from the management office, get my apartment set up, and get back here in time for the moving truck.

I was only moving twenty miles away, but to a new and mostly undeveloped part of town no one ever visited. Being unfamiliar with southeast Orlando, I Googled the nearest Publix on Narcossee Road. It was a little further down the two-lane road on Lee Vista, about seven minutes from my office. Narcossee reminded me of Tuskawilla in the late 1980s, with tract homes under construction in between long stretches of road where livestock still roamed.

My new apartment was a blessing. I had never lived in an apartment before—not even in college. It was a little out of my price range, but I'd heard stories of women becoming depressed after divorce because they had moved into grimy one-bedroom apartments with roach infestations and leaking roofs. If I was going to have a mental breakdown, I wanted to have it next to the pool with a view of the lake.

Coincidentally, it was the only apartment they had available at the time my dad called and it happened to be a one bedroom. It was an undeservedly gorgeous sanctuary. The bedroom had a huge walk-in closet and the bathroom had a soaking tub. New carpet had just been laid and the crown molding finished off the apartment beautifully. Tall, narrow windows lined the wall by the lake in both the bedroom and the living room, which had a little fireplace and mantel.

After I went by the manager's office to pick up my keys—the keys to my freedom—I wanted to stock the fridge with some groceries while I still had the emotional composure to do so.

I parked my car in the large strip-mall parking lot and walked into the shiny, oversized grocery store. I grabbed one of the little green shopping baskets, but then returned it for one of the larger carts. This wasn't a weekend retreat. I was starting over and would need a bigger basket.

As I strolled the aisles with complete lucidity, a rush of power surged within me. I was really doing this. I was really going to get away from him.

Rushing down the last few aisles, I finished up shopping and headed back to my apartment. It would take me twenty minutes to get home, leaving me only twenty minutes to unload everything and get stuff set up for tomorrow. As I put food into the narrow pantry and loaded frozen dinners into the freezer, I oscillated between feelings of joy and trepidation. If I was really doing the right thing, why did it hurt?

I sat against the back wall in the living room, staring at the 500 square feet of empty carpet between me and the fireplace at the other end of the room. In less than eight hours, this apartment would be filled with furniture and boxes. And Figment. I was definitely taking Figment. She would like this place. Plenty of low window sills to watch the birds and lizards in the bushes outside.

When I got back to my house, the moving van was already there, and so were my parents. My friends had not shown up yet. If they had, they might have been able to stop the chaos I saw unfolding in front of me.

"What are you doing?" I yelled as I entered through the wide-open front doors.

Two bulky men were carrying the camel-colored leather

couch into the truck while my mom dumped all the silverware into a large duffle bag. None of this was in the plan.

"We're helping you move," said my mom, not pausing to look at me. It was like she was on a game show and could keep whatever items she could bag in a limited time frame.

"No, this isn't helping! This is going to piss him off. He's going to think we've been robbed."

The plan had been to change as little as possible so he could keep living his same life and just let me out of it without upsetting him. I watched as the two movers carried the black leather recliners up and out of the family room. I wanted to scream, Put those back! But I couldn't form the words.

"Honey, he doesn't deserve any of this," Mom said. "He doesn't deserve you or any of this."

"But Mom, I don't want it," I argued back. "This is just stuff. It's going to be baggage for me. I don't need any of it. I just wanted a bed and a couple of chairs!"

"What about your closet?" Dad asked emerging from the master bedroom.

"Okay, yes, I want everything that's in there," I said. "But nothing else!"

I went and found the cat carrier and scooped up Figment. I dumped out her litter box and put it in my car. I was headed back in for my bathroom stuff when I saw the movers trying to figure out how to get the flat screen TV off the wall. I couldn't help but laugh out loud.

"Leave it," I told them.

"Here's the paperwork from the attorney," my dad said, handing me a folder with white papers neatly stacked together with a metal binder at the top. Several pages had been tabbed with a "Sign here" sticker. At least Duncan would appreciate how organized it all was.

I looked around the house and hated how empty it looked

without the furniture. I wanted it all put back so the only thing missing was me. I called my friends and told them to just meet me at the apartment to unpack. It was too late to help out here.

My parents told the movers to follow them. My dad went out through the front door and got in the Oldsmobile. I put Figment in the car and went out through the garage. Just as my parents were pulling away, my cell phone rang. It was Duncan. I wasn't sure if I should answer it, but I needed to know why he was calling.

"Hello," I said, almost as a question.

"Are you at home?" Duncan asked.

I didn't know how to answer. I watched my parents disappear down the road with the truck close behind.

"No, why?" I said, hoping I sounded convincing.

"I just got a call from the police," he said. "The alarm is going off at our house."

My dad must have punched in the wrong code. Or left the door open.

"Oh, I'll run by and shut it off," I said.

"No, it's okay. I'm almost there already."

There was only one way in and out of our development. My only hope at this point was that he didn't see the moving truck or my parents' car as he drove in. I could have pulled away at that moment and raced out before he realized what was going on, but I didn't. I sat there in my car with Figment in the carrier on the passenger seat. I put my hands on top of the steering wheel and rested my forehead on my hands. I closed my eyes and told myself to take a deep breath, because it was time for me to rage.

I went back inside and picked up the divorce papers from the counter. As I headed back outside, I ran right into a police officer who had been sent to check on our house. Duncan had paid extra for this service to protect his precious toys. Now I was going to use it to protect me.

"Officer," I said confidently. "Thank you for coming out, but

I'm afraid it's a mistake."

The officer looked around the house, suspicious at its emptiness. He would get it in a moment.

"You see, I am leaving my husband because he is abusive," I said, his eyes putting it all together. "He doesn't know it yet, so I would appreciate it if you would stay while I hand him these papers. It will only take a moment. Then I'm going to get in my car and drive away."

The officer nodded and stepped back outside. He said something into his radio and I walked outside with him.

Duncan's car pulled around the corner. He parked in the driveway and got out. He looked at the cop, then at me. He moved very slowly. I marched up to him and handed him the papers. He took them, but did not take his eyes off the cop.

"Crystal," he said quietly. "What the hell is going on here?"

"Duncan," I said, just as quietly. "Sign these divorce papers. I'm leaving you, you lying asshole."

"Are you kidding me?" he asked, finally looking down at the papers. "Why is the cop here? Why did our alarm go off?"

"The movers left the door open when they left," I said. "It must have gone off when I reset the code on my way out."

Duncan went to grab my arm and the officer coughed loudly behind me.

"You don't get to touch me anymore," I said staring him in the eyes. "Sign the papers. Put them in the mail and don't show up for the court date. I will go. It will be uncontested. Agree to the terms and I won't say anything about anything. I just want out."

I turned around and headed to my car. Duncan went to get back into his car, but the officer walked over to him and stood right behind his Range Rover so he couldn't back out until I was safely gone.

28

DUNCAN

August 4, 2002

"Sucks for you, son," Pa said.

He was sitting on a small green plastic chair facing mine. We watched the traffic flow through the apartment's parking lot from his tiny balcony three floors up. Tenants came and went below us like ants. Mum came out and sat down in the chair next to me. She lit a fag and blew her smoke away from my face.

"Rory's not answering his phone, love," Mum said. "Should I try to ring him on another number?"

"No, Gale," said Pa. "Let me clear me head and think for a moment."

Pa had on the same white undershirt and jeans he had worn all week. Mum wore a long brown skirt and silk blouse, which was silly since she never went anywhere.

"We have to sell the house per the terms of the divorce," I said. "Which is fine. The money's going into a fake account anyway."

"Where are you going to live?" Mum asked. "I can make up the couch here if you like."

"No, Mum. I'm buying the house across the street. The owner told me she hasn't officially put it on the market yet. If I can get a deal on it, I'd like to stay in the neighborhood. It's nice."

I didn't want a two-story house with a big mortgage anyway. This one-story house would be better for me as a bachelor. Didn't want my parents moving in with me again, though.

"What about the lawyer, Duncan? Has she told the lawyer about you? About us?" Pa rarely had such a serious look on his face. He was really worried.

"No, she promised not to tell her lawyer nothin'. I told her she could say I cheated on her if they needed a legitimate reason."

I was only offering the truth. My cell phone rang but I didn't answer it. It was the first time I had ever ignored a call from the office.

"Just give her whatever she wants in the divorce. With any luck, she'll meet someone and forget about you straightaway."

"Well, thanks, Mum," I replied. "She knows I don't have my citizenship. She knows I am supposed to go back in order to keep working here legally. If she tells my boss, I'm dead. They'll look into me. They'll look into everything. She's best friends with the boss's daughter!"

"I plan to go home," said Mum, completely disregarding the urgent information I was telling them.

"Are ye deaf, woman?" Pa said, turning around to stare at her like the idiot she was. "We can't go back. Not now."

"Why not? We've waited ten years. Surely they've forgotten by now."

Mum sat up on the edge of her chair, sticking her chest out at Pa. He raised his hand in a back-end motion, but then lowered it to his side again.

"Shut yer trap," Pa said, taking the final puff from his fag.

"Both of you shut up! You're not listening to me!"

I shook my head. Their phone rang. Mum jumped up to answer it. She returned to the balcony, cordless phone in hand.

"It's Rory."

Mum put the phone firmly into my hand and stared me down.

"Just keep an eye on her," I said into the receiver without breaking eye contact with Mum. "Tell me everything."

I went inside, placed an envelope on the bar and picked up my car keys. Maybe I should go by her parents' house. See if her car is there. If not, I should pay a little visit to her office tomorrow, remind her that I could find her if I wanted to.

On top of everything going on at work, now I had to deal with this. At the mere mention of work, my bloody cell phone rang again. It was William.

"Hey, man," I tried to sound happy.

"Where the hell are you?" he yelled into the phone. People were shouting over the music in the background. "We're all over at the Irish pub. Thought you'd be here by now."

"I don't know if I can make it. Crystal left me today. Took all the furniture out of the house while I was at work."

"Oh," he said, "sorry to hear that. You're not going to take any time off, are you? We're heading into our busiest week, you know."

"Yeah," I sighed into the phone. "I know."

"That's why you've got to pick one that's pretty, but not so smart, like I did."

"Yeah, Crystal's not stupid. That's for sure."

"Come on. Meet us. I'll buy you a beer. You could use one."

"Sure thing. See you in a few."

I hung up the phone and left the apartment.

At least Crys left our bed. Didn't want to sleep on the floor when I came home drunk. And if I planned to do anything right now, it was to get sloshed. Pa had the wrong approach to this, as usual. I would play the nice guy to Crystal. I'd tell her she had to pay for the divorce since it was her idea.

It was kinda funny, actually. Tried to keep her quiet in the marriage. Now I was trying to keep her quiet in the divorce. High-maintenance little bitch. If she told the judge I was not a legal citizen, I would lose everything. Bollocks. Maybe I should let Pa handle it his way.

My head was sweating something awful. Before running into the pub, I tried smoothing down my hair, what was left of it anyway, with a comb. Couldn't meet any new chicks with a bald head, now could I? I put the comb back in the glove compartment and got out of the Rover. I tucked my shirt in and locked the car. It really sucked losing Crystal today, but at least I still had my job. Didn't know what I would do if I ever lost that.

29

LYSSA

September 22, 2002

DENNIS YONDAY'S REPORT EMERGED PAINFULLY SLOWLY, ONE LINE AT A TIME FROM THE INK-JET PRINTER ON MY DESK. If we could make bomb-disabling robots, we should be able to make a printer that went faster than a 1970s fax machine. I tried reading it upside down as the black ink formed words that became sentences. Any minute now, Jodie was going to remind me I was late for our briefing.

The cover letter was done and I ripped it off the printer and shoved it into a manila envelope before anyone could see. The second page started to emerge. It said Dennis was backing off the investigation. In his two decades of experience, he had never encountered anything like this. He had to stop because he felt his own life, and the lives of his contacts, were in danger.

He also thought his identity may have been compromised.

I dialed my dad's cell phone number faster than the printer could spit out rows of horrible news. The endless ringing sounded in my ear. Pick up, pick up, pick up.

"You've reached the voicemail box of Anthony Vargas." Ugh! "Please leave a message at the sound of the tone."

"Dad, please call me back as soon as you get this. Please call me back. It's urgent."

"Lyssa," Jodie's voice ripped me back into reality. "Is that the Afghanistan briefing?"

I looked down, almost forgetting what was in my hand.

"Um, no. No, it's not. Why? Did you need a copy of it?"

"Yes, remember, you said you would run it by me before giving it to Ron? I wanted to make sure you included the name of that imam from Paris."

I shook my head as if I had been asleep for days.

"Right," I said. "I'm sorry, I'll print that out and leave it on your desk before I go to lunch."

"Lunch is at the White House today. Don't forget."

Jodie whipped her ballerina-bunned head around and went back to her closet-sized office.

I should not have read this report in my office, but my curiosity won out over my rationality.

My stomach hurt. If didn't know any better, I would say I was having contractions. Suddenly, Ron walked up behind me and tapped me on the shoulder. I jumped as high as a pregnant woman can, looking like a whale breaching in slow motion.

"You don't plan to keep the president waiting, do you?"

He was pulling on one of the dark-blue blazers he kept in his office for White House lunches. I stood up from my desk and folded the back of his collar down. The whole office had already cleared out and I had yet to deliver the Afghan report to Jodie's desk.

"I'll meet you there," I said to Ron, throwing Dennis's report into my purse. I ran off one report for Jodie and another one to take home with me, just in case I didn't come back here after lunch. These meetings were long and arduous. At least I would get to see Graham and show him Dennis's findings. I grabbed my Burberry purse and headed out into the moist summer air.

When I arrived at the side entrance, a cluster of Secret Service men stood guarding a set of double doors behind the metal detectors. I could not get through security until Graham showed up with my pass. A few moments after I removed my cardigan, he darted from behind the double doors.

"You're late," he said with a smile.

Graham handed my pass to the security guard, who passed it to me through the metal detector. I put the lanyard around my neck, set my purse in the basket, and walked through to Graham. I wanted to wrap my arms around him and make out with him right then and there, but this was a Republican White House. Such a public display of affection might elicit a few stares. I just smiled at him and retrieved my purse. We darted down the north corridor and I pulled Dennis's report from my bag.

"This came in today," I said, walking as fast as I could with an extra thirty pounds strapped to my belly. "I haven't had a chance to read it, but it doesn't start well."

Graham took the report from my hand, not looking down at it.

"So, you decided to bring it here and hand it to me in front of White House security cameras?" His sense of humor was always so dry.

When we got to the conference room, Graham pushed open the double French doors and we took seats in the back next to the American flag. A long silver tray of sandwiches stuffed with shredded lettuce was placed in the center of the table. Graham leaned forward and selected a few pieces. A tall, thin man in a white shirt silently handed me a couple of sodas. Jodie and Ron were seated near Condi. Hopefully Ron wouldn't notice I was wearing a temporary security pass. Not that he would care, but I wanted to avoid that conversation for now.

A loud cell phone ring interrupted the speaker and the blood instantly drained from my head. The ringing was coming from my purse. A look of horror came over Graham's face, and he took my sandwich from my hands as if this were a routine experience.

"Must be Bush calling to say the plane's late leaving the ranch," shouted an older military officer from the front of the room.

As I went to turn the phone off, I saw that the call was from my dad. Hmm. The president or my dad. Tough call. I rolled my chair back from the table and ducked outside the French doors.

"Dad," I whispered.

"Lyssa, I can't hear you honey."

"I got the report back from the investigator," I said. "It doesn't look good."

"What did you say, honey?" he asked.

"I haven't finished reading it, but they are calling it off, something about . . ."

I couldn't finish my sentence. A sudden pull of my insides took my breath away and I dropped my phone. I tried to inhale, but before I could exhale, my water broke and I found myself standing in a puddle in the East Wing. There goes my Junior League induction.

Graham had come into the hallway to find me when he saw me standing there, dripping. He rushed to my side after a brief pause of shock.

"Baby's coming!" I said.

30

CRYSTAL

September 22, 2002

WHEN I WAS A LITTLE GIRL, MY DAD WOULD TAKE ME SWIMMING AT A LOCAL **YMCA.** The smell of chlorine was strong enough to singe your nose hairs. What I remember most was the water's reflection on the walls and ceilings. Wavy lines of light danced up and down inside a rectangular shape.

When my eyes opened that first morning in my new apartment, the refracted sunlight bounced off the lake and up onto the ceiling of my bedroom. For a moment, I just lay on my back, staring at the liquid sunshine zig-zagging around inside the window shaped box on my ceiling—a sign of hope. I had made it. Sometimes your heart has to break into a million tiny pieces so it can escape through the bars and be free.

Duncan was more pissed about the furniture than the

divorce, but he signed the papers and sent them in. For the first time, I had him on his heels. Once we sold the house, I would have some cash in my savings account. My dad called it the year of Jubilee, the year the slaves in the Old Testament were forgiven their debts.

The day after I moved into my new apartment, I didn't think I would ever get organized or unpacked. My books took up more room than my clothes. Dad wanted my car parked in the garage the first night, so we had to pile all the furniture into the living room. He was worried about me being alone all the way across town by the airport. Nothing but cow pastures lined the streets between my apartment and my new office on SR436. It was peaceful and quiet out here. I liked it. I wanted to be alone.

This morning, Dad came over pretty early to check on me and bring me a Starbucks gift card. He had meant to give it to me the day I moved in, but had forgotten about it, understandably. He had also taken my MFA diploma to get it framed. He wanted me to hang it up in my new place. I only wished I had used my maiden name on it.

"What do you think?" Dad asked, holding the frame above the desk in my bedroom. "Right here?"

"Yep," I said. "That's perfect."

He tapped the nail into the wall and hung the frame lightly on top of it. I gave him the thumbs up and we walked into the living room. He put his hands on his hips and surveyed the apartment.

"Do you think this is enough to help you start over?" he asked.

"This is too much, actually. I really just need my cat, my books, and some coffee," I joked. I sat down on the couch, my left leg folded under me.

"Crystal, I want you to know something," my dad said, coming over to the couch to sit next to me. He put his hand on my right knee. "If I ever did anything . . . to make you want to run into the arms of this man, elope with him, I want you to know . . . I'm sorry."

My jaw dropped open. I've never had a good poker face.

Wow, I thought. Just, wow.

He must have read the disbelief on my face for what it was.

"I mean it," he continued. "I'm apologizing for not having been a better father. I could have hugged you more. I could have just spent more time with you."

His eyes were red, bloodshot. Tears fell down my cheeks. While it was satisfying on many levels to hear him say those words, they'd come too late. The damage was done. The walls were built. Those pivotal years were gone.

"I'm sorry, Crystal. I'm so sorry. I don't know what I would do if anything ever happened to you." He leaned in and hugged me, a long hug.

"It's okay, Dad," I said, squeezing him back. "Thank you for telling me that."

We sat in that hug for a few long moments under the tall, nine-foot ceilings of my new apartment. I released my arms and wiped my eyes.

"I have to go into the office today. It's my first week on the new job, so I better get ready," I said.

"I guess the apple doesn't fall far from the tree," said Dad.

Let's hope it falls a bit further, I thought.

We said good-bye. I took a shower and got dressed, appreciating every moment of having my own space.

It was freakishly warm, even for September. The low-lying morning fog spread out like a spider's web above the expansive green pastures along Narcoossee Road. Rolls of hay sat several hundred yards apart, yet to be discovered by the hungry cattle. This was probably what most of Central Florida looked like in the 1980s. Hardly a car on the road, the morning dew on the fields holding the sparkling of the morning's light in its clear orbs.

I decided to use my new gift card to get coffee before work. I hit the drive-thru Starbucks and ordered my usual, a grande coffee with a shot of peppermint. No cream. I loved my coffee. I loved my apartment. I loved my new job. My dad had apologized to me. I was feeling lucky enough to buy a lottery ticket.

When I sat down at my desk and checked my email, I found more than 200 messages waiting for me. The art director kept dropping slides off at my desk with a giant smile on his face, which meant we were behind schedule on the new issues of the magazine.

The production manager came by every two hours, leaving more proofs for me to check. My inbox swelled with sheets of paper awaiting the wrath of my red pen. Stacey Smith, the other associate editor, brought me a peanut butter and jelly sandwich for lunch. She was a tall, cute blonde with an infectious smile, and one of the most amazing human proofreaders I'd ever met.

"Peanut butter and jelly," she sang as she handed me the sandwich. "Tastes so good in my belly."

"Gee, you'd never guess your parents used to own a daycare."

"Can you tell I used to sing that song every Friday when we served PB&Js?" Stacey leaned against my desk as we chowed down on our sandwiches. "It was much better than leaving your kids at a 'dayscare'."

"Okay, then you must remember the song about the ghost of John?"

"No daycare is complete without it," said Stacey.

"Long white bones with the skin all gone," I started singing when the production manager, Jenny, came in with the last stack of proofs.

"Hey," said Jenny. "That's no way to talk about our cover model."

We laughed, but she was right. Our cover model did look anorexic.

"Once you guys are finished with this stack, you can go ahead and go home. Yippee, right?"

"You forget we have like ten other stacks before we can do those," Stacey reminded Jenny. "We'll be lucky to get out of here before dark."

"Let me know if you want another coffee run," said Jenny. "I'm leaving in an hour and there's only two guys in the back working in production. Whoever leaves last has to lock up the front and back of the building. Don't forget."

Twelve stacks of magazine pages later and Stacey and I were the only ones left in the office. Stacey was married and had a dinner party to attend, so I offered to proof her last stack. Single people were always expected to work later than married people.

Night had fallen outside and I was getting hungry. My sister had called twice, but I didn't have time to call her back. Giving only a light edit to the last few spreads, I returned the final edits, heavy with red ink and yellow tabs, to Jenny's desk. She would have to deliver the bad news to the designers on Monday. There were too many edits still to be made and we were so close to deadline. I grabbed my purse and car keys and locked up the rear entrance doors. Setting the alarm at the front door, I rushed to shut the front lights off, duck outside, and lock the door behind me.

As soon as I was outside, a brick of strong wind blew right through me. I hadn't even thought about checking the weather this morning. For a moment, I debated darting back inside and grabbing my sweater, but a split second later large drops of rain were pelting my backside. I decided to make a run for my car. When this type of rain started, it only got worse the longer you waited. I looked down and ran. With each step, the sheets of rain came down harder.

I got to my car and reached for the handle to the driver's side door when somebody slammed up against me. Before I could turn around, the person grabbed my hair like a horse's mane and pulled my head back and down. I wanted to scream, but could not bring enough air into my lungs. He bashed my forehead against the roof of my car. Blood ran down my left temple and I collapsed to the ground; my keys skidded under the car. I tried to crawl underneath to reach them. The gravel from the pavement scratched the skin on my cheek. My hand landed on my car keys and I struggled to press the panic button.

His hands pulled me out from under the car by my leg. When my hand holding the keys was in plain view, his boot crashed down on my clenched fist. I let out a howling scream; it felt like my bones were being crushed.

"Help!" I screamed.

I heard cars driving by on Semoran Boulevard. I wanted to get up and run, but everything was so blurry. My head burst with pain. The man latched on to the bottom of my shirt, twisting it to pull me up from the ground. I reached for the keys with my left hand, curling my hand into a fist so each key poked out between my fingers.

I tried to see his face, but the rain blinded me as I looked up. As he spun me around to face him, I kicked him in the groin and swung open my car door. I pulled the door shut as quickly as possible and fumbled for the ignition key. I heard a tap on the window as I put the car in reverse and turned to see a gun pointed right at me. Slamming on the gas, my car flew backwards.

Weaving in and out of the office parking lot, I heard the sound of a motorcycle rev behind me. The bike quickly caught up to my bumper and flashed its high beams. I plowed into the two-way traffic, realizing I had left my purse and phone behind.

It was late on a weeknight and none of the stores were open. I didn't know where to go. I couldn't go home, and I had no idea where a police or fire station was nearby.

The airport. It was less than two miles ahead. I drove through the red lights and sped around slower cars ahead of me. If I could make it to the departure ramp, I knew there would be a cop there. There was always a cop there. I flew past the other cars and it dawned on me that the man who attacked me didn't want my purse. He didn't even want my car. He was coming after me.

My mind raced with possibilities of who would want to hurt me. Was this a friend of Duncan's? It didn't make sense.

My Mercedes hugged the turns leading up to the departure ramp like a race car. The motorcycle pulled up along the right side of my car. The wipers were completely ineffective, just pushing the deluge from one side of the windshield to the other.

I followed the airport's sinewy path up to the departures ramp as the bike, now in front of me on my right, forced my car closer to the sidewall. Before I realized that I could have just turned my wheel right into the bike and struck him, I hit a puddle and hydroplaned. I lost control of the car and went into a tailspin. The rear bumper smacked the back tire of the motorcycle, kicking it into a summersault and sending its rider over the ramp.

My head slammed against the driver's side window. I gripped the wheel and prayed.

A police officer opened my passenger's side door. The salt from my tears stung the open wounds on my face.

"You alright, ma'am?" the cop asked, shining his flashlight in my face. "I saw that guy chasing you. Did you know he had a gun?"

"I can't breathe," I said in a whisper.

He must have seen the blood on my head and radioed for medical help. I heard the other officer radio in the description of the white truck.

"Is this your car?" he asked, still shining the light in my face.

"Yes," I whispered. "Is he gone?"

"Do you know who was on the motorcycle, ma'am?"

I tried to shake my head, but it hurt too much to move.

"No," I said. "No idea."

They turned their flashlights away from the interior of my car. One of them appeared to be my age. His hair was shaved pretty short, but I could tell he was blond. He said something into his radio and then turned around to face me.

"They're sending a medical team up," he said with a slight Southern accent. "Just sit tight, okay?"

I really couldn't move if he asked me to. I forced my eyes open and saw that the rain had stopped.

"Do you have any identification on you?" he asked. I shook my head. That hurt.

"I dropped my purse," I told him. "Back at my office."

The cop stood there looking at me. I was worried I might be in worse shape than I felt. A few medics ran out of the airport and over toward my car. I closed my eyes and laid my head back on the headrest. While they touched up my bloody forehead, I looked over to see the blond cop waiting and watching. He seemed overly concerned for airport security.

Once they were done with the bandages, they made me sign a waiver that I was declining a trip to the emergency room.

"Excuse me, officer," I yelled.

He walked up to me and leaned into my open driver's side door.

"Yes, ma'am," he said.

"Could you please give me a ride back to my office?" I asked. "You can bring me right back here. I just need to get my phone and my purse and don't want to go by myself."

"I can't take you in a squad car, but I'm done with my shift, so I'll take you in my car if that's alright with you," he said gently, probably not wanting to be overheard.

"Yes, that's fine," I said. "Thank you."

I looked over at the motorcycle as if seeing it for the first time. It was a blue R1 Yamaha. My stomach sank. I forced my feet to walk over to the side wall and looked down. Before my eyes lay my ex-husband, head twisted unnaturally to one side. The rest of his body imprinted against the ground as if a magnet had attracted each limb separately. Shock gave way to relief. Those hands, now curled and smashed beneath me, would not strike anyone ever again. The thought filled me with an almost sadistic jolt of energy in my arms, which wanted to raise up in praise-like form to the sky. Instead, my knees buckled. I crashed to the cement barrier wall in front of me and cried. I had killed Duncan.

31

LYSSA

September 23, 2002

"Push!" Graham held my hand and yelled. He stood beside me in blue scrubs, watching as the doctor cradled the baby's head in his hands. "You're almost there, sweetheart, just one more."

Wet hair clung to the sides of my face and sweat rolled down my chest. I could not catch my breath long enough to give a good push. It felt like I had been pushing for twenty-four hours straight.

"Push, Lyssa, push!" the doctor commanded from behind his silver-framed glasses.

"I'm pushing!" I cried. "Augh!"

I took one last deep breath and screamed, contracting my stomach muscles as hard as I could. Then I heard it. The most beautiful sound in the entire world. The first cry of my baby. I looked down at my spread-eagled legs as the fluorescent hospital light illuminated my child's slimy skin.

"It's a boy," the doctor said, handing him to Graham while the nurse cut the umbilical cord. "It's a perfect boy."

I cried as I watched Graham hold him delicately in his arms. Time paused for us in that brief moment. I was amazed at the love I felt for someone I had never seen before.

They cut the umbilical cord and handed our son to me. I sat up, numb from the pain and the painkillers. He was so tiny. So precious. *What a gift of life!* I was humbled by the presence of such a miracle in my arms. The nurse needed to rinse him off and take his vitals, but I begged for just one more second with him. His fingers were barely large enough to fit around my thumb. When the nurse left with my baby, another nurse came up and asked Graham for the baby's name.

"Randall," I said, looking at Graham. "Randall Jennings."

"Are we going to call him R.J.?" Graham asked.

"We could make him a Junior."

"Indiana was the dog's name," Graham said in his best Sean Connery voice.

We laughed, and the phone beside my bed rang in a horribly coarse tone. It was more of a clanging sound than a crisp ring. One of the nurses came in to change my IV. Her pale blue scrubs matched the pallid color of paint on the walls of my incredibly small room.

"Randall's daddy speaking," Graham answered the phone. He could be such a goof.

"Who is it?" I asked.

"It's Crystal," he said.

Graham handed me the phone.

"Lyssa," Crystal's voice was calm. I cried at the sound of it. "Lyssa, are you a new mommy now?"

"Yes, I am. He's perfect, Crys," I could barely speak. "Perfect little fingers and toes. I wish you could see him."

"I will," said Crystal. "I'm coming. I'll be at your place when you come home. I love you."

"I love you, too."

I handed the phone back to Randall. There was something strange in Crystal's voice, but before I could say anything about it, my parents came barreling in.

"Where's our grandson?" Mom asked, arms extended.

I handed Randall over to Mom and smiled with pure joy.

Once I was released from the hospital, we drove home as a new family. After being in a stuffy hospital room for two days, I savored the fresh air. We had just finished the nursery. Graham loved baseball, so we decorated the room in pinstripes and baseball caps. Mom even found a cute little rug that looked like a catcher's mitt. Crystal gave us tons of children's books, some of which were the Little Golden books she had held on to from our childhood.

That night, I sat with Crystal, drinking milkshakes in the family room. Randall was asleep on the Boppy pillow in my lap. Mom and Dad were in the guest room in the basement. Crystal had prepared the pullout couch for them and she took the daybed in the nursery.

I put my hand gently on Crystal's back and gently rubbed from left to right, like our mom used to do when we had upset stomachs. She looked at me and gave me a forced smile.

"Are you okay?" I asked, staring at the bandages on her face and hands. "If you want to talk about the accident, I'm here for you."

"I talked about it with the police so much that I don't want to talk about it anymore," she said. "At least, not now."

I smiled at her and nodded with understanding, even though I was dying to know more details.

I looked at Graham and wondered if he was thinking the same thing I was. I didn't even have to ask.

"Lyssa, I think it's time we told her," he said.

Crystal's smile faded. Her eyebrows lifted with curiosity.

"Tell me what?" Crystal set her glass down on the coffee table and folded her arms under her chest. She looked like an angry Buddha sitting on my couch, but a skinny one. I exchanged glances with Graham and he got up from his chair to go get Dennis's report.

"Crystal, Graham and I hired a private investigator to look into Duncan and his family."

"You what?"

The high pitch of Crystal's voice awakened Randall. I handed her my glass, then lifted him up gently and switched his position to the other side of my lap.

"Shh!" I put my finger over my lips, reminding her to keep it down.

"Sorry," she said, lowering her voice to a whisper while still speaking angrily. "You what?"

"Lyssa's security clearance was denied earlier this year," said Graham as he re-entered the room. He put the report down on the wooden coffee table. Crystal put down my glass and picked up the report.

"Which was odd," Graham continued. "But it's not totally uncommon. We asked around and thought Duncan's profile might have been inconclusive, so we had a former agency friend reach out to his friends. Turns out the FBI was looking into a thread of "recycled" Social Security numbers, and my contacts connected the dots from there. They were both looking into the same person who was connected with the same group of people—Brits who end up in the U.S. drawing down someone else's retirement funds and lines of credit."

Crystal's face was shifting from an intense scrunch of her eyebrows to a wide-eyed look of concern. She looked down at the report in disbelief.

"Your sister was worried about you," Graham said. "We were both worried."

"So, you investigated him without telling me?" Crystal asked, but it was more of a statement. She threw aside the report, stood up and began pacing by the couch.

"We didn't want you to accidentally tell him during the divorce proceedings," Graham said, taking his place in the leather chair again. "We thought it might put you in danger if he knew you suspected anything."

"Hmm," Crystal mused with sarcasm. "Danger like a man might attack me as I'm leaving work one night?"

"I went into labor!" Now I was shouting.

Randall started crying. I tried to soothe him, but I couldn't calm him and Crystal at the same time, so I handed him off to Graham.

I walked over to Crystal and took both her wrists in my hands. I looked her straight in the eyes.

"Crystal, please don't be angry with us," I said looking into her eyes, which were now starting to well up with tears. "We had every intention of telling you once the divorce was over."

"But you started this before I went to Mom and Dad's house, didn't you?" said Crystal. "You called that investigator before I even knew I was going to leave him. What if nothing came of the report? Would you still be telling me right now?"

She was right. I felt so busted. I let go of her hands and went to take Randall back from Graham's cradled arms. It looked like this baby was going to be a good sleeper. He was out like a light.

"The report was fairly inconclusive about Duncan," Graham

said quietly. "The real danger seems to lie with his father's family in Scotland."

Crystal finally picked up the report and began skimming through its pages.

"Organized crime ring!" Crystal gasped. "Are you kidding me?"

"The report is legitimate, Crystal," Graham explained. "Dennis is one of the best in the business. The Douglas family, or whatever their names are, have been selling IDs to people in Scotland a handful at a time, which is probably why they've never been caught. It was never meant to be a large-scale operation. There was some kind of feud. The Douglas family lost, and rather than be killed, they snuck out of the country."

Crystal didn't speak. She stopped on one of the pages and stared. Tears fell down her cheeks as she read. I tried to put my arm around her, but she leaned away. I reached down to the floor and pulled baby wipes from the turquoise container. Crystal took them from my hand and wiped her face.

"Ew, these are wet," she said looking down at the wipe.

"Sorry, I think we're out of tissues," I said and laughed. That was probably the first time Crystal had ever touched a baby wipe.

"So, if Duncan Douglas isn't his real name, then what is?" she demanded.

"We don't know," said Graham. "Dennis had to call off the investigation before he could find out. His identity may have been compromised. Duncan probably knew a U.S. agency was on his trail."

There was a pause. I thought Crystal might ask why, but she didn't. She just stared at me, her eyes now raw and red.

"I know you never liked him," Crystal said.

"No, I didn't," I replied. "From the first moment I saw him walk through our door, I thought he looked like a used car salesman. His hair was slicked back, his little gold charm getting tangled up in the black chest hair popping out from his shirt."

"His hair was not popping out of his shirt . . . that couldn't've been all of it," said Crystal. "You've dated some slimy guys too."

"Hey, now," I argued. "That was just my first impression. Then he insults me in front of you and you pretend like you don't hear it. You haven't been acting like yourself for years."

"He did?" Crystal questioned.

"Several times. And that's not like you. I didn't like how he controlled you. Then he refused to become a U.S. citizen and it basically confirmed he was shady. If it wasn't for Graham, I wouldn't have had the resources to do this . . ."

Crystal looked down in shame.

"Honey, I'm not sorry we did this. I'm only sorry it took me so long to figure this out. You should have left him years ago."

"I know," Crystal said sadly.

"Well, why didn't you?" I asked, honestly perplexed at how such a strong woman could tolerate Duncan for so long.

"It's not easy, Lyssa," Crystal said. "First, I had to even contemplate the possibility of it. I mean, we're Christians and we're told that God hates divorce."

"God hates abuse, Crys," I explained.

"Let me finish, Lys. Once I broke the barrier of those thoughts, I had to figure out what a life would be like without him. I would be alone. What would be my purpose when I came home from work every day?"

"Crystal!" I said, dismayed. This wasn't the sister I thought I knew.

"What? You try working so hard for something for so long! You don't just want to get up and walk away from it—the house, the mutual friends, the holidays—you're splitting one life into two. Not to mention how convinced I was that no one would ever want to be with me."

I couldn't stand to hear anymore. "Crystal, you are stronger than that. He may have told you otherwise for years, but you'll bounce back. You're a warrior, and warriors never forget who they are. Graham and I love you. We can't wait to see how much joy your life will be filled with when you remember who God made you to be." I tried not to get ahead of myself. "But first, you need to read that whole report."

Crystal continued to stare at the report in disbelief. "So, the last four years of my life . . . my in-laws . . . my marriage certificate . . . it's all fake."

"Not all of it," I said, tucking my sister's hair behind her ear. "The real Crystal is still inside there. I know it. Just be your amazing self again. We love you. Your family loves you. That's real. Your talent, your degree. Those are all real. Even if you never knew about this report, you still should have left him because of how he treated you. But we wanted you to make that decision on your own. We wanted you to be free from him inside your head. Now that he's dead, that's really the only place where he can still hurt you."

Crystal blew her nose, and I pulled out another wipe for her. I put both my arms around her shoulders and laid my head against hers. I had been so fascinated with the mystery surrounding Howard and Gale, I'd failed to anticipate the emotional implications for my sister. My heart broke for her, but at the same time, I was so incredibly relieved.

32

CRYSTAL

October 1, 2002

Fall in Washington D.C. felt refreshing. I was not used to wearing sweaters and boots and driving through crisp fallen leaves like I was in a car commercial. The sky became a cool blue color, providing a sharp contrast for the red and yellow trees swaying in the crisp breeze. The restaurants here had fire pits outside where you could sip your wine and people watch all afternoon. I tried to imagine living here, being near my sister and the baby.

I decided to stay a few more days after Randall was born. My new job was letting me work remotely. I told them I was just staying temporarily to help my sister out with the baby, but it was more so because I couldn't get out of bed the first few days. Then a few days turned into a few weeks. Ironically, staying in the nursery did not bother me. I seemed to be experiencing the same sleeping patterns as a newborn. When he woke in the middle of the night, I would grab a bottle and tell my sister to go back to bed.

In some strange way, I felt like little Randy's birth into this world had freed me from the one where I had been trapped. By the time my nephew grew up, he would have no idea about what happened the day he was born, or about any of the sad events leading up to it. Randall was only going to know me as the "the cool aunt." I would make sure of it.

"Crystal!" Lyssa yelled from downstairs. "Dad's on the phone! He needs to talk to you!"

I laid on my side in bed and opened one eye. The sunlight pierced through the rectangular gap around the blackout roller blinds in a crooked U pattern. Nothing in these old houses seemed to fit modern decor perfectly.

"Coming!" I shouted back.

I thought maybe if I said it out loud, my body would follow instructions. But it just lay there. I used my right leg to kick the covers off so that my bare legs were exposed to the chilly air. As I lay on my left side, I looked down at my right thigh rising up like a small hill that jutted out from the waistline of my short white tank top. My right hip bone nearly showed through my skin, indicating how much weight I had lost since coming to D.C. I still had a pretty solid tan line across my navel area. I wondered if anyone would ever notice these parts of my body again.

"Crystal!" Lyssa shouted again. "Today already!"

"Fine!" I yelled back.

I slid on the gray sweatpants that were on the floor next to the bed and sauntered down the narrow staircase in the back of the house and into the kitchen. Lyssa stood up against the sink washing dishes with Randall strapped against her body like a kangaroo with a baby in her pouch.

"What is that?" I asked looking at the swaddle. I had only seen that thing on women in Africa.

"It's a Moby," Lyssa replied and handed me the phone.

I gave her a strange look in response and took the phone.

"Hi Dad," I said, pretending to be more awake than I really was at the moment. "What's up?"

"Look, I know you've been through a lot, and I'm glad you've been with your sister and the baby, but there are some things here that need your attention."

I'd known this conversation was coming. I was actually surprised it hadn't happened until now.

"Like what?" I joked.

"Don't be smart. Your mother and I have been taking care of our house and your apartment and your cat. We sold your car at a loss, just to get rid of it for you. We don't mind helping for a little bit, but we need to know what your plan is. You should come back to Orlando and decide what you're going to do."

I was listening to the words he was saying, but I did not have a response to give. There was a pause.

"You need to get this over with so you can move on."

"Fine," I said. "I'll call you when I have my flight information. And, Dad, thank you. I appreciate everything you and Mom have done to help me."

"Of course, Crystal, we love you," he said.

"Love you, too," I replied, but it felt like I didn't mean it.

I hung up and handed the phone back to Lyssa. She had finished with the dishes and was feeding Randall.

"What did Dad say?" Lyssa asked.

"He said I need to figure out what I'm doing next with my life."

"What are you going to do?" asked Lyssa.

"I don't know," I replied.

I reached over and smoothed the fuzzy black hair on Randall's head. My hand had healed almost completely, but I could still see a few scrapes on my knuckles.

"I know I can't impose on you guys any longer. At some point, I need to shower and get dressed before noon. You've been a saint letting me stay here right after having a baby."

"Nonsense," said Lyssa. "You've been a huge help. And no matter what you decide, you are always welcome here. And I haven't showered in three days, much less before noon, so no judgment there."

We both laughed and Lyssa put Randall up against her left shoulder to burp him. I marveled at how instinctively delicate she was with him. I never felt like that came naturally to me. While I was incredibly happy for my sister as she started her new family, I couldn't help but think that was the furthest thing from what I wanted right now.

"Speaking of showers," I said, "I'm going to go upstairs and take one. Then I'm going to decide what to do next with my life."

I smiled genuinely and started backing my way out of the kitchen while Lyssa smiled back at me.

The knobs on Lyssa's shower were the old white antique handles with left and right dials. I got the water to the scalding heat I needed and then stepped under the drops like entering a waterfall.

I closed my eyes and saw the words that were in that report in my mind's eye. I saw Duncan twisted below me on the ground. My stomach turned. Had he come after me because he knew he was being investigated? Would he have left me alone otherwise?

Was it Lyssa's fault I almost got killed? I would never know. I would have to get out of this shower and get on with my life and I would never know. Unanswered questions like these would be a scratch on a record that would cause a needle in my mind to loop over and over again. The investigator was stumped. I was stumped.

I had to let it go. I had to lift my mind up and get over it. I didn't feel a need to bring the rest of his family to justice. I just wanted out. And I was. What was done and gone had to be released. I was alive and free and thankful. That seemed as good a place to start over as any.

I knew I couldn't go back and change the decisions I made in 1998, but what I could control was every decision I was making from now on. This was the emotional place I wanted to be in, and I had to forgive myself for not being here five years ago. It was not going to happen overnight. In fact, I might struggle with it for a long time, but I was never going to stop trying.

EPILOGUE

International terminals at airports were usually very busy. Today, Dulles was unusually quiet. The bright sunlight from the noon sky outside came in through the large angled windows above the ticket booths and reflected with extreme intensity off the shiny tile floor. An automated announcement came over the loudspeaker, and I sat my bag down on the ground so I could switch hands.

I hadn't been through international airport security since 9/11 and barely recognized things. I knew the government was taking over and adding additional rules about what you could bring on an airplane, but this set-up reminded me of buildings my dad took me to in Germany right after the Berlin Wall came down. Lots of gray. Lots of metal. No one smiling. I was lucky I wasn't flying out of the domestic terminal today. That part looked like a zoo. Nobody seemed to know what was going on or what the rules were.

I pulled the crossbody strap of my purse over my head and got my passport from my wallet. I looked down at it and smiled upon seeing "Crystal Vargas" as my name, though I still didn't recognize myself with blonde hair. I felt in my canvas pants pocket for my plane ticket and lifted my black duffle bag up with my other hand.

Considering how long I would be gone, I was fairly proud of myself for packing this light. I seemed to remember it being easier to do as a kid when I was traveling with my parents, but now that I thought about it, they'd probably put some of my stuff in their bags. People thought traveling with babies was bad. Try traveling with a teenage girl.

Before I could enter the black ropes leading to the screening, a young couple, who were clearly on their honeymoon, darted in front of me. I didn't think they were being rude. I didn't think they saw me, or anything other than each other. They looked like they were in their late twenties. He was Filipino. She had lighter skin and could almost be Irish, with her curly hair and freckles. He had a brown leather bag slung over his shoulder and she was wearing sandals and some kind of resort wear. My guess was that they were headed to a tropical resort. What was amazing was that I didn't feel pangs of jealousy or wonder if I would ever feel what they were feeling. I was happy for them, albeit a little annoyed that they got in front of me in line. Not that I was in a hurry. I'd gotten to the airport with plenty of time to get to my gate.

As I thought about the journey ahead of me, my stomach became surprisingly queasy. This wouldn't just be my first trip overseas in ten years—this would be my first time writing about it for a paycheck.

I kept trying to tell myself it wouldn't be much different than the assignments I did for the WHERE magazines. In fact, it would be a lot more exciting than the travel junket I'd done to Thomasville, Georgia, with its "blackened catfish" featured at every meal.

The thought of doing another one of those trips made me cringe. Back then, I had to call the airlines, make them look up my "media rate," and still had to pay the balance out of my own pocket. Getting to Thomasville hadn't been easy either. They'd flown us into Tallahassee and then shuttled twelve of us strangers over the border into Bulldog territory, where they'd put us up in bed and breakfast places that looked like miniature dollhouses inside. I never played with dolls as a kid, so none of their fine china tea parties appealed to me. But I hadn't been writing for me. I was writing for the fifty-five-plus demographic who were starting to buy their first RVs and wanted to see "this great country."

As I made my way through the scanners and collected my bags on the other side, there was nothing I wanted more than to leave "this great country." My parents wanted me to stay and go to a therapist, but I wanted to snuggle up in a window seat and watch the runway lights grow smaller until everything looked like a giant Lite-Brite set thousands of miles below me. That sounded therapeutic to me.

To disappear into a crowd and focus solely on what I wanted seemed like a more practical, real-world implementation of "getting over it," than sitting in an oversized chair talking about my feelings. Counseling didn't do me any good when I was married. It certainly wouldn't do me any good now that I was divorced at twenty-six. Ugh. What a typical Florida girl I turned out to be.

I got to my gate and searched for a good people-watching seat. With over an hour before boarding time, I wanted to do some people watching. After so many years of Duncan making me feel like I was invisible, I was now going to put those acquired skills to some use and eavesdrop on the conversations around me. They said Nora Ephron used to take phrases from other people at restaurants and get ideas for her characters. Of course, that was easier to do when you didn't have strangers moseying up to start chatting with you.

A few more people began gathering at the gate. I tucked myself away in a corner and pulled my hair over my eyes. If you didn't make eye contact, people would be less likely to strike up a conversation with you.

When I sat down, something fell out from one of my cargo pockets. When I saw what was lying on the floor, I almost left it there. It was the cigarette lighter with the lightning bolt on it. The one I'd first found in the coffee shop in San Diego. Guess it had been awhile since I'd worn these pants. I reached down with my left hand and picked it up, examining it as if I had never seen it before.

If it had been an omen, I would not have wanted to take it with me. But it was a reminder. A reminder of that coffee shop I missed dearly. A reminder of my beloved afternoon thunderstorms. A reminder not to drift through life, falling victim to other people's decisions or intentions for me. From now on, I was going to be the lightning. I had a fire inside. What could have been the end of me would be my beginning. I was going to let it be a spark that led to the flame that fueled my journey. I tucked the lighter back into my cargo pocket, this time using the button to keep it from falling out again.

After writing in my journal for an hour in the corner of the airport where no one could see me, my flight was ready for boarding. I shoved my things back inside my bag and threw it over my head so it slung diagonally across my chest. I pulled my ticket out of my pocket and headed towards my future.

I followed the other passengers into line and heard the popping sound of the stub coming away from the rest of the ticket. Once I heard that sound, I knew there would be no turning back. That sound meant I was getting on that plane.

As I stood in a line of people in the jetway, I thought about my graduation day. I thought about the sad, lonely girl who couldn't lift a fork to her mouth. I saw myself sitting with Duncan in the rain on the steps of Knowles Chapel. I saw myself being hurled onto the living room floor. Then I saw Duncan's body beneath the departures ramp.

The line moved forward slowly as people began to take their seats, and I entered the plane's oval doorway as if it were an escape hatch. Instead of ducking inside an aircraft, I was emerging up through an opening. I looked around at the other passengers, some of whom looked back at me. They had no idea who I was. Or what I had just done.

I found seat 27A and threw my duffle bag into the overhead bin before sitting down. I removed my crossbody purse from over my shoulder and slid it under the seat in front of me. I sat back, closed my eyes, and set my mind on saying goodbye to a version of myself I did not like.

As I opened my eyes again, I thought about holding baby Randall and the feeling of this freedom being like the gift of a new life. I smiled, buckled my seatbelt, and couldn't wait for the plane to take off.

ABOUT THE AUTHOR

Becca Bredholt is an award-winning poet and writer who began her career in print editorial in Orlando before moving to Washington, D.C. and launching her marketing career. *Huffington Post, Yahoo Travel* and *Orlando Magazine* are a few of the dozens of publications that have featured her writing. She previously starred in a reality TV series on ABC hosted by Marla Maples called *The Ex-Wives Club*. Becca currently writes short stories, directs short films, and pens a wine blog for women. She completed her master's degree in Liberal Studies at Rollins College and has her undergraduate degree in journalism from Point Loma Nazarene University. Becca is now married and living in Maryland as the mother of two dragons.

f ⊚ beccabredholt
www.beccabredholt.com